"When will it be a good time?" The sarcasm in Mike's voice rang out loud and clear. "You've told me that you want to get your life back. Part of that should be having a relationship of your own. I'm available, interested, and ready for more than friendship with you. Tell me what I have to do to get us there."

Drained from skipping around the real issue, Jordan decided to be honest. "Mike, you're a former student. Do you really think we have anything to build a relationship on?"

"Yes," Mike answered without a moment's hesitation. Challenging, he asked, "If I didn't know better, I'd say you were scared. Is that what's going on in your head? Are you afraid, Jordan? Is that why you won't go out with me?"

She whipped around and lifted her chin, ready to do battle. "No. Why would I be afraid of you?"

"That's my question."

In a near panic, Jordan said, "Talking to you is not working, so I'm going home."

With one hand at the small of her back, he encircled her with his arms, pulling her into his embrace. "Don't be afraid," he whispered into her hair, "I'm here. I'll always be here for you."

Mike's touch was firm, but gentle. His eyes filled with deep longing and need sent her skittish heart into a gallop. Silently, he drew her to him, wrapping his arms around her waist, holding her close. She melted against the solid warmth of male flesh.

He brushed a gentle kiss across her forehead. "There's something between us. It has nothing to do with my teenage crush. It's about you, the woman I know now and care for." His voice dropped to a husky purr as his hands tenderly stroked her back. "Let me show you."

Love Changes Everything

Karen White-Owens

BET Publications, LLC
http://www.bet.com
http://www.arabesquebooks.com

ARABESQUE BOOKS are published by

BET Publications, LLC
c/o BET BOOKS
One BET Plaza
1900 W Place NE
Washington, DC 20018-1211

All Kensington Titles, Imprints, and Distributed Lines are available at special quantity discounts for bulk purchases for sales promotions, premiums, fund-raising, and educational, or institutional use. Special book excerpts or customized printings can also be created to fit specific needs. For details, write or phone the office of the Kensington special sales manager: Kensington Publishing Corp., 850 Third Avenue, New York, NY 10022, attn: Special Sales Department. Phone: 1-800-221-2647.

First Printing: November 2005

10 9 8 7 6 5 4 3 2 1

Printed in the United States of America

I would like to dedicate this book to the many teachers that work so diligently to educate our children. Despite overcrowded classrooms and a lack of supplies and textbooks, you continue to do your job in the most effective and efficient manner possible. Thank you.

ACKNOWLEDGMENTS

I'm a firm believer that books are a collaborative effort. *Love Changes Everything* is no exception. I want to thank my editor, Demetria Lucas, for all of her hard work on my behalf. Science teachers Laurel Peterson and Cheryl Terrell for their help sorting out the technical stuff. Darlene House and Patricia Walker for helping me through the final process of putting together this manuscript. My critique group for their support and the many hours they listened to me ramble on about this story as I tried to come up with a plot that would interest and surprise my audience. My husband for his continuous support and my family for always believing in me.

Prologue

A strangled cry of alarm pierced the quiet hallway of Randall High School. En route to the copy room, Jordan Anderson stopped. She scanned the area with a Styrofoam cup of hot chocolate in one hand and her students' final exams in the other.

Jordan caught a glimpse of a lone figure shooting from the boys' bathroom. As she moved closer, an invisible band tightened around her heart at the expression on Mike Walker's face. He looked frightened and frantic, causing her apprehension to shoot up a notch.

"Ms. Anderson. Ms. Anderson." Mike halted in front of her, gripping his stomach. Panting, he forced words from stiff, frightened lips. "DeMarcus has got a gun."

Terror iced her skin as her greatest nightmare became a reality. The cold edge of fear touched her spine. "Are you sure? Did you see it?" Jordan asked in an anxious whisper.

Mike nodded. "He's in the bathroom."

His words propelled her into action. The exam pages slipped from her fingers, slowly gliding through the air and landing on the floor. Hot chocolate splattered the rust-and-tan flooring, creating abstract images on the tile.

"Find the principal," she commanded, dashing in the direction of the bathroom.

"Okay." The boy shot down the opposite corridor.

Hands clenching and unclenching, Jordan stopped outside the bathroom door, silently hunting for the correct words to defuse this situation. The cynical voice in her head questioned, *what are you doing?*

Jordan flattened herself against the wall outside the bathroom, trying to calm the accelerated beat of her heart. She peeked around the doorway, searching the black-painted walls for the young man. Cowered on the floor under the lavatory's single window, he wept. A silver revolver was firmly clasped in his hands.

In a slow, but deliberate movement, she stepped away from the door frame and moved inside the lavatory, hovering inside the room. The combined odors of urine and air freshener made her nose twitch and she grimaced. "DeMarcus?"

"Stay out!" he ordered through his tears.

Equal doses of adrenaline and fear pumped through Jordan. She took a step closer to the young man, determined to resolve this situation. "I want to help," she said softly.

"You can't." Tears streamed down his cheeks. The misery in his voice broke her heart and her teeth sank into the tender flesh on the inside of her cheek. "I hate this school. Nobody likes me."

"Hate? Why?"

"They treat me like I'm crap. Nothing," DeMarcus spat.

Uncertainty surged through Jordan and she gnawed on her bottom lip, taking a hard look at her options. Maybe she needed to stay out of this, or wait until a more experienced and authorized person arrived.

Mike called her from the doorway. She glanced beyond him, expecting to see the principal. Her hope died a quick and painful death. "Don't come in here."

"Ms. Anderson, I couldn't find Mr. Jones." His eyes glazed over wild and frightened. "I found Ms. CeCe at her desk, so I told her."

A jolt of alarm zapped her. His words sealed her fate. There wasn't anyone else. Jordan put a finger to her lips and shushed the boy, focusing all her energy on DeMarcus.

She probed gently, "What happened? Who hurt you? Threatened you? Is that why you've got a gun? To protect yourself?"

DeMarcus's tears doubled with each question. His sobs tore through the room. But he held on to the gun. "They stuck my head in the toilet and dumped my food in the trash." His eyes glittered with hard determination. "No more. I hate 'em. It's my turn."

Pain resonated from DeMarcus's voice, and Jordan's heart reached out to this tortured kid. His anguish made tears pool in her eyes for all that he'd suffered and filled him with such intense and vengeful rage.

Jordan shook her head, moving slowly and deliberately across the floor until she stood in front of him. "No, it's not. I won't let you end your future this way. Everything is ahead of you. Don't destroy your future because of a group of dummies."

"I don't care."

"Well, I do!" She extended a hand, coaxing softly, "Come on, honey. Please. Give me the gun."

As he responded to the command in her tone, De-Marcus's eyebrows bunched together while he rose from the floor. Jordan reached for the gun. He shrank away, crying. "Stop! No! Stay away! Get back!"

"Don't," she pleaded, hearing the quivering note in

her voice and hoping that DeMarcus didn't. "Come on, son. Please, give it to me."

"No! No!" he cried, using the back of one hand to wipe away his tears. Then he aimed the gun in her direction.

Jordan quit breathing. Gentling her voice, she said, "Kids are cruel, vicious to each other. Mean and spiteful in ways that I don't understand. Sometimes adults are the same way. But you're not alone. You have friends and me." She paused, gathering her thoughts. "No one should have to deal with that kind of torture. I wish I had soothing, encouraging words and sweet guarantees. I don't. This may happen again."

DeMarcus watched her with rapt attention. A mixture of hope and distress glittered from his pain-filled eyes. She held his gaze, willing him to understand and make the right decision.

"I can promise you that things won't always be like this. Life . . ." Jordan moved a step closer. "Will . . ." She gripped the barrel of the gun. "Get better."

Hesitating, he lowered the weapon, but refused to release it.

Her tongue slid across her dry lips. "A gun won't prove a thing. It'll help you get jail time. While you're in the penitentiary another group will form and continue to terrorize the remaining students. Don't go out that way."

Softening her voice even further, she continued, "If you do this, they've won. All the pain and humiliation you endured will make other students believe those bullies are stronger and smarter. They'll own the school and do whatever they want without any consequences. Don't let that happen. They don't deserve that much power. Show them that you are made of tougher stuff."

Seconds passed in taut silence. Jordan's gaze never wavered, silently willing the young man to weigh his options, to make the right choice. Perspiration slithered down her spine as she waited. Fear clogged her throat. Using her best teacher's voice, she added, "You're too smart for this. Hand me the gun."

With a cry of defeat, DeMarcus released the weapon.

Weakness invaded Jordan's limbs and she staggered against a stall door. She shut her eyes and let out a huge sigh of relief. "Thank you. Thank you." Jordan made sure the safety was on the gun before stuffing it into her pants pocket and reaching for DeMarcus's arm, helping him to his feet.

Tears spilled down his cheeks, DeMarcus wrapped his arms around her, sobbing uncontrollably. She held him close, offering soothing support. Once DeMarcus's tears subsided, Jordan led him from the bathroom and with a heavy heart into the hands of the police.

Chapter 1

Twelve years later

A colossal wave of panic swept through Jordan Anderson as she turned into Anthony Pierson High School's parking lot. Her heart raced and perspiration led a path down the narrow slope of her neck.

Jordan pulled her silver Saturn SUV into an empty spot and turned off the engine. She collapsed against the cloth-covered seat, unconsciously stroking the incision on her right wrist.

The time has come, she thought, studying the red-brick building with incredible amounts of trepidation. Today started an important journey to recapture the joy of teaching. No longer a starry-eyed baby teacher fresh out of college, Jordan sought enjoyment and fulfillment in her chosen profession. She needed to dispel the sense of panic and apathy that had violently crept into her life and took control.

I can't hide in the car forever, Jordan rationalized, opening the door and swinging her legs onto the concrete-paved ground. The sun's summer rays caressed her skin as she unlocked the back door. She dropped her

scarlet Kenneth Cole shoulder bag inside the card-
board box nestled in the backseat and removed the box
overflowing with the tools of her trade. With a gentle
nudge of her hip, the door swung shut and she crossed
the parking lot.

Memories of the previous twelve years twisted her
gut into knots. Jordan felt as if she'd been in the trenches
of a war instead of working in her chosen profession.
Rude parents, unruly students, and an uncompromising administration contributed to her disheartened attitude. She ended the last school year emotionally
drained, physically battered with her spirit broken. Although she still loved teaching, she craved a break from
the emotional baggage that accompanied her career.

Turning in the direction of her car, Jordan hit the
black car remote on her key chain. The SUV chirped
and the headlights flashed, arming it.

Mindful of the weakness in her wrist, she gingerly
shifted the box from her right to her left arm and
reached for the door handle. She still had trouble
handling heavy items. After six months of physical
therapy, the doctors had declared her as fit as she
would ever be.

Inside the building, she sighed, enjoying the sense of
space and quiet. These were the final days of summer
and Pierson High School remained a kid-free zone.
Everything would change two weeks from today with the
start of the new school year. Every available inch of
floor space would be occupied by students, crowding together in social groups to discuss the highlights of their
summers.

She cut through the empty kitchen, strolled across
the cafeteria and down the main corridor. The sil-
houette of a tall teenager detached itself from the
wall and took shape as she approached him.

Jordan's eyes narrowed. A man stood in front of her, not a boy. She gauged his age to be anywhere from the mid to the late twenties. A tiny smile formed on her lips as she admired the tantalizing picture he presented.

He's definitely a cutie, she thought, giving him a thorough once-over. This man stood way over six feet with the solid, muscular frame of an athlete. A long, oval-shaped face framed sparkling coffee-brown eyes that danced with golden flecks. Jordan giggled and shook her head, knowing full well that he might be handsome, but he was still a tenderoni and one step away from jailbait.

Admiring his skin, Jordan smiled. Each year women eagerly paid millions to cosmetic companies to achieve his blemish-free bronze complexion. His broad smile revealed even white teeth as he came near her with an outstretched hand.

Jordan took his hand in a firm handshake. An electrical charge zapped her. Time halted as they gazed into each other's eyes. Finally, she pulled her hand free, rubbing it against the soft fabric of her black linen shorts.

"Hi," he greeted in a deep baritone voice. "I'm Mike Walker. I've been waiting for you."

Unable to resist the appeal of his smile, she grinned back. "Hi. Jordan Anderson. I'm starting here as a teacher this semester."

"I'm your welcoming committee." He removed the box from her hands. "I'll take you to your classroom, and then we'll need to get to the staff meeting."

An uncertain smile wavered on her lips. "Thanks."

Mike cleared his throat and ran a hand over his wavy sable hair. "No problem." He took her arm in a loose grip, creating a new assortment of sensations. "The science classrooms and labs are grouped together. You and I are neighbors. That way we can help each other, when necessary."

"Good."

"Yeah. It helps." He smiled, guiding her down the hallway.

Each time Mike smiled, an invisible string drew Jordan closer to him.

"By the way, I teach biology, earth science, and astronomy," Mike said.

Jordan thrust a finger at her chest and responded, "Physics, physical science, and chemistry."

"I know." Mike stopped at a wood door with the number 15 marked in big black letters. A ceiling-to-floor windowpane filled the left portion of the entrance.

Mike pulled a gold ring of keys from his pocket, chose one, and turned it in the lock. Opening the door, he peeled the key from the ring and handed it to her.

Jordan stepped into the room, taking her first look at what would be her workplace for the new school year.

This classroom resembled others that she'd occupied. Beige walls, mud-brown and white tile flooring, and rows of blue and gray desks stuffed the room. Ceiling-to-floor windows ran the length of one wall. A teacher's workstation guarded the front door.

He placed her box on a nearby desk. "Walker Moving Company is at your service. Do you have anything else to bring in?"

She shook her head. "No, this is it. Later this week I'll probably bring in more stuff."

Nodding, Mike reiterated, "Just remember, my offer to help you move in is available anytime."

"I appreciate it. Thank you."

Depositing her purse on the desk, Jordan examined the room.

Mike took her arm and guided her to a door at the

rear of the classroom. "Let me show you around. We share a lab. This door leads to it. The key I gave you will open your room, my room, and the lab."

Jordan stepped through the entrance, glancing around the lab. Gleaming state-of-the-art equipment stood ready for use. Every possible piece of equipment needed to perform experiments waited. Bunsen burners, beakers, and microscopes lined the black marble tabletops.

"I'm warning you in advance, Debbie, our department head, will go ballistic if you don't lock up the lab whenever you use it. It took lots of persuasion to get our administration to let go of the bucks to build these labs. So be careful."

"Noted. I'll keep it in mind," she promised, tapping her forehead with a finger. She made her way around the lab, touching items as she moved between the aisles.

Mike pointed at a wooden door at the far end of the room. "My room is on the other side of that door. That's room fourteen."

They returned to her classroom a few moments later when Jordan had finished surveying the room. Mike perched on the edge of one of the desks. Disappointment lurked behind his dark lashes, partially hidden, but visible if she looked closely. "You don't remember me, do you?"

Jordan studied his face. "No," she answered, slowly shaking her head. "Should I?"

He stood, shoved his hands into the pockets of his jeans, and moved across the room to the windows. "I hoped you would. You taught at Randall High School, correct?"

"Yes. What about it?" Jordan moved closer to him.

"I'm Mike." He emphasized his name as if she should recognize it.

"Mike?"

"Remember DeMarcus?"

That name clicked in her head, conjuring up the boy's tortured face and Mike's shocked expression.

Her mouth dropped open and eyebrows shot up. "Oh my," Jordan muttered, turning away as those old memories crystallized. "Oh my," she repeated, cupping her cheek with her hand. "Good grief. You've grown up."

"Yes, I have." Grinning, he softened his voice to a whispered purr. "I'm not sure if you're aware of this, but the way you handled DeMarcus always stuck with me and inspired me to become a teacher."

Flattered, she mustered a faint "Really?"

"Mmm-hmm. You safely negotiated a situation that could have had a very different outcome."

"That's what they paid me for," she said flippantly.

He moved aimlessly around the room. "And more, I say. I admired you for the way you stood by and helped DeMarcus. Jordan, up to that point, I had no idea what my future held. My agenda included college, but that ended it. I felt confused and uncertain. That incident grounded me and gave me direction."

"Thank you." A sad little smile switched on and off her face like a lightbulb. "I needed to hear something good about my days at Randall High."

"You changed my life."

They studied each other across the length of the room. The silence grew taut and she felt compelled to break it. "Do you enjoy teaching?"

"Yes. Very much," he answered quickly. "I found the place where I'm needed." Mike glanced at his watch. "Whoa, we better get moving. The meeting starts promptly at nine."

Jordan nodded and dropped her purse in her desk drawer. As she crossed the room, she grabbed her portfolio and a pen from the box. "How long do you think our meeting will last?"

He shrugged, opening the door. "Couple of hours. We'll meet at nine each morning until the semester begins. Lunch happens at noon and we return around two-thirty for a daily wrap-up."

"What happens after lunch? Are there additional meetings?"

With a hand at Jordan's elbow, Mike guided her down the corridor. She tried to ignore the warmth of his touch against her skin. The tingling sensations spread from the top of her spine and hustled down her back.

"No. Generally, we work in our rooms, unless Chet or our department head schedules a guest speaker."

"Sounds good." Jordan stuffed the pen into the side pocket of her shorts. "What about the staff? Is it a good team?"

"Yes, they are." Gazing down at her, Mike smiled. "You'll see for yourself." His eyes darkened and his voice turned conspiratory. "Here's a word of advice. Don't let them intimidate you. They love doing that."

She let out a shaky breath. "I am intimidated and nervous."

"Don't be. You'll do fine. Besides, you've been teaching far too long to let them get the upper hand." His warm palm shifted from her elbow to the base of her spine, leading her with gentle firmness. "We'll meet in room one each morning."

"Who besides the teaching staff attends these meetings?"

"The principal and assistant principal. Some of the maintenance people return when we do and the administrative staff generally attend some of the meetings."

"What kind of stuff will we be covering?"

"Team teaching is one of the concepts we're ex-

ploring this year. By the way, we do lunch together as
a department."

"Okay."

"Here we are," he announced, opening the door.

Jordan preceded him into the room. The occupants
quieted and turned to watch them. She felt like a
specimen from a museum on display as she crossed the
floor and sank into a blue plastic chair at the back of
the room. Mike followed, settling in next to her.

A thin woman with coffee-colored skin and narrow
shoulder-length blond braids stood behind a podium,
motioning for Jordan to join her at the front of the
room.

"People, this is Jordan Anderson. She's joining the
science department this fall. Please welcome her to our
Pierson family."

As he swallowed the last drops of Gatorade, the smile
on Mike's face refused to disappear while he scanned
the information he had picked up when he entered the
room. Jordan Anderson had arrived and she looked exactly the way he remembered. Tall and willowy, Jordan
displayed the grace of a dancer. Skin the color of rich
unsweetened tea and almond-shaped eyes the color of
espresso coffee, she was beautiful. His heart almost
exploded from his chest when she strolled down the
hallway like a queen, checking out her kingdom.

Since his department chair had mentioned Jordan
was joining the Pierson High School staff, he'd been
waiting for her to put in her appearance. Finally, after
weeks of anticipation, she had arrived. His eyes swept
over her once more. Jordan was beautiful and she was
finally close.

Mike snatched a quick glance at the woman sitting

next to him. He drew in a deep breath of air, inhaling her fragrant scent. Her unique fragrance perfumed the air with a rich combination of exotic fruit and sensual promise.

A red elastic band held her auburn, wavy ponytail in place. It swung from the crown of her head, resting between her shoulder blades. He studied her profile a moment longer, fighting the urge to run his fingers through her soft mane.

Eyeing her covertly, he considered how his image of Jordan had changed as he matured and became a man. While he was a student, all the guys had drooled after Miss Anderson. They talked about how she filled out her sweaters and about that dimple in her left cheek that seemed to wink at them when she smiled. He didn't participate in locker room antics, but he recalled more times than he could count that Ms. Anderson had been a hot topic of discussion in the gym. Sometimes his buddies would take bets on who would make her smile and fantasized about what life would be like with her.

Mike knew it was a lot to expect, but he couldn't help feeling disappointed that she hadn't recognized him. On the other hand, they had plenty of time to get to know one another now. And he planned to make good use of his time.

Chapter 2

Overwhelmed, Jordan sat at her desk, stunned at the amount of paperwork she had received during this morning's faculty meeting. She thumbed through the material, absorbing a fraction of the information.

Rules, regulations, and outlines for the coming school year were among the data available in her new three-ring binder. She sighed, flipping through the pages. Curriculum maps, lists of science textbooks, and the new procedures for disciplining students were stuffed into the blue binder.

A tap on the door drew her attention. The door opened and Mike poked his head inside. "Hey, you." He moved across the classroom and perched on the edge of a student desk in front of her.

The warmth of his voice and smile sent a shiver of delight surging through her. Unable to resist Mike's smiling presence, she grinned back. "Hi. What's up?"

"We're heading out to lunch. Do you want to join us?"

"Who's we?" Jordan asked.

"Science department."

Jordan pursed her lips, considering the invitation.

It was too soon for her to do lunch with the staff. She needed some time to adjust to her new surroundings.

"Nah." She shook her head and placed a hand on her binder. "I'm going to get acquainted with my room and review some of the info we got at the meeting."

"You sure?" Mike shoved his hands inside the back pockets of his jeans.

"Yeah. Enjoy."

"You've got to eat," he reminded her. "Plus, this is a good chance for you to meet the department faculty."

"To be perfectly honest, I'm not ready. This morning floored me. I need a little time to regroup and mentally prepare for the next session."

Mike raised his hands in an act of surrender. "No problem. Trust me. I do understand."

"Thanks for thinking of me."

He ran a keen eye over her lean frame. "Can I bring you something back?"

"No. I'm fine. Go have a nice lunch."

"Will do." Mike started for the door, stopped, then turned to her. "Before the school year starts, you'll have to come out with us."

"It's a deal," she promised. "See ya."

The door closed quietly behind him and she returned to her binder.

He's nice, Jordan thought. *Cute, but way too young. If he were a bit older I might see what comes next.* Chuckling, she had an image of herself, wrinkled and gray haired at eighty with a young man hanging on her arm, or rather holding her up. She erased the mental picture from her mind and refocused on the work in front of her. The cutie that had just left faded from her thoughts as she concentrated on the binder.

Fifteen minutes later, Mike returned, strolling through her door. "How's the reading going?"

"Slow," Jordan admitted, sniffing the air. She recognized the enticing aroma of chicken.

He deposited a white paper bag on her desk and dug inside.

She tilted her head to one side. "What's this?"

"Lunch," he announced, removing the items from the bag as he identified them. "Chicken salad on toasted wheat and balsamic vinaigrette for your salad, correct?"

Amazed, she asked slowly, "How did you know?"

Heat flushed Mike's cheeks. Embarrassed, he ducked his head, saying, "All those years ago, I remember seeing you eat this. Plus, this. Hot chocolate, right?" He grinned as he offered her a white Styrofoam cup.

Nodding, Jordan took the cup from his hand. She removed the plastic lid, sniffed appreciatively before sampling the mixture. Her eyes drifted shut as she rolled the hot chocolate around her tongue, savoring the taste of warm milk and chocolate. "Mmm. This is heavenly. Thank you."

"My pleasure," Mike responded.

She opened her eyes and reached for her purse. "What do I owe you?"

"Nothing. My treat."

Ready to protest, Jordan closed her mouth, deciding to use a different approach. "Okay. But next time lunch is on me."

"Deal. For now, do you mind if I share my lunch period with you?"

Silently delighted by the idea, Jordan agreed, "No. Not at all. That would be nice."

Mike glanced around the room, spotted a stool, and pulled it to her desk. "That's me. Nice." He reached into the bag and removed a grilled chicken breast sandwich, strawberry-flavored bottled water, and an apple.

They sat in comfortable silence, munching on their lunch. After taking the final sip of hot chocolate, Jordan sighed contentedly. "That hit the spot. Thank you."

"No problem." He bit into the apple.

She wrapped up the remains of her lunch in a paper napkin and tossed it in the trash.

Without warning, he ran a finger across her bare left hand. His touch burned her skin. "No ring. You were Ms. Anderson at Randall. Is there a Mr. Anderson?"

Reluctant to reveal her nonmarried status, she debated telling him a lie. Instead, she opted for honesty. "No. I came close. But never made it down the aisle."

"What happened?"

"The job got in the way."

He nodded. "Kids?"

"It never happened for me."

"I'm surprised," Mike muttered thoughtfully, absently stroking her ringless finger. His voice turned husky as his gaze slid over her. "You're an attractive woman."

Thrilled by the compliment, Jordan allowed his words to float over her. While the sensible side of her realized that they were only words, they were very pretty words coming from a twenty-eight-year-old male.

"Thank you," she said. "Marriage and a family would have been great. But I'm content. I enjoy my life the way it is."

"You've got time," he said. "The right man is going to come along. I can feel it."

Her eyes widened a fraction and her heartbeat sped up. This conversation had ventured into territory that felt way too personal for her taste. She decided to steer the discussion in a different direction. "What about you? Are you married? Involved?"

"Nooo. Not married." He dropped the apple core in

the bag and wiped his mouth with a white paper napkin. "So far the right woman hasn't come along."

"Really!"

His answer surprised her. She felt certain that Mike had many opportunities to meet and establish relationships with the opposite sex.

He stretched, then resettled on his stool. "For the present moment, my life is good the way it is."

"Why?" Jordan asked.

"I'm not in a hurry to settle down. My great love is out there somewhere and I want to find her. Someone I can share everything with. A person that I don't have to hide any part of myself from." Mike smiled. "My soul mate."

"That's a big order. Do you really believe it's possible to find your soul mate? Or that you even have one?" Running her tongue across her lips, she said in a skeptical tone, "After all, it's a huge world." Jordan held her breath, waiting for his answer. For a reason she refused to question, Mike's answer meant a great deal to her.

When he spoke, his deep voice resonated within her, resurrecting a surprising level of longing inside her. "Anything is possible. And I do believe she's out there. I think she's waiting for me just like I'm waiting for her. We just have to connect."

Mike's sentiments were beautifully expressed. Jordan found herself wondering if she had a soul mate in the world searching for her. An awkward silence settled over them.

"You were bound for Michigan State when you left high school," Jordan said, feeling the need to break the uncomfortable quiet. "Is that where you got your degree?"

"No. Things changed. I went to Eastern Michigan University," he stated proudly, sitting straighter on his stool.

"Good!" she exclaimed. "Eastern is one of the premier teaching universities in the state. Are you working on your graduate degree?"

"I finished it two years ago. I wanted to knock it out. I didn't want to spend the next five years working on a degree part-time. I went straight through."

"You've got that right," Jordan agreed, leaning back in her chair. "I completed mine while working at Randall. It took a lot out of me, working all day, then going to school at night. Honestly, I've never regretted completing it as soon as I could."

"Speaking of my alma mater, why did you leave Randall?"

She shrugged, a bit uncomfortable with the question. "I was on the fast track to an administrative position. Soon after that, I became assistant principal at Benton High School. It didn't take long for me to realize that I was in the wrong place. I belonged in the classroom." A self-mocking smile flirted across her face. "Crazy, huh?"

"Not at all. How did you end up here?"

"Kids and parents had almost burned me out. I needed a change of scenery to get my equilibrium back."

"That's understandable. We're in a high-stress profession."

"Yes, we are," Jordan agreed. Her thoughts turned inward. One of her more challenging and difficult moments from the previous school year flashed into her head.

"Hey." Mike waved a hand in front of her face. "Earth to Jordan, where did you go?"

Blinking, she returned to the present. "Sorry."

"Don't worry about it."

She brushed a lock of hair from her eyes. "I have to be honest, I remember you as a jock. Basketball, if my memories are correct. I would have thought you'd be a member of the Pistons with a girl on each arm. How did you end up teaching science?"

Mike laughed loud and hearty. He linked his hands together and placed them on top of his head. "You just summed me up. I did go to Eastern on a basketball scholarship. My counselor kept telling me to study something that would get me a job. Trust me, the Pistons never called. So I finished my degree." He waved a hand at the classroom. "Here I am."

"Your counselor gave you good advice."

"Yes, he did. To stay on the team, I had to maintain a 2.0 GPA. You won't believe this, but my first biology class fascinated me and I took another and another. Before I realized it I had a major in biology with a minor in chemistry."

Jordan grinned back at Mike. "Unbelievable."

"Yeah."

"How long have you been at Pierson?" she asked.

"Six years. I came here right out of college."

"I'm proud of you." She laid her hand on top of his, smiling into his captivating brown eyes.

"Thank you. You helped to make me the man I am today."

The door opened and the pair turned. The science department head, Deborah Rucker, entered the room. She stopped in her tracks, zeroing in on their linked hands, and her eyes widened, then turned cool as she surveyed the intimate scene.

Laden with a stack of manila folders, Debbie resumed her trip across the floor. She halted at Jordan's desk and stood authoritatively over the pair before turning to Mike. "Hi."

Jordan eased her hand from Mike's.

"Hey, Deb. Here, let me get those for you." He rose, offering their supervisor his chair.

"No, I've got them. I thought you went to lunch with the rest of the department," she stated brusquely.

"I decided to spend some time with Jordan."

"Mmm," Debbie muttered, taking a hard look at the desk. She touched the white bag that minutes ago had held their lunch. "You brought lunch back?"

"Yeah. We've been talking about back in the day." He turned to Jordan. An engaging smile spread across his face. Unable to resist, she grinned back.

"Back in the day?" Debbie inquired, looking from Mike to Jordan.

"Jordan taught at my high school," he replied with a friendly rejoinder. "I learned chemistry from her."

Debbie smiled, revealing a large number of teeth. Unfortunately, no true warmth reached her eyes. "You didn't tell me that. Interesting." She stepped around Mike and slipped onto the stool that he'd relinquished, and speared him with a glare. "If you'll excuse us, I need to talk departmental and human resources business."

"Sure. No problem." Mike scooped up the white bag and dumped the remains of his lunch inside. "Jordan, thanks for the walk down memory lane." He gave them a two-finger salute and dropped the paper bag in the trash can on his way out. "I'll see you ladies at the afternoon meeting."

Silently, Debbie and Jordan watched Mike leave the room. Debbie pulled the stool closer to the desk. "This is the best time for us to talk. There's been a lot of information thrown at you today and I thought we could spend a little time deciphering it."

"That would be good," Jordan answered cautiously. Debbie's demeanor made her feel uncomfortable. Although her tone remained professional, it lacked the encouraging warmth Jordan had encountered during her interviews. Today, ice coated every word.

She handed Jordan a manila folder filled with forms. "These are your personnel forms. Tax and insurance information. Fill them out and get them back to me before the end of the week. Put them in my box and I'll pass them on to Human Resources. Receiving your first paycheck depends on how fast we can get everything processed."

"I hear you." Jordan flipped through the papers before placing the folder on the opposite side of her desk.

"I have your schedule and class lists," Debbie added, offering Jordan a second folder. "There are six one-hour class periods. Five classes will be your responsibility. In addition, you have a prep period and a half hour lunch break."

"Okay."

The department head toyed with a blond braid, continuing, "To help accelerate and smooth your adjustment period, Pierson offers teacher-to-teacher mentoring. Your mentor will be available to answer any questions and help you with small issues that might crop up during the course of a school day. Mike volunteered for this assignment." Her eyes narrowed. "If you'd prefer someone different, we can accommodate you."

"No, no. I'm fine with Mike. I like him."

"He's a good *kid*," Debbie stated in a voice that carried admiration and a hint of something more. "It surprised me to find Mike in here. You guys must have really hit it off."

Jordan studied Debbie for a beat. The voice in Jordan's head whispered *be careful*, as a chill slowly slithered down her spine like the cold scales of a snake.

"He's been pretty helpful," Jordan offered.

"How long ago did you meet?"

Jordan shrugged. "Twelve, almost thirteen years ago."

Debbie nodded. "Were you a new teacher? Or had you been working awhile?"

"New teacher. Right out of college."

Debbie flipped a handful of braids over her shoulder and added, "He's a good *kid*. The students love him, probably because he's not much older than them. You know, more of a contemporary than a disciplinarian."

"Mmm." *Point scored,* Jordan thought. Clearly, Debbie was warning her about Mike. What was this woman up to? That was the second time Debbie had referred to Mike as a kid. *I get it,* she thought. *You're not too happy about what you just saw.*

"After all, he just finished facing some of the challenges of our students."

Is there something going on between Debbie and Mike? Jordan wondered, taking a quick glance at the other woman's ringless left hand.

It didn't matter, she thought. *Mike was not on her agenda.*

Jordan smiled her most pleasant smile at Debbie. *No need to worry about me, I'm not interested in a relationship with him.*

Chapter 3

The strong stench of paint filled Mike's nostrils while the jazz saxophone of Dave Koz touched his ears. An imaginary lasso roped him, halting him in his tracks. He retraced his steps and peeked through Jordan's classroom window.

Chuckling, he stepped into the room. "Hey, you."

Jordan stood at one of the tables, sorting through a series of charts and posters. A blue lab coat swallowed her slim frame. Pink, green, and yellow paint dotted the front of the garment.

She swayed to the music, rocking from side to side. Under the lab coat, a crème body-hugging top and scarlet capri pants covered her willowy frame. She glanced in his direction and smiled. "Hi, Mike."

Enthralled, he felt his heart rate accelerating as he watched Jordan. An invisible string pulled him across the floor to where she stood. Her single dimple winked at him. "What ya doin'?" he drawled as he stared pointedly at the newly painted storage cabinet.

She turned a chart of the solar system toward him. "Decorating. I want to make my classroom reflect some of the stuff I plan to teach this term."

"Do you need help?" He stopped next to her. The combination of Jordan's warmth and her fruity fragrance enticed him.

"I'm fine right now. But I could use your expertise." She tapped the table loaded with charts, maps, and posters of inventors. "I plan to have my room in order before classes start next week. Which would you suggest I use?"

He shifted through the pile, separating several he found interesting. "These work for me."

Nodding, Jordan gathered the charts Mike chose and placed them on her desk. The CD player hummed and shut off.

"Where are you on your way to?" she asked.

"Lunch. But I heard the music. I wanted to check it out." With a knowing smile, he removed the CD from the player and took a look at it. "I love Dave Koz. *Saxophonic*. Correct?"

Surprise lit up her eyes. "Correct. Now I have a question. How does a guy who should be listening to Jay-Z and Eve know about Dave Koz?"

"One good question deserves another. What do you know about Jay-Z or Eve?"

She giggled. The wickedly enticing sound danced along his skin like a caress. "You can't work at a high school and not know the latest artists."

"True." Mike flipped the CD over in his hands. "I'm not denying that I listen to Jay-Z or Eve, but I was raised by my grandparents and jazz was definitely part of our lifestyle."

"Grandparents? Wait a minute, I vaguely remember seeing a young woman pick you up from school the day DeMarcus got in trouble. Wasn't that your mother?"

"Nah. That was our neighbor."

Jordan perched on the edge of her desk. "What about your parents?"

"Mom died from congestive heart disease when I was eight. A year later, my pop died during a rescue in an abandoned building. He was a fireman."

"Oh, I'm sorry," she said, rubbing her hand up and down his arm.

Mike smiled. He appreciated her sympathy, but he didn't need it. He was well past the grieving process. "Don't be. It all happened a long time ago. What about you? Do you have any family here?"

"No. My parents migrated to Arizona about eight years ago. I was tempted to follow, but Detroit is my home."

Mike nodded and then asked, "Siblings?"

"One. A sister, Joi. She lives in Tucson. That's why my parents moved that way. She has twin boys and needed some help."

"That's nice that they went out there to be with her."

"Joi's alone. Her husband had a stroke and died a few years ago. She needed the support and my parents were ready to retire and leave the city."

"That's tough for a woman with children."

"Yes, it is." She glanced at him with curiosity in her eyes. "So your grandparents taught you about jazz?"

"Granny Beth and Grandpa Roy loved Coltrane, Ellington, and Dinah Washington. That's what played at our house. When I switched on rap, they almost went into a dead faint, then tried to reeducate me to the finer points of jazz."

Jordan's face lit up and she laughed. "You are funny."

Mike leaned back and grinned, taking pleasure in being near Jordan. He loved seeing her smile. That single dimple fascinated and drove him crazy in equal portions. Seeing her so open and without the caution that controlled every word she uttered was a treat. It felt good to see her happy, if only for a few minutes. Her smile chased away the demons he sometimes noticed in her eyes. Sometimes he saw shadows and deep emotional pain behind the mask she wore.

"It was pretty cool. We would have these cultural exchanges of information. They'd listen to my music and then they expected me to listen to theirs." An image of Grandpa Roy's record collection sprang to Mike's mind. "I still have most of their albums."

"They take up a lot of space?"

"I live in a huge house in Indian Village. Heck, the place has seven bedrooms," he muttered, visualizing Jordan firmly planted in his home.

"It must be wonderful to have that much space available to you."

"I found it difficult at first. The house seemed too big. Plus, I'd never lived alone. After all, it was my grandparents' home. At one point, I had a couple of buddies move in with me. It didn't work out. Now I live alone and enjoy my Coltrane, Ellington, and Dinah Washington whenever the mood strikes me, plus OutKast."

"Good for you."

He shrugged. "What about you? Do you live in the city?"

Jordan nodded. "I have an apartment in Rosedale Park."

"That's a nice area." His brows wrinkled. "I didn't think there were any apartments in Rosedale Park."

"Very few. I found one that maintains its classical charm. I've lived there for a few years and I don't think I'll be moving any time soon."

"No hankering for your own home?"

She scrunched up her nose. "Not by myself. It's too much work and responsibility for me."

Since Jordan seemed so receptive, maybe he'd push a little further and see what happens. "Since I'm here, why don't we finish up your room, and then grab some lunch."

"Lunch?"

"Consider this part of the grand tour. It's time for you to sample the local cuisine. Besides, I don't like to eat alone. I do enough of that at home. Turnabout is fair play. I help you, then you have lunch with me."

"I guess I don't have a choice. I can't have you eating alone," she teased. "I mean, it would be bad for your digestive system."

"You're right about that. What do we need to do?" He waved a hand around the room.

Jordan dragged a stepladder from the closet. He rushed to her side and removed it from her hands. She pointed at a spot above the window. "I want to paint a border, and then I'll add the posters from my desk."

Mike studied the spot. "Let's get this done. Where's the paint?"

Jordan strolled down the dark, near-empty corridor of Pierson High School to her classroom. She drew in a deep breath, inhaling the odor of pine cleaner and floor wax. An hour from now everything would change. The chatter of students, hustle and bustle of teachers making their way to their rooms, and staff members patrolling the hallways would light up the building, bringing the school to life.

She stopped outside room 15, unlocked the door, stepped inside, and switched on the lights. Reaching for her fragile control, Jordan leaned against the door, shut her eyes, and breathed deeply, combating the tight knot of anxiety that so often took possession of her body.

Different school, different students, maybe she'd find a spark of interest in her pupils. Maybe at Pierson High School she could make a difference.

Showing more determination than she felt, Jordan straightened her navy blue jacket and smoothed the wrinkles from her matching skirt. She tapped the On button for her CD player, adjusting the volume. Instantly, the violin strings of classical music filled the air, calming her frayed nerves.

She marched across the room. Her face scrunched up and her lips pursed. There was something on her desk. A long stem, yellow rose waited. *Who sent this?* she wondered, reaching for the note tucked under the flower.

Happy first day at Pierson, Mike, she read, picking up the rose and smelling its sweet fragrance. She stroked her cheek with the soft pedals. *He's such a sweet guy,* she thought. This was so nice. Some young woman would be lucky to have him.

There was a tap on her door and Mike entered from the lab. Dressed in a periwinkle-blue dress shirt, charcoal-gray trousers, and a tie with blue, green, and dove-gray geometric squares, he looked quite handsome.

"Good morning," he muttered in a husky bedroom whisper that sent shivers up and down her spine.

"Hi," she muttered back, confused by her reaction. She lifted the flower. "Thank you."

"You're welcome. Yellow represents friendship and I consider you one of my friends."

"Thank you again. I feel the same way about you. It is a beautiful gesture that makes me feel as if I belong here."

"Of course you belong. But hey, I'm just your mentor. Everyone needs a little encouragement the first few days of school. The students tend to overwhelm us. And administration can be just as bad. Just remember, I'm here." He pointed a finger at the door to the lab. "All you have to do is knock on my door, come and see me, or send a student."

"I will. I really appreciate the support."

"That's my job." Mike sauntered across the room and picked up a stack of papers with green lines from her desk. Scanning the pages, he said, "Uh-oh."

Jordan's brow furrowed over her brown eyes. "What?"

"You've got Paradise Simpson and Erin Hill in your first-hour chemistry class. Those two were in my biology class last year." He blew out a hot puff of air. "It can be a challenge to maintain control with those two in your class. Paradise and Erin are a handful when they're together."

"Oh, really?" She felt some of her good cheer drain away. She didn't expect every student to be perfect, but two outrageous kids in one class could really destroy the atmosphere of learning.

He nodded. "Yeah. They're best friends and clown around together. Don't let that fool you. They can be really cruel sometimes. Last year, we had a new student, Kira Scott. Paradise and Erin teased her unmercifully. Kira's parents were at Pierson all the time. Two suspensions didn't slow them down. But those Saturday detentions did the trick. They finally left Kira alone."

Jordan said, "Shades of DeMarcus."

"You've got it," he agreed. "I was really surprised to learn that she's coming back this year. Be careful. Paradise and Erin are pros at double-teaming a teacher."

Jordan nodded, taking note of his comment, putting those names in her memory bank for future reference. Some students always required delicate handling. The sooner she identified the troublemakers, the sooner she could settle them down, or get them out of her class. "What do they look like?"

"Both are cute. Short. Paradise wears glasses and Erin is the more aggressive of the two. Along with being the big mouth, Erin is also the oldest of the pair. At eighteen, she terrorizes the younger students. I heard somewhere that she got kicked out of her last school because she beat another student with a brick. She's on probation."

"Sweet kid."

"Yeah. Erin has some anger management issues. But she is really quite bright. If you can get her focused on her work, she can be fun to have in a class. The important phrase here is focused on her work."

"Oh mentor man," she teased with a smile on her lips and a bow of her head, "how do you suggest I handle the dynamic duo?"

He chuckled. The rich sound drew her closer to him. "Separate them. No doubt about it. Put Erin right in front of your desk. You need to keep an eye on her." He pointed at her desk. "Then park Paradise in the back of the classroom as far away from Erin as possible. That's the only way you're going to maintain control in your class."

Jordan's gaze swept the room, mentally placing Paradise and Erin at the suggested locations. Nodding, she decided to give Mike's suggestion a try if the young ladies got out of hand.

Mike rested a hand on Jordan's shoulder. She drank in the comfort of his nearness. "I meant to mention this yesterday, but we were so busy with our rooms that I forgot. If any student gets to be too much, you can give them a time-out by sending them to me and vice versa. That way you defuse the situation and keep the rest of the class on task."

"That's a good idea. If they get out of hand, I think I'll use it."

Mike asked with a trace of concern in his voice, "Are you ready?"

"No."

"Yes, you are." He placed a hand on her shoulder and squeezed. "You'll do fine."

Jordan offered him a tiny, uncertain smile. Her insecurities crept into her tone as she said, "I hope you're right."

"Just remember, I'm next door and the staff is behind you. Send any problem kids to the dean of student discipline, Jefferson Thurman. He'll handle things. That's his job."

"Will do," she said. "Thanks for the heads-up."

"Do you need anything from me before I go back to my room?"

"No." Jordan shook her head. "I think I've got everything."

He secured the tie at his throat. "Let's do our thing. Hey, why don't we go to lunch? If you need anything, we'll be able to discuss it then and get the problems solved ASAP."

Jordan hesitated for a moment, gnawing on the corner of her lip. She didn't want the school gossip mill to start talking about them, linking them together romantically, but Mike had a perfectly legitimate reason to get together.

"Sounds good to me," she answered.

Mike took her hand and stared into her eyes. The chemistry between them crackled. The slight connection zipped through her, causing every nerve to tingle.

He appeared equally moved by their shared moment. Clearing his throat, he dropped her hand and slipped through the lab door.

Jordan sighed contentedly. Once this first week of classes ended, she'd make every effort to keep some distance between them. *He's too young and too appealing for someone like me,* she thought, mentally preparing herself for the day ahead.

Chapter 4

Jordan stood outside her classroom, monitoring the hall traffic. The first bell rang and the students sprang into action, taking off in every direction. Five minutes later the tardy bell signaled the start of first period.

She followed the stragglers into the room, shut the door, and turned to her first-hour class. The school day and year had officially begun.

Jordan drew in a deep breath, gnawing on the corner of her bottom lip. Mindful of Mike's warning, she took a moment to examine her class.

Erin and Paradise were easily identifiable. The dynamic duo had sauntered into the classroom with their arms linked, strutting across the floor as if they owned the building. The pair were dressed in the teenager uniform of tight slacks or jeans, petite breast-hugging tops, and expensive name-brand sneakers. Both stood barely over five feet. One had an angelic, heart-shaped face with walnut-colored skin. Dark brown bobbed hair framed her face. *You must be Erin,* Jordan realized.

Jordan remembered Mike's comment regarding Paradise, noting the fashionable black-rimmed glasses that added maturity to her youthful round face and caramel-colored skin. She wore her sandy-brown hair in a ponytail that swung from the crown of her head.

Each girl teased and insulted their classmates as they headed to the back of the room. Paradise snatched a cap off a young lady's head. She tossed the cap to Erin, starting a game of "give me back my cap." After several moments of running between desks, the girl gave up and returned to her seat.

Jordan sighed deeply. They were going to be a handful. "Give it to me."

Erin strolled to the front of the classroom and presented the cap to Jordan as if it were a trophy.

Jordan moved down the aisle and halted next to the student that had lost her cap. "What's your name?"

"Kira Scott."

Nodding, Jordan returned the cap. Poor thing. It looked as if Erin and Paradise were planning to pick up where they had left off the previous school year. *Not in my classroom,* Jordan promised silently. She didn't want another DeMarcus situation.

Whether she liked them or not, they were her students and she had to make the best of this situation. Maybe she could soothe the savage beast with music. Jordan strolled to her desk and turned up the volume on the CD player. The soft violin strings of the Detroit Symphony Orchestra circulated throughout the room.

"Everybody find a seat," she stated in her most authoritarian voice. "After we get through the attendance, we can discuss my class requirements."

Silently waiting for her students to settle down, she grabbed the class roster and moved around the edge of her desk to stand in front of her pupils.

"I'm Ms. Anderson. This semester you'll be learning the fundamentals of chemistry."

Heavy sighs, moans, and groans followed this announcement. Jordan waited a moment longer for them to settle down. She cleared her throat and casually strolled between the rows of desks.

With a knowing chuckle, Jordan said, "Come on, people. You made it to room fifteen, so I'm pretty sure chemistry didn't magically appear on your schedule this morning. But I'm certain it wasn't a surprise that you have to take it."

A few appreciative chuckles followed her statement, but the general consensus stayed the same.

Nervous, Jordan ran a hand over the front of her jacket. "Let's make the best of this school year," she suggested, scanning the class list. "I'll try to make this as interesting as I can and you can try to learn it. I think that's a fair trade."

There was a knock on the door. A young man entered the classroom with a basketball tucked under one arm and his backpack tossed over the opposite shoulder.

"You're late," Jordan said.

"I'm sorry." He strolled across the room and handed her a pass. "Mr. Bartholomew had me in his office. He screwed up my schedule."

Nodding, Jordan took the pass and glanced at it. "Take a seat."

"Hey, babe, back here." Paradise waved a hand in the air. The young man broke into a trot, bouncing the basketball.

"Jarell." Jordan waited until he stopped and faced her. "Put the ball away or it's mine."

"Okay, Ms. Anderson, I'm gonna put it away," Jarell answered, bouncing the ball once more. Jordan held out her hand. The boy muttered under his breath, but returned to the front of the class and handed it over.

"I'm sorry. I didn't mean to do it. My reflexes kicked in," he explained.

"That's not fair," Paradise snapped, jumping to her feet. "That's his ball!"

"Life isn't fair," Jordan countered, holding the younger girl's gaze. "Besides, this conversation is between Jarell and me."

"He paid for that ball," Erin added loudly.

With a grin, Jordan said, "And the boy's home I'll give it to will greatly appreciate Jarell's kind gift."

Paradise shook her head. "No, no. That ain't right."

"It's one of the rules for my class."

"This is lame. You wrong, Ms. Anderson."

"Actually, you're wrong," Jordan said, meeting Jarell in the center of the aisle. "This is a schoolwide rule. No basketballs outside the gym. You should not have had it outside your backpack."

Maybe she should cut this guy a bit of slack and put an end to this useless debate. They had more important matters to discuss. Besides, Jordan didn't want to start the school year off with a lot of unnecessary animosity between herself and her students.

"This is the first day of school and first period. I'm sure no one has gone over the rules with you. So I'm going to give you a break this time. Don't let me have to remind you again," Jordan warned, returning the ball to its owner.

"Thank you, Ms. Anderson," Jarell muttered, stuffing the ball into his book bag.

"You're welcome. Now let's get back to chemistry."

Erin raised her hand and asked in a tone laden with attitude, "What's that noise?"

Annoyed, Jordan maintained her professional facade with hard-won effort. *Erin's trying to get to me. Calm down,* she thought. "That's not noise. It's classical music. The Detroit Symphony Orchestra to be exact."

Erin shrugged and scrunched up her face as if she'd

smelled something unpleasant. "Do we have to listen to it? I mean, it's so lame."

"Which means what?" Jordan asked.

Erin shrugged. "Not popular or cool."

Jordan nodded, moving among the rows of desks. "Well, it's on because it helps with the creative process."

"Whatever," Erin muttered, flipping her hand in the air.

"It's been documented that listening to classical music enhances the thinking process." Jordan's voice lacked the necessary authority needed to control her class as she returned to the front of the classroom. "I figured it couldn't hurt."

"It's not fair."

"How so?"

"This is *our* class. Why should you get to choose the music?"

"People, this isn't a democracy. It's a dictatorship. And I'm the dictator. I'm the queen in this classroom," Jordan responded softly, tapping a red marker in the palm of her hand. "My CD player and my CDs. We do things *my* way."

A roar of disapproving voices verbally knocked the wind from her. She flinched at the tone of their voices.

"We're the ones that have to listen to it."

"Why can't we listen to Jay-Z? How about Kelis?"

"I want to hear OutKast."

Her students' demanding tones pushed Jordan over the edge. Suddenly, she felt cold and hot all at once. A thin layer of perspiration coated her back, making the lining of her jacket stick to her skin. She glanced at the marker in her hand, surprised to find her hands were trembling.

Jordan gazed out the window, reaching for control. Short gasps of air burned her lungs as she frantically worked to regain her illusive calm. *This has got to stop. I'll never get through the year at this rate.*

A student squealed, "Ms. Anderson, Ms. Anderson. Are you going to cry?"

Lost, Jordan scanned her desk and fixed her gaze on the rose. The stress eased as she focused on the yellow flower. *Mike believes I can do this and I can,* she realized, turning back to the expectant faces of her students.

"I'm fine," Jordan answered, regaining her equilibrium. "We need to get back to my class rules. Okay, folks. No OutKast. No Eve or Jay-Z. This isn't a negotiating point."

Groans and moans filled her room.

"Sorry, kiddos. This is my classroom and we're here to learn chemistry. And incidentally, I play what I believe is appropriate. For now, I'm going to play classical music."

Omega's Coney Island was one busy restaurant. It catered to the teaching staff of Pierson and all the businesses along the Detroit-Southfield border.

Single patrons lined the counter, eating lunch, reading newspapers or books. Servers dressed in white polo shirts and black skirts hurried from booths to tables, taking and delivering orders.

Jordan followed Mike through the eatery to an available booth. She slid onto the beige vinyl bench, placing her purse on the empty space at her side. Mike handed her a colorful laminated menu.

"Thanks." She glanced at her watch. "Are you sure we'll be able to get back to Pierson in thirty minutes?"

"Don't worry about it. You're one of the lucky ones. Your prep period follows your lunch. That gives you a total of ninety minutes."

"I don't want to make a habit of using my prep period this way. But for today, it works." She opened the menu, perusing the restaurant's offerings. "What do you recommend?"

He opened the one in front of him, scanning its enticing pages. "They have great salads. Greek, cobb, and antipasto are the best. I got your chicken salad sandwich last week from Omega's."

Nodding, she closed the menu and returned it to the metal holder sitting on the table. "I want a cheeseburger and fries."

After the server took their orders, Mike leaned back in his chair. "So, how did your morning go?"

She sighed, massaging her forehead. "Rough."

"How so?" He reached across the table and gave her hand a sympathetic squeeze.

"You were right. Paradise and Erin are a handful." Jordan ran her fingers through her wavy hair. "I don't think I handled them very well. Actually, I think I acted sort of stupid."

Mike's hand rested on top of hers. "Jordan, it's the first day of school and this is your first semester at Pierson. Cut yourself some slack. The kids are going to test you. You know this. Give yourself time. It'll all smooth out."

"I hope you're right, because I'm feeling really slow today. I let them get to me." She studied their linked hands, feeling comfort in Mike's reassuring touch mixed with a surge of excitement.

"Hey, stop beating yourself up. It's a new school, different students. It'll take a while to get used to Pierson and the kids."

"Maybe you're right." Jordan drew in a deep breath of cleansing air.

Silently, Mike studied her. "There's more, isn't there?"

Jordan nodded.

"You want to talk about it?"

"I don't want to play true confession." Her voice wobbled. "It makes me feel like I can't handle my life."

Mike smiled sympathetically. "Don't worry about that. We're friends. You can tell me anything."

"I have panic attacks," Jordan admitted.

"Why? What happened?"

She fiddled with her silverware, wiping it clean with her napkin, then moving the fork from one side of the table to the other. "One of the parents at my last school attacked me."

His alarmed gaze slid over her, searching for residual injuries. "Attacked?" Mike prompted softly.

"He broke my wrist. Gave me a black eye."

Mike looked at her arm, taking note of the inch-long incision at the base of her wrist. He stretched out a hand, running a light finger across the slightly raised ridge. "I'm sorry," he whispered in a voice laced with sympathy. "That should never have happened."

"No, it shouldn't."

"But?"

"It did. And since then I've had trouble returning to a classroom."

"I'm sorry."

Ashamed, Jordan focused on the window, studying the traffic. "You didn't do anything."

"I know. But you shouldn't have to deal with idiots like that. What happened?"

"He cornered me in my room one day after school. I couldn't get away." She shut her eyes, experiencing all the fear and pain a second time. "He kept shouting, what was wrong with me? Didn't I realize that his daughter deserved an A? How did I expect her to get into college with grades like this?"

"Did she deserve a better grade?"

Jordan shook her head sadly. "The D-minus I gave her was a gift. She refused to do any of the work."

"Ouch."

"Yeah. The bone pierced my skin, so I had to have surgery and I was off work for six weeks. I couldn't make myself go back. I got out of the rest of the school year on stress leave."

"What did you do this summer?"

"Tried to pull myself together for this semester. Fight the attacks. I thought I had them beat until today."

"It sounds like such a difficult time. I feel bad that you suffered through that alone. Things will get better for you. Trust me on that. I have faith in you. I've seen you stare down the barrel of a gun and come out on top." He smiled at her. "A few rowdy students won't keep you down, at least not for long."

"They did today. They beat me down," she whispered in a tiny voice.

"Today is half over. You've got the full afternoon to get back on track. Remember, they are still just kids, don't let them push your buttons."

"How am I supposed to prevent it from happening?"

Mike reached across the table and covered her hand. "Well, the next time focus on a pleasant memory or something fun, then refocus on your class. That'll get you over the hump. Can you do that for me?"

When Mike spoke to her like that, showing such compassion for her needs, she believed she could do anything he asked.

"I did it today," Jordan admitted.

"How?"

"I focused on the rose you gave me. When I got upset, it gave me the strength to keep going."

"There you are. Something to focus your energy on." He held her gaze with his own. "Promise me that you'll try."

The concern in his eyes reached her and before she realized what was happening, she nodded. "I will."

He patted her hand. "Good."

The server pushed plates of hot food in front of them.

"Let's eat," Mike suggested, plucking a French fry from her plate and biting into it.

Giggling, Jordan nodded, turning her attention to the meal in front of her.

Chapter 5

Relieved, Jordan sighed, watching the last student grab his book bag and hustle out of the classroom. The first school day had ended and she'd survived. Granted, there had been a few scary and unsettling moments, like the panic attack she experienced during her first period. If she put that incident aside, Jordan felt as if she'd recovered and gotten back into the swing of teaching and running a class.

She glanced at the white clock hanging from the wall at the front of her classroom, calculating the amount of time left to her. The first faculty meeting of the school year began at 3:30. That left her exactly twenty minutes to clean her room, organize her desk and get to room 1.

With long, purposeful strides, she moved between the rows of desks, checking for student valuables that might have been left behind. No items were revealed, so she returned to her desk to sort through her notes and glance through her students' suggestions for experiments they'd like to conduct.

Mike entered the room after knocking on the door.

"Hey," he muttered in that husky voice that she automatically responded to.

"Hey, yourself," she answered, reading what her third period believed were chemicals found in some of the food they consumed. "What's up? Are you my personal escort to the staff meeting?"

"Nah. You're a grown woman. I think you can find your way down the hall. If you can make it through your first day of classes, the rest is easy," Mike teased, smoothing his tie into place.

His gaze slid over her, touching all those feminine spots. A sharp sensuous current passed between them. He rubbed a hand up and down her arm, sending a wave of sensations through her limb. "I didn't get a chance to drop by and see how you were. How did the rest of the day go for you? Any more attacks?"

Embarrassed by her lunchtime confession, Jordan ducked her head. Heat surged into her cheeks. "I did fine."

"Good. Were there any students we need to talk about?" He perched on the edge of her desk, stretching his long legs in front of him. "Do you have questions that you'd like to ask?"

Jordan pursed her lips, doing a mental shuffle through her day. She smiled, feeling a sense of accomplishment as she realized that this day hadn't been any different from any other school day she'd survived.

"Classes went much better after my first period. Don't get me wrong, they weren't beating down the door to learn about the periodic table and chemical compounds, but they weren't rude. A couple of kids tried to disrupt the class, but I shut them down pretty easily. I think I'm getting the hang of this teaching thing again. The rest will come."

"It will," Mike encouraged, watching Jordan. "Just give it some time."

Sorting her student profile sheets and class work into separate piles, Jordan eyed Mike. The mischievous twist to his lips hinted at something more. "Okay, you. What's going on? What's on your mind?"

"Nothing," he answered like a little boy ready to explode with a secret he promised not to tell.

"Right." She emphasized the word, folding her arms across her chest. In her best teacher's voice, she said, "Michael Walker, tell me another one. You've got the same expression on your face that I saw hundreds of times when you were my student. I can read you like a book."

"Maybe so. But I'm an adult now."

His declaration hung in the air.

Yes, you are. And a handsome one at that, Jordan agreed silently, deliberately keeping her eyes on his face when she desperately wanted to take another look at the hard, sculpted body that was still evident under his dress shirt.

Mike cleared his throat and ran a hand over his hair. "I thought about what you said at lunch. How you focused on the rose when you had that panic attack."

She peered at his face. He almost looked sheepish. Stains of scarlet colored his cheeks. *What's going on here?* she wondered.

"I've been thinking of ways to help you. Give you a boost when things get a little hairy. And then I thought of this." He revealed a green stuffed animal from behind his back. "This is Sarah."

Jordan glanced at the toy and laughed out loud. Sarah, the T-Rex, wore a white T-shirt and a blue-and-white-checked shirt. *Girls Just Want to Have Fun* appeared on the front of the T-shirt in bold red letters.

"I had my appendix removed during my freshman year of college and my grandparents bought Sarah."

Jordan's eyebrows rose inquiringly.

"Don't ask. Let's say my grandpa Roy got a little confused and picked up the wrong gift. It became a family joke that we all enjoyed." He shrugged. "Any-hoo, I thought of you and I want you to put Sarah on your desk in a place of honor. Whenever you feel blue or a panic attack makes you doubt your abilities, step back from the situation with a glance at Sarah and refocus."

Touched by Mike's kindness, Jordan knew that she must refuse the toy. Strong sentimental values were connected to it and it wouldn't be fair for her to take it. "Oh, Mike, this is so sweet of you. But I can't take it. I mean, your grandparents gave it to you."

"First of all, I didn't say that I'm giving it to you."

Jordan blushed. "Sorry."

"No problem," he said with a wave of his hand. "This is a loan until you become one hundred percent. And I expect to get Sarah back in the same condition that you received her. Understood?" he chastised, pointing a finger at her. He destroyed the severity of his admonishment with a broad grin.

"Yes, sir," she answered in a mock meek tone.

"Good. Now, let's find the perfect place for Sarah." He rearranged her desk so that he could position Sarah. "She needs a spot where you can see her at all times."

After trying several locations, he decided the place of honor would be between the stapler and the tape dispenser. He patted Sarah on the head and said, "You be good for Ms. Anderson. She needs a little encouragement to help her over the rough periods and I know you can do it."

Jordan laughed for the first time that day. Unconsciously, she slipped her hand through the crook of his arm and steered him toward the entrance. Her hand dropped away as he reached for the doorknob. "Thank you. I really appreciate it. Come on, you. We have a staff meeting to attend."

"No problem," Mike answered, placing his hand over hers. "That's what mentors do." He glanced at his watch. "We've got about five minutes. I've got to lock up my room. I'll see you at the meeting." With a wave of his hand, he slipped out of the room.

Jordan entered room 1 quietly and found a chair at a table near the back of the room. She leaned her elbows on the tabletop.

Principal Chet Bartholomew addressed his team of teachers with the ease of someone that had done so for many years. He had the expertise of a well-established orator. His fingers stroked the mustache curling over his upper lip as he touched on the important agenda items.

Chet stood a smidgen under six feet tall. His jovial manner and body weight were more in line with Santa Claus than a high school principal. Unlike St. Nick's flowing white hair, a fine thatch of reddish brown peach fuzz covered his head as he peered at the staff through gold-rimmed square-framed glasses.

His portly frame stood at the podium. "This year . . ." He paused. "Pierson will be taking a different approach to extracurricular activities and programs. Instead of a sign-up list, I've taken the liberty of assigning each teacher an activity related to their program area of expertise."

Mike snuck into the room and snagged a copy of the agenda from the table at the rear of the room. He scooted into a chair next to Jordan, twisted off the cap of his Gatorade, and took a long swig. His unique scent wafted under her nose, intensifying her awareness of him.

Leaning close to Mike, Jordan whispered, "What extracurricular activities?"

"He's talking about after-school programs like chess clubs, cheerleading, baseball in the spring, and stuff like that. Normally, he takes volunteers. This is new."

Jordan's eyebrows rose. She didn't like the direction things were going. What if she got stuck with a program that didn't fit into what she knew? Did she have a choice? Was she allowed to reject the activity and get something else?

"Take a look at the list." Chet continued his monologue, drifting through the aisle of desks, handing copies of his list to the staff. "If you have a problem with your assignment, try to swap with someone. Otherwise, consider this as the gospel according to Bartholomew." He flicked his tongue across his thumb and separated two stubborn sheets of paper, continuing to distribute the list among the instructors.

Jordan glanced down at the typed sheet in her hands, and her eyes widened and her heart dropped. Cheerleading? Chet must be crazy! She taught science, not phys ed.

Chet rolled the remaining sheets into a tube, then strolled up and down the row of desks. "I expect you guys to start preparing for the program as soon as possible. Activities should be up and running before the end of the month." He slapped the tube of paper against his leg. "If you need help, contact the teacher that ran the program last year and see how that person arranged the activity. We have kids who need something to do after school. I don't want them aimlessly wandering the building. They get in trouble without something structured to keep them occupied."

Jordan studied her colleagues, searching for a willing soul to take this cheerleading project off her hands. No one met her gaze and she had the distinct impression that no one wanted this job.

"One final point," Chet said. "We practice energy conservation at Pierson. At the end of the day make sure all equipment is shut off and that your doors and windows are locked. Remember, kids will be kids. An unlocked, unsupervised room is a place for something unfortunate to happen."

"I'm done with my agenda." Chet threw his hands in a wide arch. "Is there anything else that we need to discuss before we conclude this meeting? Is there anything else for the good of the order?" He waited for a moment, waved at the teaching staff, and headed for the door. "Good-bye. We'll see you tomorrow."

Jordan rose from her chair, weaving her way through the aisles. She wanted to talk with Chet. The extraordinarily long line made it obvious that others were unhappy with their assignments.

When her turn came, she pointed at the list. "Chet, cheerleading is not my strong suit. Is there something else you can assign me to that will be a better match and use of my skills?"

"Jordan, last year Debbie coached the team. Now that she's department head, she doesn't have the time to take on this activity." The principal blew out a hot puff of air and drew an arm around her. She felt as if she had been swept up by a politician, trying to sway her vote with double talk. "Plus, Mike is your mentor. He's the coach for the basketball team. You'll be working together once the basketball season starts. It seemed like the correct mix. He can help you and you can help him."

"But . . . but," Jordan stammered, mentally scrabbling for the right words to explain her dilemma.

"You and Mike will be partnered. Plus, you'll be cochairing the Science Olympiad. I figured you would have new ideas about how we can win this program. To tell you the truth, I'd really like to see us display a trophy in the main corridor." He patted her shoulder reassuringly. "It's going to be fine."

Oh yeah, definitely a politician. He had the demeanor and persuasive air of the best George W. Bush impersonator.

Chapter 6

Two weeks later, Jordan waited for her cheerleaders to appear for the season's first meeting. She scratched her ear, wondering for the hundredth time why she'd stopped protesting about being assigned to this particular after-school activity.

Standing at the gym's double doors, she waited with a boom box clutched in her right hand and a gym bag in the left. Dressed in purple leggings, a silver short-sleeved T-shirt, and white socks and running shoes, Jordan worried about conquering the intricate details of coaching the cheerleading squad.

A yell of victory snagged Jordan's attention and she glanced inside the gym to find the basketball team moving to the far side of the gym. After a great deal of discussion and compromise, she and Mike had agreed to a schedule for practices in the gym.

The basketball team used the facility daily, but her cheerleaders needed a workout three days per week. On the days when they both required practice time, a designated portion of the facility would be available for Jordan's squad, while Mike's basketball team used the hoop and floor on the opposite end of the court.

Although she'd requested a different assignment, Chet refused to listen to her appeal or make any changes to his schedule. With no alternative, she'd taken the initiative and boned up on everything available regarding cheerleading, making herself an informed instructor, ready to lead this team.

Her gaze landed on Erin, Paradise, and Desiree as they sauntered down the hall. *Oh no,* Jordan cried silently as the first wave of panic hit her like a punch to the gut. She almost doubled over when her stomach muscles tightened painfully. *Please let the dynamic duo plus one be on the way out of the building. I don't want them on the squad.*

No such luck. They strolled past Jordan, entered the gym, and crossed the floor.

Her hands trembled as heat flooded her body while perspiration dotted her forehead and cheeks. She leaned against the cool wall for support, drawing air deep into her lungs.

If she didn't make an effort to take control, the panic attacks would consume her and leave her with nothing. Fighting the edge of hysteria, Jordan pulled herself together, muttering, "This is not going to happen today." With superhuman resolve, she shook off the panic twisting every nerve ending, beat down her feeling of helplessness, and gained control. Still a bit shaky, but recovering, Jordan pushed away from the wall.

With renewed determination, she strolled across the polished wood floor and paused in front of her team. She cleared her throat, waiting for the students to quiet down and give her their full attention. After a moment, the group calmed and focused on Jordan.

She fixed her gaze on each girl for a beat, evaluating her strengths and weaknesses. A motley crew sat before her.

"Okay, ladies. Let's get started. I'm Ms. Anderson and I'll be your cheerleading coach this year." Jordan opened her gym bag and removed a set of multicolored folders. From a red folder she withdrew and passed a group of forms to the twenty-odd young ladies. "This is a permission slip for your parents. We can't allow you to participate on the cheerleading squad without the approval of your parent or legal guardian. Also, you must have a physical on file," she explained in a strong voice. "If you haven't already done so, call your doctor and get it done ASAP."

The ladies grumbled as they reviewed the forms.

"The permission slip and the physical must be on my desk no later than Friday morning. Ladies, I'm in room fifteen. Put it in my mailbox or leave it in the main office. Practice sessions will begin at three-fifteen on Tuesdays, Wednesdays, and Thursdays. After the basketball season begins, we'll cut practice to two days per week, Tuesdays and Wednesdays." She raised her hand, drawing their attention. "By the way, ladies, the school's policy on tardiness applies to this activity. I only want people willing to commit to the team and its rules."

As she felt stronger, Jordan's voice grew more powerful. "Here's my final point. Should your name appear on the ineligibility list, you *cannot*, let me repeat that, *cannot* be on the cheerleading squad. Actually, you're not allowed to participate in any extracurricular activity. If you have three or more failing grades, now is the time to leave, because once I get the list, we're going to have a serious talk."

The students huddled together on the bleachers. They spoke in tones far too low for Jordan to hear the details of their conversation. She suspected whatever their topic, she would end up with a problem.

Desiree raised her hand. "Ms. Anderson?"

Jordan folded her arms across her chest, and her eyebrows rose questioningly. "Yes?"

"We want to know more about you. What's your background?" Desiree stood with the hint of a smirk on her lips. "How did you get this job? Have you ever coached a team before?"

Quickly hiding a smile, Jordan hooked her thumbs into the waistband of her leggings. Anticipating this kind of revolt, she had prepared herself. "Mr. Bartholomew assigned me this project. No, I've never coached a cheerleading team. This will be my first time."

Agitated, Paradise planted her hands on her hips and struck a defiant pose. "Why should we follow you? You don't know any more than we do."

"That's not true. A big part of coaching involves understanding teamwork, being able to support and work with you as a group. My job is to teach groups of students every day. There's very little difference. I can do this," Jordan answered honestly.

With plenty of attitude to go along with her height a young lady with a ponytail stood and added, "How do we know you're the right person to lead us? I mean, you're new to the school and nobody knows what you can do."

Jordan glanced at the young lady perched on the top row of bleachers, taking note of Erin's, Paradise's, and Desiree's wide-mouthed grins.

"Yeah, do you know any cheers or the moves?" shouted a dark-skinned student sitting on the second row.

This mini revolt had the dynamic duo's signature written all over it. They had started the fire, then stepped back to steer clear of the sparks. Jordan expected challenges to her authority and now she needed to squash them.

She tapped a finger against her lips and moved

around the gym. She'd been assigned to lead the team the best way she knew how. If the students were unwilling to accept her as their leader, fine, she'd get a new team. But first, she planned to try to win their trust and salvage this team.

Folding her arms across her chest, Jordan pierced each girl with a steady glare. "I see. What you're trying to say in your indelicate way is that you want me to audition for my job as coach. Am I correct?"

A low rumble of uncomfortable agreement and nodding heads rippled through the ranks. Obviously, she'd found the source of the problem. Well, she had a few surprises for them and she knew the perfect way to start.

"I see your point." Jordan stretched her arms above her head to warm up her muscles. She spread her legs wide and rocked back and forth, loosening up. "Why should you follow the advice of someone who doesn't know what she's doing? Correct?"

Twenty-odd bobbing heads sat before her.

"Okay, let's talk about cheers. How many of you can do splits?" she asked, sliding into a perfect split without breaking into a sweat. She rolled to one side and stood, smoothing the wrinkles from her T-shirt. "Or cartwheels?" Without a word, she spun into a cartwheel, flipped in the air, and landed on her feet in front of the group that now sat openmouthed with shock.

Jordan continued her impromptu audition with a combination of midair flips and turns. She ended her performance in a standing position, arms extended and legs braced for another set of convincing flips. Amid the applause and cheers, she turned to grab her towel and noticed a tall, male figure standing in the coach's open door.

Mike! Her heart danced in her chest.

His arms were folded across his chest and his eyes followed her every movement. Suddenly, a wide grin spread across his face as he gave her the thumbs-up signal.

With a slight dip of her head, she acknowledged him as her pulse quickened. Breathing hard, she stood before her team, waiting for their verdict.

They didn't have a clue how hard she'd worked on learning those moves. Nor did they know that she'd spent several nights per week perfecting the cartwheels and splits. And the thing that she absolutely refused to tell them was how much her body ached after doing all of those stunts to impress them.

After she got home, she planned to soak in a tub of Epsom salt and hot water to soothe her tender and strained muscles. For now, she planned to appear unaffected and in complete control of her body.

"Wow!" exclaimed the student from the upper bleacher. "Ms. Anderson, that was soooo sweet!"

"Yeah!" shouted another girl.

Draping the towel around her shoulders, she felt it absorbing the perspiration glittering on her brown skin. She watched the stunned but admiring expressions on the team members' faces. Eyebrows curved over her questioning eyes, she asked in a smug tone, "Did I pass?"

Applause and cat whistles followed. Several young ladies gave her a standing ovation. Her eyes landed on Erin and Paradise. Jordan wanted to laugh, but restrained herself in front of the team. The dynamic duo's sour expressions illustrated how unacceptable they found this turn of events. Dismissing them, Jordan concentrated on the other members of the team. What they felt did matter. Jordan had proven herself to be a knowledgeable leader.

Smiling at her team, she tossed the towel aside and said, "Okay, ladies, let's get started."

A couple of hours later, Jordan stood at the entrance to the gym, a damp towel wrapped around her neck. After her demonstration, practice ran smoothly. By revealing her knowledge and skills, she'd gained the respect and trust she needed to lead this team.

Paradise and Erin were different. They weren't ready to surrender. The duo needed a little extra time to make the adjustment. Jordan didn't have any problems with that. Eventually they would adjust if they planned to remain on the team.

"Ladies, we'll meet again on Wednesday. Don't forget to bring your permission slips, your physicals, and some loose-fitting, comfortable clothes for our workout. Your Britney Spears wear is not going to work for cheerleading practice."

The tall student with the ponytail stopped in front of her. "Ms. Anderson, I'm really glad you're our coach."

"Thanks, Tia."

"I think this is going to be our best year."

"I hope so. I'm going to do everything I can to make that happen. I'll do my best and I expect the same from you."

"You'll get it," Tia promised.

Jordan's voice rose above the chatter of the team members to make another announcement. "Don't forget, if you are on the ineligibility list, please don't come to practice. I'd hate to have to ask you to leave. It embarrasses me and you. So let's avoid that."

After the last student disappeared out of the main entrance, she returned to the gym for her things. Exhausted, Jordan shoved her belongings into her gym bag, doing a mental check of her refrigerator at home, searching for something for dinner. A soft touch at her elbow got her attention.

Mike grinned down at her. Dressed in a pair of faded wide-leg jeans, a black silk shirt, and a pair of white Air Force One sneakers, he looked gorgeous. In contrast, she felt grimy and sweaty.

"Your moves looked pretty good." He winked at her, then added, in a tone filled with admiration, "For a woman who claimed she didn't know anything about directing a cheerleading team."

"Thanks. I've been working on those moves since the staff meeting." Jordan pushed a strand of hair behind her ear, warmed by the compliment. "Don't tell the team, but every muscle in my body is protesting."

Chuckling, Mike scooped up her bag and slung it over his shoulder. "You looked terrific. I'm proud of you. Even the dynamic duo failed to find an unkind word to say. Although I'm sure they worked hard on that. You gave the pair a surprise they weren't expecting. Shutting them down is a major accomplishment."

"Yeah. I liked that part," she admitted, bumping against him playfully. "When they stepped into the gym, I panicked," she confessed, glancing around to make certain that no one heard her. "I wanted to run in the opposite direction and let somebody, anybody else deal with those two."

Mike placed a hand on her shoulder and squeezed. "But you didn't. You fought back and regained your composure and the team's respect. Be proud of that. That took a lot of courage."

"I am. I just wish the panic attacks would stop," she confided, embarrassed by her lack of control. "For a minute there, I didn't think I'd be able to make it through the practice."

"Give it time, Jordan. Don't beat yourself up if you have a slight relapse. You're doing everything right. Two weeks ago you didn't think you were going to finish your first day of classes. Now you're in control and coaching the cheerleaders. It's all coming together." He picked up the boom box and they started toward the door. "What do you have planned this evening? How about dinner?"

Halting, she echoed, "Dinner?"

"Yeah. You know, food? Generally the last meal of the day. Dinner."

"Thanks, but no, thanks. I'm tired." She reached for the boom box. "A nice hot bath is calling me."

"Come on." He squeezed her shoulder, sending her skittish pulse racing. "Dinner will relax you, then you can go home to your hot bath."

She stopped in the middle of the gym and turned to face him. "Mike, you don't have to buy me a meal. I'm fine. Besides, you feed me lunch every Friday."

He shifted the boom box to his left hand and cupped her elbow with the right, guiding her across the wood floor. "I'm your mentor and we haven't talked this week. It's my job to find out how things are going for you and help in any way I can. It's been a long day for you and me and I'm ready for a meal. And as I've told you in the past, I hate eating alone."

An unidentifiable element in Mike's voice made her hesitate. This felt more like a date request than two colleagues getting together to discuss work.

Before she could explain how it happened, Mike had maneuvered her into the parking lot. They stood next to a late-model midnight-colored Mustang convertible. He removed a remote from his pocket and popped the locks. A second later, the car gave off a soft chirp and the engine roared to life. Mike ran around the back of the car and stored her gym bag and boom box.

"Wait," she cried, hurrying around the car to stop him. The trunk closed with a decisive snap and he glanced at her.

"What?" he questioned innocently.

Pointing at the trunk, she said, "Mike, my stuff."

He took her arm and guided her to the passenger's door. "Come on. Dinner. Talk. After we're done, you can go home and feed your cats."

Her eyes narrowed and her temper flared. Was he implying that she acted like an old maid that raced home each evening to be with her pets? "I don't have animals. And I resent your placing me in that category."

Surrendering with a lifted hand, Mike apologized, "Whoa! My bad. I didn't mean to offend." He didn't seem sorry at all. In fact, he opened the door and propelled her forward. "Just teasing, honestly."

"I don't appreciate the implication."

He took her hand and kissed the palm, gazing at her with big brown eyes that begged her to forgive him. "I'm sorry. Forgive me?"

Shaking her head, Jordan laughed out loud. Mike was such a character. "Sure. Okay. But I have to go."

"Jordan, unless you have dinner with me, I'll think you're still mad at me," he said in a contrived tone.

She rolled her eyes before climbing into the bucket seat and accused with a smile that belied the harshness of her words, "You are such a con man."

A triumphant grin spread across his face as he softly shut her car door. She leaned across the seat and opened his door, catching his softly muttered words. "But I got what I wanted. Dinner with you."

Yeah, you did, Jordan thought as she buckled her seat belt.

As they zoomed out the gate, she noticed Debbie crossing the parking lot. From this distance, Jordan felt the tentacles of the department head's disapproval. Her instincts warned repercussions would follow. Debbie would be the one behind them.

Jordan decided to enjoy her dinner with Mike and let go of her fears. Debbie and her reaction to their dinner could wait for another day. Besides, school ended hours earlier and they were on their own time. Jordan planned to enjoy herself and have fun.

Chapter 7

Mike zoomed down Telegraph Road into the parking lot of Meriwether's, Chuck Muer's seafood restaurant. He halted at the entrance to the white tower accentuated with dark wood beams.

The valet opened Jordan's door and extended a hand to help her from the Mustang. Hurrying to her side, Mike rested a possessive hand at her elbow and guided her into the restaurant's lobby.

An auburn-haired hostess dressed in a white button-down tuxedo shirt, black bow tie, and ebony tailored trousers stood behind a dark wood podium. "Good evening, welcome to Meriwether's," she greeted with a big toothy grin. "Will that be two for dinner?" She gazed from Mike to Jordan and back again.

"Yes," he answered, retaining a warm hold on Jordan's arm.

The hostess retrieved two menus from an over-stuffed wooden slot attached to the podium. "Right this way. Watch your step," she warned, leading them down two steps to the sunken dining area.

Romantic and intimate described the ambience. The hostess escorted them to a secluded booth set apart from the main dining room. Dark wood beams traced the line of the room.

They slipped onto the benches covered in soft tan vinyl. A wide table covered with white linen separated them. On the table, a lantern burned. The flame bounced off the surfaces of the crystal and silver table settings, shedding an intimate glow over the booth.

Jordan examined the décor and came to a quick decision. She leaned forward and said in a worried whisper, "Mike, seafood isn't cheap. I don't want to break you. Let's go dutch."

He shook his head, pursing his lips. "No. I invited you and I'll pay for the meal. Don't worry about the cost. It's on me." With that said, he picked up his menu and studied it.

Yeah, that's what worries me, she thought, taking another visual sweep of the room, feeling worry tug at her heart. Where was all this leading? What did Mike really want from her?

Okay, she'd noticed the admiring glances that he tossed her way, not to mention how difficult it felt to resist the invisible string that drew them together. Mike was a baby, for goodness' sake. A handsome baby, but a younger man, nevertheless.

No matter what she felt, she didn't plan to act on it. She had arrived at Pierson's door determined to get her career back on track, not romance the help.

He should be romancing some sweet young thing straight out of college. Instead, he sat across from her trying to soothe her older, wrinkled, panic-attack-having butt.

Mike lowered his menu and asked, "How about oysters on the half shell for an appetizer?"

His clear, expectant gaze took her breath away and she found herself at a loss to remember why she had been fighting him about accompanying him to dinner. She raised a defeated hand. "Whatever you think is fine with me."

He ordered a bottle of Riesling and the oysters and then they got down to the business of selecting their entrees. Once they completed the process, Jordan stole a glance at Mike and found him studying her. His eyes were compelling, magnetic, and she instantly glanced away.

Heat burned her cheeks bright red. Mike looked as if he could devour her. Uncomfortable with the silence, she searched for anything intelligent to say, something to draw his attention away from her.

"Chet mentioned something about you and me working on the Science Olympiad together. Have you been part of it before? How does it work?" She shook out her napkin and laid it across her lap.

Mike waited patiently as the server filled their glasses with Riesling. He lifted his glass. "Science Olympiad is one of the fun programs that I do. This will be my fourth year doing it. We recruit students and then enter them into the statewide competition."

"Statewide competition?"

"Yeah. All the local high schools get a chance to participate. They compete against the champs from other schools, then it steps up to the state level. It's fun. The competition includes all types of things." Mike's eyebrows furrowed above quizzing eyes. "Jordan, you've never been involved in the Science Olympiad?"

She couldn't help smiling. He looked like an adorable little boy when he frowned. "No. It's new to me. Mr. Burke loved the program and always volunteered to run it. So I never had a chance to participate."

His mouth dropped open and his eyebrows rose. "Old man Burke is still at Randall?"

Jordan nodded. "Last time I visited."

Smiling, Mike said, "I remember that dude. Man, what a science nerd."

"And he still is," Jordan added.

"Man. Who would have believed it?" He shook his head.

"How do we recruit students? Do we ask for volunteers?"

"Sometimes I give incentives, offer extra credit if they participate. That way I always get three or four additional students for my team. It helps the kids that may not be doing well in my class."

"How many students do you need?" She brought the glass of wine to her lips.

Mike answered, "I aim for ten to twelve."

Her eyes widened. "Woo! Do you get that many?"

"Sometimes."

"What do you do after that?" Jordan sipped the smooth wine, enjoying its crisp, fruity favor as it washed over her tongue.

"We prepare our team. The committee gives us a choice of projects. We can have the students build something, or solve a forensic puzzle. Remind me and I'll pull the info from last year. I might have a videotape from last year too."

"Fair enough."

During their discussion the server maintained a silent vigil, refilling their wineglasses, removing empty dishes, and adding ice water to their goblets.

Jordan began to relax and enjoy the food and her dinner companion. Her guard dropped and she spoke freely about her day and the things she wanted to accomplish during her tenure at Pierson.

Their meals were superbly prepared. They started with seafood chowder and Martha's Vineyard salads.

Coconut shrimp and swordfish with scalloped potatoes, and sautéed green beans followed.

Conversation continued between them as they enjoyed their meals. Thirty minutes later, Jordan leaned back and sighed, resting her hands on her full belly. "That was wonderful."

Mike wiped his mouth on the white linen napkin and smiled back at her. "I told you, you'd enjoy it. So, what do you want for dessert?"

"Dessert! I don't think I have room for anything more."

"Nonsense. This is dinner and we're going to enjoy the full experience. Now, I'm partial to the triple strawberry mousse cake with vanilla bean ice cream. It's my favorite."

"Mmm," she moaned, envisioning the scrumptious confection. "That sounds heavenly. I couldn't eat a goodie like that by myself."

"No need. You know I'm always here for you. I'll help," he offered. A devilish twinkle sparkled from his eyes.

Barely able to contain her laughter, she muttered in a silky tone, "Aren't you the sweetest thing?"

He shrugged. "I aim to please. Whatever you need."

She ignored his double-edged innuendo, although her racing pulse refused to calm itself.

The server set a plate of the heavenly confection before them. Jordan's eyes widened as she took in the six layers of yellow cake, separated by fresh strawberries and whipped cream generously sprinkled with brown sugar. She spooned a tiny portion of the dessert between her lips and shut her eyes as the cake practically melted in her mouth.

Mike grinned at her. He retrieved his spoon and took a generous helping of the cake and ice cream.

They worked their way through the dessert talking about miscellaneous topics. Years had passed since she enjoyed a dinner and her companion so much. Again, she felt the edge of something more. The beginning of a relationship that went beyond friendship.

Mike made her feel many things that she didn't want to think about. She felt emotions that were forbidden and she'd believed lost to her. What a shame that she found this kind of kindred with someone that was too young to ever truly be hers.

She sighed contentedly. "That was wonderful."

"Told you. It's almost impossible to leave Meriwether's without sampling their desserts. Next time we come here you have to try their chocolate cake. It has eight layers and I go home with an extreme sugar buzz."

Next time? Jordan's eyes popped wide open. Next time. Mike acted as if they were a couple and would indeed go on more dates. She placed her spoon on the table, trying to come up with a way to put this evening in the proper prospective.

Although she enjoyed her time with him, she refused to allow herself to get too attached to Mike. That would lead her down a path of disappointment and pain. Whatever Mike's plans, she didn't have to go along with them.

Once the bill had been settled, Mike cupped Jordan's arm and they left the restaurant. The valet brought the Mustang almost instantly and they were on their way back to Pierson within minutes. Ella Fitzgerald's sultry voice cooed from the speakers and lulled Jordan into a mellow mood.

They rode in silence for a bit until Mike took one hand off the steering wheel and squeezed hers. "Jordan, thanks for having dinner with me. I really do hate to eat alone."

His touch sent wild sensations up her arm. "Thank

you. I've never been to Meriwether's. It was quite an adventure."

"Maybe we can have a few more adventures," Mike suggested slowly.

She paused to catch her breath. Her misgivings were gaining energy.

Mike continued without waiting for an answer. "You know, I had quite a crush on you when you were my teacher at Randall."

"Did you?" Jordan asked, plucking at the seat belt strap pressed against her breast.

"Mmm-hmm. I thought you were one sexy woman." He took his eyes off the road, gazing at her. "You still are."

Her heart began to thump in her chest. She needed to divert this discussion to something less personal. "Thank you, I think."

"No thanks needed," he said in a tone laced with sensual promise. "It's the truth."

Nervously fidgeting with the seat belt, Jordan faced Mike. "What are you saying?"

"I liked you then and I like you now," he whispered into the darkness of the car, "and I want to go out again. Whenever. As often as possible. I want to get to know you in all the ways that count." Using his free hand, he reached for hers, linking their fingers.

Although she'd half expected something like this to happen, Jordan still wasn't prepared. If Mike had been ten years older, she might have taken the plunge.

She drew her tongue across her dry lips, unlinked their hands, and folded hers in her lap. "Mike, I like you too and I really appreciate all the help and encouragement you've given me since I came to Pierson. I consider you one of my friends. The type of friend that I'd like to have for a long time." She sighed. "But I can't get involved with you."

"Why?" he shot back.

Shocked at the way he seemed to be ignoring the obvious, she said, "I have issues that I'm trying to resolve. Plus, we just reconnected. I don't want to jeopardize our friendship."

"Let's start with your issues. What about them?"

"Mike, I'm having panic attacks. This is my first year at a new school. I'm trying to get my life back."

"Why can't you handle all that and have a relationship too?"

"Because I can't. I need to do these things alone."

"You don't have to be alone. I'm here for you," he promised.

"I'm sorry, Mike. I can't."

"Can't or won't?" he questioned. "You've talked about issues and doing things on your own. What you haven't said is how you feel about me." He leaned close to her. In the confined space, she could feel his warm breath on her skin and the touch of his hand as he caressed her cheek. "I'm not talking about being friends. Right now, I care what you think of me and how I can convince you to give us a chance."

Mike pulled into the school's parking lot and stopped next to Jordan's SUV. She reached for the door handle, eager to escape. He caught her arm, holding her in place.

"What about dinner next week?"

"I don't think it would be a good idea. We have to work together." She shook off his hand and hurried from the car. He followed, running around the hood to help her out.

Frowning, he said, "That's not good enough. What's really bothering you?"

"Mike, I like you. I really do. But I have enough on my plate right now without adding a romance to everything that's going on. It has nothing to do with you and everything to do with me. I'm sorry, it's not a good time for me to get involved with anyone."

Ready to end this conversation, Jordan pushed past him. His arms reached out and held her firmly, forcing her to look at him. She saw the confusion in his eyes, and her heart ached for him. She wanted to smooth out the wrinkles marring his face and hold him close.

But she couldn't be what Mike wanted. He should find someone closer to his age, maturity level, and background.

"When will it be a good time?" The sarcasm in his voice rang out loud and clear. "You've told me that you want to get your life back. Part of that should be having a relationship of your own. I'm available, interested, and ready for more than friendship with you. Tell me what I have to do to get us there."

Drained from skipping around the real issue, Jordan decided to be honest. "Mike, you're a former student. Do you really think we have anything to build a relationship on?"

"Yes," Mike answered without a moment's hesitation. Challenging, he asked, "If I didn't know better, I'd say you were scared. Is that what's going on in your head? Are you afraid, Jordan? Is that why you won't go out with me?"

She whipped around and lifted her chin, ready to do battle. "No. Why would I be afraid of you?"

"That's my question."

In a near panic, Jordan said, "Talking to you is not working, so I'm going home."

With one hand at the small of her back, he encircled her with his arms, pulling her into his embrace. "Don't be afraid," he whispered into her hair, "I'm here. I'll always be here for you."

Mike's touch was firm, but gentle. His eyes filled with deep longing and need sent her skittish heart into a gallop. Silently, he drew her to him, wrapping his arms around her waist, holding her close. She melted against the solid warmth of male flesh.

He brushed a gentle kiss across her forehead. "There's something between us. It has nothing to do with my teenage crush. It's about you, the woman I know now and care for." His voice dropped to a husky purr as his hands tenderly stroked her back. "Let me show you."

Gently, he traced her lips with the tip of his tongue. The touch of his lips created delicious sensations, making her crave more. Then his mouth covered hers, seeking entry, and she complied. He explored the recesses of her mouth, savoring the sweetness of her lips as she did the same. Mike shattered her resolve with the hunger of his kiss.

Lifting her arms, Jordan circled his waist, pulling him close. She returned his kiss with a passion that belied her previous tales. The crisp, fruity tang of the Riesling and the garlic from the swordfish were on his lips, combined with the delicious essence of Mike.

His tongue drank from her mouth, making it impossible for Jordan to think about anything but him and getting closer and feeling him against her. She felt weak at the knees with need. No matter how much she denied the truth, she wanted him.

Reluctantly, they parted. A few inches separated them. Mustering all the strength at her disposal Jordan turned to her car. Mike watched her with a heated gaze.

With shaky hands, she fished her keys from her pocket and hit the remote, unlocking the SUV. "Good night," she whispered and got into the vehicle.

Shocked, Mike stood at the driver's door. Disappointment and hurt were etched into his handsome features. Unable to take any more, she glanced away, turning the key in the ignition. The engine fired to life and she drove off, leaving him standing alone in the school parking lot.

Chapter 8

The referee blew his whistle, calling a time out for the Pierson Jets. Jordan pointed at the court, and her cheerleaders took center stage. Standing at the foul line, she directed the girls as they performed a selection of loud, slightly sensuous, and aerobic cheers.

Unable to resist, she stole a glance at the people several spaces away. Mike and his assistant coach, Kevin Mallard, were huddled in a circle with their players.

Dressed in a tailored navy blue suit, crisply pressed white shirt, and striped mint-green and navy blue tie, Mike oozed professionalism. His stance and demeanor conveyed a no-nonsense, let's-get-this-thing-done approach to the game.

He lifted his head, letting his gaze skip along the foul line until he reached her. The cold and distant expression held her gaze.

Flinching, Jordan broke eye contact, rubbing her hands up and down her arms, fighting off the chill created by Mike's expression. *That's what you get,* she chastened herself. *You wanted him to leave you alone. Well, he's doing just that.*

It had been two weeks and four basketball games since

their interlude in the parking lot. Ten school days crammed with tension and uncomfortable silences. She felt miserable and she missed Mike. Somehow between the beginning of the first day of classes and now, Mike had slipped beneath her defenses.

She missed the friendship that went along with their morning hot chocolate and Coney Island lunches. Those little getaways centered her and kept her focused on her students and the job.

Mike's voice rose above the crowd. "Jarell, I know you're good. But you have to work as a member of the team. Pass the ball, man. Don't try to make every shot yourself. There are five players on the court. You don't own the court."

"I can't help it if the rest of ya can't keep up. It's not my fault. I'm here to play ball," Jarell announced smugly.

"You're right, we are here to play the game. But you can't win the game alone. Everyone"—Mike made eye contact with each member of the team before spearing Jarell with a stern glare—"and I mean everyone must work together. I don't care how good you think you are. This is about winning the game, not about your personal preferences. Deal with them on your time. Understand?"

Kevin added, "No one plays alone. Don't forget it. Stay focused. Now get out there and score some points. Win the game."

The buzzer blared throughout the Jersey Bulldogs' gymnasium. Mike and Kevin exchanged high fives with their team as they trotted back onto the court while the cheerleaders returned to the sidelines.

The teams resumed their respective positions. The referee tossed the ball to a Pierson player and the game commenced.

Arms folded, Kevin paced the foul line. Mike returned

to his position on the bench, a constant and assessing eye on the game. His arms rested on his thighs while his tightly linked fingers swung between his spread legs.

The cheerleaders roared from their spot on the bench, drawing Jordan's attention. Curious, she tuned into the game just in time to catch Jarell slip behind a Bulldog player and steal the ball. From the corner of her eyes, she watched Mike jump to his feet, his hands clenched into tight fists. He marched along the narrow space, tossing coded messages to his players.

Paradise jumped to her feet, shouting from the cheerleaders' bench, "Yeah! That's my babe. That's the way I like to see you play. You're on, babe. You're on."

Surrounded by Bulldog players, Jarell dribbled, searching for a way out.

Paradise clapped loudly. "Come on, Jarell. You can do it."

Jordan twisted around to face Paradise and shook her head. She refused to accept this highly unsportsman-like behavior. Sulking, Paradise flopped down on the bench and pouted.

"Don't screw up," Mike warned, tapping a nervous hand against his thigh. "Come on, pass it. Omere's open. Pass the ball to him."

Trapped, Jarell stood in center court, weighing his options. Omere crouched, arms extended, fending off the Jersey player, waiting for an opportunity to receive the ball. Without warning, Jarell jumped, attempting a three-point shot.

Spellbound, a hush came over the audience. The ball circled the rim, hovered on the edge, then tilted away from the basket and dropped to the floor. The Bulldogs didn't waste a minute. The player scooped up the ball and dribbled his way to the opposite end of the court.

Mike's expression turned thunderous. For a moment,

Jordan wondered whether he would go onto the court and physically remove Jarell. Getting control of himself, Mike ran an agitated hand over his hair and returned to the bench.

Pierson recaptured the ball after a failed attempt by the Bulldogs to score. The next few plays occurred in a blur of activity. A volley of exchanges ensued, resulting in the ball switching teams several times before Pierson came out victorious.

Jarell stole the ball from a teammate and dribbled his way to the basket, ignoring the cry of protest from his team members. He completed a dunk, hanging from the hoop, suspended in the air before dropping to the wooden floor. The crowd howled, loving his antics.

"Stop hogging the ball, Jarell," Mike yelled, a sheet of crumbled paper in his fist. "We're a team. Pass the ball, man."

Jarell ignored Mike's request. Slipping between the Bulldogs players and past his own team members, he continued until he reached the opposite end of the court and made another shot. His antics held everyone on the edge of their seats.

Agitated, Mike paced back and forth, looking as if he wanted to pull out his hair. If Jarell had more sense he would fear for his life.

The game belonged to Jarell. He worked his magic up and down the court, making shot after shot.

The halftime buzzer rang and the team filed off the court. Five sweaty young men trotted passed Jordan. She wrinkled her nose, lifting her hand to ward off the overpowering odors.

Mike gave Jarell a new rendition of his earlier speech. In her mind, Jordan knew Jarell was having the time of his life and didn't intend to stop unless Mike benched him.

The Pierson Jets' cheerleading squad took their place and performed a variety of routines. Jordan's squad did her proud as they gyrated to the music, ending with a standing ovation.

Minutes later, the buzzer sounded and the game resumed. Mike took up his vigil on the foul line, his gaze glued on his team.

Jarell seemed on a high. Nothing stopped him. After another steal from a Pierson player, he shoved a Bulldog player out of his way, and the referee called a foul. The young man began to argue with the ref, getting in his face.

Mike formed the time-out symbol with his hands, waving the team off the court. When Jarell reached the bench, Mike put an arm around his shoulder and steered him away from the audience and teammates, speaking softly to him.

The younger man shoved Mike away, shaking his head and shouting, "No!"

Silently nodding, Mike pointed at the bench.

Jarell refused to comply. "You're wrong, man. You know you are."

"I'm sorry," Mike muttered.

"I'm the best player you got."

"Yes, you are. But you're nothing if you are a team of one. I kept you in as long as I could. But you're jeopardizing the game and the team. It's time for you to sit on the bench. Calm down. Get your perspective again." Again, Mike pointed toward the bench. "Have a seat."

Breathing hard, Jarell shoved Mike. "To hell with you and the Pierson Jets. I don't need them," he shouted, stomping to the locker room.

The bus's engine hummed softly. Black exhaust fumes billowed from a tailpipe at the rear as the team filed onto the bus, ready to go home. Jordan followed, climbing the steps and glancing around.

The team was dead tired. They'd fought a difficult battle, but emerged victorious after Jarell's exit from the game.

In contrast, Eve's lyrics exploded from the interior. Arms were raised and hands waved in the air, chanting, "Go, Pierson! Go, Pierson!"

The heavy odor of perspiration rose from the young men while loud cheerleaders sang their victory song as they packed the rear of the bus. Jordan stood near the front, silently doing a quick body count. Her eyebrows furrowed over her eyes. She'd made a second head count. A few stragglers hadn't found their way to the bus.

Jordan stood in the middle of the aisle and did a third cheerleader head count. She hoped she'd miscounted, but she knew that she hadn't. Eyeballing the occupants, silently she noted that half of the dynamic duo was missing.

Paradise had found her way to the bus. She sat with an arm curled around Jarell, muttering soothing words of sympathy into his ear.

Pursing her lips, Jordan studied her watch, then returned to the front of the bus. The game had ended more than thirty minutes ago. All of the Pierson students should be seated and ready to go.

Kevin sat in the front row, his head down and his arms folded across his chest. If she hadn't known better, she would have suspected that he'd fallen asleep. But no one could sleep with the combined lyrics of Eve and the student's high energy level. The bus practically throbbed with the music.

Jordan approached him, placed her hand on his shoulder, and shook him. "Do you know where Mike is?"

Kevin hunched his shoulders. "He's probably in the gym."

"I'm missing a student. I'm going back inside to search for her. Tell the bus driver, okay?" She tossed her purse strap over her shoulder and headed for the door. "I'll be right back."

He nodded, slumped deeper into the seat, and shut his eyes.

She hurried across the parking lot and entered the main hallway, dodging the custodian's broom as he swept up the trash left from the game. Reduced lighting cast eerie images on the walls as she half walked, half sprinted down the hallway to the gym. She opened the door and peeked inside, expecting to find Erin with one of the basketball team members. Except for the cleaning crew, the gym was empty.

Not sure what to do, she returned to the main hallway, considering her next move. Should she go back to the main office and have someone make an announcement over the paging system? She passed the boys' locker room and halted, drumming her fingers against the wall.

What were the odds that Erin had found her way into the boys' locker room? Jordan let out a self-mocking chuckle. Erin was shameless. She could be anywhere, doing anything.

Jordan gnawed on her bottom lip. Should she barge in? Erin was Jordan's responsibility, so she'd better check every location. She hesitated at the door, offering herself silent encouragement. Newswomen did it every day.

Her heart danced in her chest when she pushed open the swinging door and stepped inside. The locker room was dark. A mist hung over the room, dusting its surface as the lingering fragrances of deodorant, soap, and soft voices filled the air.

Quietly, she inched her way between the lockers and benches toward the voices. Jordan felt certain she heard Erin, but she didn't recognize her male companion. It was probably a player from the Bulldogs' team. Someone the girl didn't want the Pierson Jets to know about.

Cautiously, Jordan halted and glanced at the pair from behind a series of lockers. Her eyes widened and her mouth dropped open. She felt as if she'd been run over by a Hummer.

Shocked, she shook her head, trying to dislodge the image. Mike! What was he doing here with Erin?

Even at her distance, Jordan could feel the waves of anger bouncing off the pair. Erin's hand lay intimately against Mike's chest as the teenager gazed into his eyes. He removed her hand, stepping away from her.

"No," he said in a loud, final tone. "My decision stands."

Jordan's feet were rooted to the tile floor as she watched them.

"Why won't you reconsider? This is important," Erin insisted, talking fast and furious.

Mike held his body as far from Erin's as possible. The narrowness of the space between the bench and the locker made it difficult. *Lovers' tiff?* Jordan wondered, noting his body language.

I shouldn't be here, she thought, observing the intimacy between Mike and Erin. This situation went way beyond the teacher and student relationship. Shaking her head, she started for the door. *Mind your own business, Jordan. Butt out,* her mind screamed.

But the professional in her knew this situation felt wrong. She didn't want to get Mike in trouble, but she would have to talk with him after they returned to Pierson. Warn him against placing himself in a position that could be misconstrued.

Jordan turned away and practically ran out the door. She'd ask the main office to page them, before returning to the bus.

Minutes later, Erin boarded the bus, followed closely by Mike. Erin joined her friends at the back and Mike snagged the seat next to Kevin.

Jordan sat in stunned silence. Why did he find it necessary to jeopardize his career with a student? Erin was loud, vocal, and untrustworthy. The teenager would blab to her friends with total disregard for Mike's life and livelihood. His career would be toast.

What about us? Mike had said that he wanted her in his life.

Her head throbbed with tension and she rubbed her hand across her forehead, trying to relieve the pain. There were so many questions and she didn't have any answers.

Once they returned to the school, she planned to take Mike aside and speak frankly about what she saw, make him understand that his career was at risk. What he was doing was very dangerous.

Chapter 9

The school bus pulled into the Pierson High School parking lot followed by a sea of cars. Like Indians circling the wagon train, they surrounded the bus, parking haphazardly as they waited for the team, cheerleaders, and staff to disembark.

The door swung open with a harsh gasp and Jordan hurried down the steps. She lingered at the foot completing a final head count of her cheerleaders as they puttered around the parking lot, searching for their rides.

Ten minutes later, the crowd had thinned to less than a dozen students. The bus and many of the students had disappeared and started their final journey home.

Arms folded across his broad chest and his legs braced slightly apart, Mike studied the remaining students, then turned to his assistant coach. "Kevin, you can take off." He lifted his chin toward his buddy's Honda Civic. "I'll stay until all the kids have been picked up."

"Thanks." Stifling a yawn, Kevin dropped a hand to Mike's shoulder. "I'm going to take you up on that offer. I'm beat."

"No problem." A half smile touched Mike's lips as he

pointed a hand at his buddy. "You can stay after the next game."

"It's a deal." Kevin scooped up his gym bag from the ground and gave Jordan a two-finger salute. "You two have a nice weekend. I'll see you guys on Monday."

Kevin hurried to a burgundy sedan and unlocked the door. He tossed the bag into the backseat and climbed inside. Within moments, he raced from the parking lot.

Mike strolled over to Jordan. "There's no need for both of us to stay. You can leave, if you want."

"Thanks, but I'll stick around." She crossed her legs at the ankle and leaned against the hood of her SUV. "It would be my luck for one of my little darlings or their parents to make some remark that gets me in trouble. Besides, you don't want to be stuck here alone with any of my girls." She pointed a finger at Erin and Paradise huddled together.

Mike followed her pointing finger with his eyes, then chuckled.

"They're probably plotting the downfall of Pierson High. It's better to have a teacher from both sexes available to keep everyone honest."

He shoved his hands into his pockets of his trousers. "True."

Silently, they stood together. The night had turned cool. She ran her hands up and down her arms, fighting off the chill.

"Cold?" he asked, removing his jacket and draping it over her shoulders.

Jordan felt the warmth of his body and smelled the tangy scent of his cologne. She started to push the garment from her shoulders. "I can't take your jacket. What about you?"

"Don't." He placed his hand possessively over hers

and whispered in a husky voice that danced along the sensitive skin, "I'm fine. Stay warm."

The caring tone in his voice appealed to her, making it impossible for her to deny his request. Conceding, she halted her movements.

"This will help until you get home." His fingers wrapped around the dark fabric, pulling it more firmly around her.

"Thanks," she said, stroking the garment with her fingers.

"No problem. You're welcome."

Wind whipped through the lot, stirring a lock of Jordan's hair. Mike lightly fingered a loose tendril. He secured the wayward strands behind her ear and ran a tender finger along her cheek. His fingers were cool and smooth as they touched her and Jordan found herself leaning into his touch.

She wanted to stay like this forever. Forget about their problems and focus on each other.

"Jordan?"

An odd note in Mike's tone caught her attention. She examined his face. "Yes?"

"I could have used your help earlier this evening."

"What?" she asked, baffled.

"In the Bulldogs' locker room." He smiled down at her. "I saw you. Why didn't you say anything when you found me and Erin?"

Her lips moved, but no sounds came out. "I—I—I—" she stammered hastily, running her fingers through her hair. His question had totally blown her away. She had no idea that he'd seen her. "I didn't want to disturb you. You seemed to be in a pretty deep, intense discussion."

"No, we weren't," he contradicted in a cool and exact tone. "Erin was in the middle of one of her tangents. I wanted her to go away. And your help was definitely needed."

"Tangents?" she asked. "Why? About what?"

"She wanted to know what I planned to do with Jarell," he explained, shaking his head. "Would he be allowed to play ball at the next game?"

"Jarell?" She shook her head. "Wait a minute. Why would Erin be concerned with what happens to Jarell?"

Jordan scratched her ear, mentally trying to put the jigsaw puzzle of information together. This didn't make any sense. If anyone, Paradise should be concerned with pleading Jarell's case. After all, Jarell and Paradise were a couple. "What does any of this have to do with Erin?"

"I asked the same question," he answered, folding his arms across his chest. "When I asked her what difference this made to her life, she told me that Paradise and Jarell were her friends and she always looks out for her buds." He shook his head sorrowfully. "Be careful around her."

He had opened the door to this topic, Jordan reasoned. Maybe she could learn more and help her friend make a better decision. She cleared her throat. "When I saw you two, I felt as if I intruded on an intimate moment. On the bus back to school I thought about what I saw and I had a speech planned to warn you against getting involved with a student even if she is eighteen."

"You don't have to worry about me. That girl frightens me." He perched on the edge of the SUV next to Jordan. "Erin doesn't care how she gets what she wants as long as she gets it. She has no morals."

"That's true. But you need to be careful. A student like her would not have a problem with destroying your career if you crossed her."

"You're right."

Jordan placed a warm hand on his arm. "Mike, watch your step. Please don't get caught."

"I got that. Don't worry. I'll keep my distance and sidestep her antics, okay?" Mike responded with a voice filled with so much sincerity that Jordan believed him. All of her worries vanished.

"Bye, Mr. Walker. Bye, Ms. Anderson." Shakeyla waved, then climbed into the backseat of her parents' car.

Jordan waved at the exiting vehicle and uttered a faint farewell. Mike did the same.

She sighed deeply. The last student was on her way home and so was Jordan. She dug in her purse, extracted her keys. "That's it. I'm out of here. Good night, Mike."

He dogged her steps. "Whoa! Good night? It's barely eight o'clock. Besides, it's the beginning of the weekend." He glanced at his watch. "You want to go get something to eat? Maybe a burger and fries?"

Surprised, Jordan stepped away from the SUV's door and studied him. "So . . ." she eyed him, waving a hand back and forth between them. "We're cool now? You're speaking to me?"

Embarrassed, Mike ducked his head and cleared his throat as his cheeks flared beet-red. He stammered, "I—I—I always talk to you."

"Sure you do. Except for the past few weeks," she responded sarcastically, cupping her cheek. "Maybe I missed something. Tell me, were you using sign language or telepathy to communicate with me? Because I don't remember us having one conversation. Do you?"

"Okay, you've got me," he admitted, shamefaced. "I didn't react real well after our dinner at Meriwether's."

"You could say that. Pissed off pretty much describes it."

Mike shoved his hands inside the pockets of his trousers, examining the toes of his wing-tip shoes. "I guess I owe you an apology."

"That would be nice," she responded.

"I'm sorry."

Acknowledging his apology with a tip of her head, Jordan said, "Thank you."

He scratched the side of his neck. "Obviously, I came on too strong. Expected way too much from you. I realized that I needed to give you some space. A chance to get to know me better and learn that I'm really a good guy."

"I already know you're a good guy."

"Yeah, but you're having trouble seeing me as more than a colleague," he whispered softly, moving a step closer.

"That's what you are, my colleague," Jordan answered in the same soft tone, inhaling Mike's cologne as it wafted under her nose.

Eyes focused on her, Mike added simply, "I want more."

Shaking her head slowly, Jordan warned in a determined tone, "It's not going to happen. I don't plan to get involved with anyone at Pierson, including you."

"We'll see," he answered confidently, dropping a reassuring hand on her shoulder and giving it a gentle squeeze.

"I mean it," Jordan reiterated sternly, spearing him with one of the looks she reserved for her most difficult students.

Mike laughed out loud. Amused, he allowed his gaze to drop from her eyes to her shoulders and breasts, then returned to her face. He did a suggestive double lift of his eyebrows, then smiled. "I know you do."

Exasperated, Jordan added, "Seriously."

Grinning at her, Mike moved closer, invading her personal space. With a gentle rhythm his thumb stroked back and forth across her cheek, caressing her soft skin. "I'm not a student anymore, Jordan. That expression worked when I was sixteen. I'm twenty-eight and I've got a few glares of my own."

Jordan remained stoically silent.

"I've said before there is something unique going on between us, special feelings that we can't ignore. I understand that you're not ready and I have no right to expect you to accept whatever plans I have. That was selfish of me," he stated straightforwardly. "So I'm going to wait. Back off. Give you a little space and time to come to terms with what's developing between us. No pressure." He shrugged, then amended, "Little pressure."

"Don't do this, Mike. You're setting yourself up for major disappointment. I like you," Jordan whispered huskily. "Maybe even like you more than I should. But that doesn't mean I'm going to let anything happen between us. I've got too much baggage and you don't need my type of problems in your life."

Leaning closer, he kissed her. Barely grazing her lips before he moved away, he muttered, "We've got all the time you need."

With one hand, he pulled her to him. She shut her eyes, savoring the tenderness of his lips. His firm mouth demanded a response and she complied, freely giving testament to the feelings they shared.

"All the time you need," Mike promised, creating a delicious series of sensations that she found impossible to resist. Her body hummed as he took command and deepened the kiss, exploring the moist recesses of her mouth. Between a series of slow, shivery kisses, he muttered, feasting on the warm flesh at the curve of her neck, "We've got time."

Slowly, Mike pulled away, gazing into her eyes as he gently caressed the moisture from her lips. She looked into his soft brown orbs. His eyes were liquid pools of longing that beckoned to her.

Jordan froze as the reality of what she allowed to happen smacked her. After all her protest, she'd given in to him without a token struggle. How was she supposed to make him understand that no matter what just happened, she didn't plan to let things go any further? Honesty seemed to be the best way to go.

Wetting her love-swollen lips, she said, "Mike, I don't want to hurt you. Don't wait for me. Get on with your life. Enjoy it."

"Nope," Mike answered, rubbing a hand up and down her arm. As usual, his touch sent currents of sensations through her. "I can wait. I've got more than enough time and patience for both of us. Besides, you can't resist me, at least not for long. We're together five days a week. After a while I'm going to look pretty good to you. Resistance is futile," he mimicked in his best Captain Picard voice.

Her heart skipped a beat as she admitted that he might be correct. She glanced at him, finding herself responding to his slow, easy expression.

Something shifted inside her. It uncoiled and released the lock that controlled her emotions. Mike had breached her defenses and scaled the walls to her heart and created a place for himself.

"Drive safely." He opened the SUV door and helped her inside. Once she settled in, he leaned inside the open window and stole a final kiss. "Don't worry about anything. We've got time. All the time in the world."

Chapter 10

Jordan slipped her arms into a navy blue lab coat to protect her black suede pantsuit. She stood at the whiteboard with an erasable marker in one hand and an eraser in the other, completing her instructions for the class project. Her chemistry students entered the room, pairing up, settling down, and preparing for their experiment.

"Okay, ladies and gentlemen," she began, popping a disc into the CD player and adjusting the volume of the opera *La Traviata*. "Let's get started." She tapped the whiteboard with her marker. "Read the instructions and begin the experiment. If you have any questions, raise your hand and I'll come over."

She glanced at the connecting door leading to Mike's room. True to his word, he'd given her as much space as he believed she needed.

Generally before assigning a project to the students, they'd brainstorm together about what experiments would help the students gain the knowledge they needed. His advice and suggestions were insightful and helpful. He still was available when she needed mentoring or advice, but he maintained his distance on all other occasions.

Jordan glanced at the lab door a second time. He must hear them. After all, her students were keeping up a steady racket, plus the music from the CD. Most times he'd peek in to be certain that a teacher presided over Pierson's wayward band of students.

Not anymore. He promised her space and time. And that was exactly what he was giving her. But she refused to admit how much she missed him and needed his reassuring presence.

With a frustrated sigh, she brought her attention back to her students, waiting patiently as they prepared to begin the experiment. "Is everyone ready?"

Her students responded with a collective "yes." Nodding, Jordan moved between the rows, lecturing. "It takes more heat energy to raise the temperature of some substances than others," she explained, tapping the marker in her left hand into the palm of the right. "Today, you are going to play the role of an investigator."

Daniel raised his hand. "Investigator?"

Jordan nodded, removing a small metal substance from a cloth pouch in her lab coat. She displayed it to the class. "Yes. You're going to determine this substance's identity by using heat energy to raise the temperature."

Studying the interested expressions on her students' faces, Jordan smiled. This was her favorite class. She received great pleasure from this group. They enjoyed exploring the scientific method and asked the most engaging questions.

At each lab station, she placed a chunk of metal next to the gas burner, then returned to her desk. "You will need the following materials to complete this experiment. I'm going to show you what each item looks like so that you can identify them. Please watch carefully. You'll need beakers." She lifted a glass beaker for the class to see. "Graduated cylinder, test tubes, glass stirring rod, clasps, stand, wire gauze, gas burner, thermometer, lead shot, our unknown substance, and distilled H_2O. Check your list against the equipment at your lab station. Everybody got a copy of the list?"

A second round of "yes" filled the room.

The connecting door from her classroom opened and Debbie Rucker stuck her head inside. "Oh, Ms. Anderson, I didn't realize you had a class in here today."

"Hi, Ms. Rucker," Jordan greeted.

Debbie stepped into the room, studying the controlled chaos. "What's going on?"

"I'll let my students tell you." She raised her voice, lifting her hand to gain the attention of her class. "Who can tell Ms. Rucker what our goal is for this experiment?"

A sea of hands wiggled in the air.

Jordan pointed at Shakeyla. "Go ahead."

"We're searching for the specific heat of an unknown metal."

Debbie chuckled, strolling to where Jordan stood. "Interesting. How are you doing that?"

"First we determine the change in temperature of the H_2O and piece of metal," Camyra chimed in. "Don't forget we calculate the heat gained by the water. But we have to remember that the remaining heat lost by the metal is equal to the heat gained by the water."

Jordan felt her heart fill with pride at the thorough way Shakeyla and Camyra described their experiment. Their answers were concise, complete, and showed an understanding of the material.

Jordan turned to Debbie with a smile of satisfaction on her face. She couldn't resist adding, "How's that?"

"Great!" Debbie answered, clamping her hands together. "You have to let me know how they do on this experiment." She gave the students a nod of approval.

Jordan smiled. "No problem. When they're done, they have to record their results and verify their findings."

Perched on the edge of her desk, Jordan studied her department head. Debbie's impromptu visit felt like a surprise observation. Jordan suspected Debbie felt she needed to check up on her. But her students were on task, doing exactly what her curriculum map and objectives diagramed.

"Ms. Anderson, enjoy." At the door, Debbie turned back to Jordan. "By the way, don't forget to lock up when you're done."

Jordan expected that. Mike and Debbie had made it very clear that this room needed to stay locked when not in use. "Don't worry, Ms. Rucker." She folded her arms over her chest. "I'll remember."

After Debbie left, Jordan turned her attention to her class, warning, "Don't forget your goggles. And if you want to keep your expensive clothes protected, put on a lab coat. One final warning, be careful with the gas burner. Please make sure that your match is lit before you turn on the gas."

Forty-five minutes later it was time to clean up. "You'll have ten minutes to wrap up and write your results," Jordan warned. She placed a hand on the black Dell monitor. "After you've finished I want you to add your findings to the spreadsheet so that we can record the class's conclusions and create a graph. Hurry up, there's only fifteen minutes left to the class period. Before we conclude today, I want to spend a few minutes discussing the experiment and your results."

She watched her students complete the experiment and begin the process of cleaning up. This had been

fun. Days like this boosted her confidence and reminded her why she became a teacher. Satisfaction
surged through her as she savored the feeling of opening and challenging young minds.

Mike zeroed in on his classroom as he eased his
way down the main corridor, dodging students and
staff. A small group of people were gathered near his
door, making a commotion.

Alarmed, he picked up his speed. *What's going on?* he
wondered. Immediately, his thoughts shifted to Jordan
as his mind took a flight of terror, visualizing all manner
of mayhem.

Drawing closer, Mike realized that he'd made a mistake. No one was at his door. They were at the lab.
Debbie, Chet, and the school's dean of students, Jefferson Thurman, were examining the door to the lab. Slim-
built, Jefferson stood over six feet with a round face and
alert, all-seeing dark eyes. A small, neat black mustache adorned his smooth dark chocolate upper lip.
Generally, Thurman appeared on the scene when situations required discipline, legal attention, or interven-
tion. The retired Detroit Police captain took a
no-nonsense approach to his role at Pierson High
School. His direct attitude intimidated most of the student body.

Mike halted, gathering his thoughts as he examined the trio. Their stern expressions kicked his concerns up a notch. "What's going on?"

His eyes narrowed thoughtfully as he watched the
group test the latch on the door. This didn't look good.

"Mr. Walker," Jefferson muttered, mindful of the
students stirring around the small group. His trained

gaze continued to inspect the lock, brooding over what he found. "Thieves got into the lab last night."

Alarmed, Mike swung his gaze to Debbie, waiting for the hissy fit to commence. Jordan was in deep trouble. After all his sweet promises, he hadn't been available when she needed him. He'd made a point of staying out of the lab yesterday when he heard Jordan and her students. But he'd checked the door on his way out of the building. It had been locked.

Buying a little time to think, Mike placed his briefcase on the floor near the classroom. "How can you be sure?"

Debbie focused on Mike. "When I got in, I checked on my way to my office. It was cracked."

Shaking his head, he disagreed, "No. That can't be. I checked last night. It was locked."

"That's not the way I found it. At first, I thought Jordan had come in early and I wanted to warn her because kids might wander into her classroom." Coolly disapproving, Debbie explained, "But I found the room empty and it looked wrong."

He swung away, hurrying into the lab with Thurman on his heels. Mike did a quick visual survey of the room before letting out a sigh of relief. Thank goodness. The room hadn't been vandalized. Jordan's CD player sat on the desk, intact, although items were missing from the lab stations.

Turning to the dean, Mike asked, "Thurman, did they jimmy the door?"

"No," answered the retired police captain. "From what I can tell, they strolled in and helped themselves to our equipment." Thurman glanced around. "Mike, I need a detailed list of any missing items from you and Ms. Anderson." With a hand on the doorknob, he said, "I'm going to call the police and file a report."

"Hi," Jordan said from the doorway. Her gaze

jumped from staff member to staff member. "What's going on?" she quizzed.

"Someone broke into the lab last night," Chet chimed in. His voice was cool and professional.

The heavy lashes that shadowed her cheeks flew up and her mouth dropped open. Seconds later, Mike noticed a fine film of perspiration along Jordan's forehead as she raised a trembling hand.

She's going into a panic attack, he thought. His resolve to give her space vanished as his protective instinct kicked in. Inconspicuously, Mike eased around the group, maneuvered his body between Jordan and Debbie. He placed his hand on Jordan's shoulder and squeezed reassuringly.

Surprised, she glanced up at him. Two deep lines of worry marred her beautiful features.

"Did you lock the door when you left?" Debbie demanded.

"Yes." Jordan's voice trembled a bit when she answered.

Debbie shook her head. "Well, I found it open this morning."

"I locked it last night before I went home." Nervously, Jordan brushed a lock of hair behind her ear.

"Are you certain?" The department head's tone contained a strong suggestion of disbelief.

"Of course. I didn't forget. We talked about locking up when you were in my classroom. I locked up." Jordan's voice rose.

Mike steered her away from Debbie's insistent probing. "Come on, Jordan. The bell is going to ring in a few minutes. Let's take a look around and see what's missing." He looked at the dean of students and added, "Thurman, we'll get a list to you as soon as possible."

Chet glanced at his watch and said, "Mike's correct.

There's not enough time to continue this discussion. But we do need to talk. Let's meet after school today. Jordan, in my office, let's say around three-thirty?"

Dejected, Jordan nodded. The downward tilt of her lips and the worried expression on her face frightened Mike.

Chet, Thurman, and Debbie weren't going to question Jordan alone. They would chew her up like a doggie treat. He planned to be right beside her.

Providing a quiet lifeline, Mike took her arm and steered her away from the lab, being careful to close and lock the door after them. "Classes start in a few minutes. Thurman, we'll do a survey of the lab and let you know what's missing during our prep period."

Automatically, Jordan responded to his tone and turned toward her classroom. Following her inside, he shielded her from the curious eyes of the students and other staff members.

Chapter 11

At 3:25, Jordan turned the key in the lock on her classroom door, taking great care to secure it. She stuffed her keys inside her pocket and started down the hall.

As she passed Mike's door, he stepped into the hallway and fell into step beside her. "Are you headed to Chet's office?" he asked.

With a stoic expression, she continued her trek down the hall. Gazing in his direction, she asked, "Where are you going?"

"With you," he answered. "I won't let you face Chet alone."

She halted and turned to him. "This isn't your battle. You don't have to do this. I know you have work to do. Don't stop your day for me."

"Who else would I stop it for?" Mike grabbed her hand and stopped her. Turning her to face him, he placed a hand under her chin, tipping it to gaze into her eyes.

"Thank you," she returned in a soft voice.

"You're welcome," he added in a gentle, caring tone. "First, I'm your friend. Everything else can wait.

You need my help. At the very least, you deserve my support."

His words warmed her heart and fortified her resolve. After the way she'd treated him, she didn't deserve his assistance. Yet, here he stood, offering his aid. She gave him a shy smile. "I really appreciate it."

"Come on. Let's get this over with." He grinned down at her, wrapped a hand around her upper arm. Together, they presented a united front as they strolled down the hall and entered the main office.

"Hi, Donna," Mike greeted.

Reluctantly, the secretary swiveled away from her computer screen and glanced at the couple. "Hi. Jordan, they're waiting for you. Go right in."

All of her fears returned with the fierceness of a punch to her gut. Her hands shook and her heart rate increased. "They?" she queried.

"Chet, Debbie, and Jefferson Thurman," Donna explained.

"Oh," Jordan uttered, fidgeting with the buttons on her jacket. A feeling of hopelessness gripped her. She'd pumped herself up to meet with Chet alone, expecting to plead her case without the watchful and hostile eye of Debbie.

Mike reached for her hand and squeezed it gently. "Remember, everything is going to be okay."

Jordan nodded, squared her shoulders, and went to Chet's office. She tapped lightly on the door before entering the room. Mike followed closely behind her.

"Here's the list of missing items." Jordan slid the sheet of paper across Chet's desk.

"Have a seat." Chet rose from his desk and waved a hand at the round wooden conference table located in the center of the room. He glanced at the sheet before passing it to Thurman.

Chet's brushy eyebrows bunched together as he studied Mike. "This is a confidential meeting."

"I know." Mike scratched the side of his neck. "But I'd like to be here for Jordan if you don't mind. Besides, it's my lab as well as hers."

Thurman turned to Jordan and said, "Mike, it's not up to me. Jordan?"

"I'd like him to stay. Besides, he may know or have seen something that I missed." Taking in a deep, shaky breath, Jordan took the chair next to Debbie and shifted away from the older woman. Mike scooted a chair between the two women.

After months of feeling as if she'd lost control of her life, she'd rediscovered the joy of teaching. She didn't want to lose her job over this incident. Studying the people around the conference table, Jordan hoped for a quick death.

"We decided to wait until the school day ended before calling the police," Thurman explained.

"Why?"

"The locked cabinet that stores the chemicals had been raided. The basic compounds used to make Pleasure are missing," Thurman confirmed.

Her heart drummed in her chest. Perspiration beaded on the base of Jordan's neck, slowly sliding down her neck. "Missing?"

"Yes."

Ohmigod! I'm not going to get out of this easily, Jordan thought, shutting her eyes against this new offense. "What does that mean? What happens next?"

Chet shook his head and let out a deep sigh of frustration. "If this had ended with the door being left open, then I'd do a verbal reprimand and be done with it. But the police had to be called. In addition, chemicals and equipment are missing. I have to discipline you beyond the reprimand stage."

Mike stepped in. "Chet, this is a first offense. And Jordan swears that she locked the lab. I checked it after her."

"I'm sorry. Ultimately, the responsibility was Jordan's. She was the only person who used the lab yesterday. Am I correct?" he asked, looking pointedly at her.

"Yes," Jordan answered.

The principal handed her a written reprimand. "Jordan, effective tomorrow you're on a one-week suspension."

"Chet, don't. This is excessive," Mike exclaimed.

Debbie stood. Her gaze slid over Jordan. "No, it's not. I specifically mentioned locking the lab when the class concluded their experiment. Too many things can happen when the proper procedures are not followed. This is an extreme example."

"This isn't fair," Jordan said. "There's been minimal investigation. What if someone else is responsible? Don't you think you're being a bit premature?"

"No," Debbie answered stiffly.

Mike chimed in, "What if I discover that someone else is responsible? What happens then?"

"We'll see," Chet promised, turning to Jordan. "I need your substitute lesson plans, seating charts, and attendance book. Give them to Debbie."

"What about cheerleading?" Jordan asked.

"I'll do it," Debbie answered.

Nodding, Jordan rose and headed out of the room. She returned a few minutes later with a package of information and handed it to the department head. Without another word, she left the room with the write-up crumpled in her hand.

Mike followed her. He stopped her as she started

down the hall. "Jordan, don't give up. I'm going to find out what really happened. I promise."

She offered him a weak smile that didn't reach her eyes. "Thanks. But I think it's pretty much a done deal. I don't want to rile them up any more than they already are. I'm going to take my suspension, then come back to work a week from now."

"You're not going to fight back?" he asked, incredulous. "File a grievance or something?"

"Mike, I don't have an answer." She ran an agitated hand through her hair. "If I could prove that I locked that door, then I would fight. Right now, it's my word against theirs." She sighed. "I just want it to end."

He gripped her arms. "What if I find something? Will you work with me?"

"Sure. Believe me, I don't want to lose a week's pay or have this in my personnel file."

"This isn't going to go away the way they want it to," Mike promised, glancing through the window at the principal. "I'm going to do my own investigation."

"You do that. I'm going home," she called over her shoulder, heading for her classroom. Minutes later, she hurried out the teachers' exit.

Mike stood in the parking lot, watching Jordan's brake lights flash when she braked on her way out of the gate. He grimaced, certain Debbie had pushed Chet into handing down the suspension. He planned to conduct a little investigation of his own. First thing tomorrow he'd examine the lab and search for clues or links to someone else.

Mike retraced his steps, stopping as he noticed the custodian moving through the hallway. His lips pursed. Lee Gardner had been with the school for years, he would probably know every student and faculty person in the building. Maybe he saw something last night.

"Hey, Lee." Mike nodded at the older man. "How are you doing?"

Lee looked up from sweeping the floor and nodded back at Mike. "Good. And you?"

"I can't complain." Mike grinned. "Besides, if I did, what difference would it make?"

Chuckling, Lee agreed. "All you do is give yourself high blood pressure."

"That's for sure. Look, I need to ask you a question."

"Help yourself."

In his eagerness, Mike moved closer to the other man, receiving a nostril full of pine cleaner and ammonia. "This morning there was a bit of commotion about Ms. Anderson. Someone slipped into the lab and stole a bunch of equipment and chemicals that can make one of those designer drugs. Did you see anything or anyone around lab fifteen yesterday afternoon?"

Lee placed the broom against the wall and stroked his chin, giving Mike's comment serious consideration. "Well," he drawled, holding a mouthful of tobacco in his jaw, "I wasn't on this side of the building yesterday. Jim kept me on the west side."

"Who worked the east side?"

"I'm not sure. Check with the supervisor. He'd have the schedule."

"Will do." Mike patted Lee on the shoulder. "Thanks, man."

"Anytime. Anytime," Lee muttered, picking up his broom.

Mike checked the time and hugged the wall as he waited for Harold Crawford to arrive. The supervisor had informed him that Harold had been the custodian on duty the afternoon of the theft.

A little after four, a short, brown-skinned man dressed in a clean and pressed pair of jeans and a Pistons T-shirt entered the building through the staff entrance.

Mike stepped away from the wall and into Harold's path. "Hi."

Harold stopped, eyeing Mike suspiciously. "Hi."

"I don't think we've met. My name is Mike Walker and I teach science here. I'd like to talk to you for a minute, if you don't mind."

"What about?" Harold asked cautiously.

"The lab connected to rooms fourteen and fifteen."

Harold's face tightened into a resistant mask and his hands shook before he shoved them inside the pockets of his jacket. He stepped around Mike and resumed his trek down the hall.

Mike followed.

Hearing the second set of footsteps, the older man stopped and faced Mike. "Look, I need a minute. It's time for me to punch in."

"Sure."

Twenty minutes later Harold returned to the hallway with a cart filled with cleaning supplies and equipment. "I haven't got a lot of time, so ask your questions so that I can get to work."

"I don't know if you're aware of this, but someone stole chemicals from the lab. Whoever it was took ingredients to manufacture the designer drug called Pleasure."

Mike watched the other man closely. He noticed a flicker of surprise in the depths of Harold's tired expression, and then it vanished. He shrugged. "Sorry, I didn't know that."

"One of the teachers got blamed for it and I'm trying to find out what really happened. Did you see anyone while you were cleaning this section of the building? Maybe there was a student that shouldn't have been here?"

"Nope. Not a soul." Harold wheeled the cart past Mike, stopping at one of the trash bins to remove the black plastic bag. He replaced it with an identical one before continuing to the next bin.

He opened the bag with a loud whoosh of air. "I didn't clean the lab."

Mike crossed his arms over his chest, watching the older man.

"Normally, you teachers let us know when you're going to use it and then I go in after you. Nobody told me nothing. So I didn't even open the door."

The lab had been cleaned and the trash pulled from the wastepaper basket. This man was lying. But why? If he was behind the manufacturing and selling of Pleasure, wouldn't he show some outward examples of prosperity? There was nothing particularly extravagant about the way he dressed.

There had to be a reason for Harold's nervousness and lies. Maybe something connected to the lab, but not the theft. What was really going on here?

"Well, thanks for talking with me." Mike offered his hand.

Harold hesitated for a minute, then clasped Mike's. "No problem. Sorry, I couldn't help," he said as he swung the broom in a wide circle on the floor.

Mike strolled to the staff entrance. The quiver in his voice spoke volumes. This man knew more than he was telling.

The time had come to talk with Jordan. Mike needed to know the details of that day.

Chapter 12

Being suspended sucks, Jordan decided as sadness and fatigue settled into her limbs. Curled in a ball on the window seat in her living room, she leaned her head against the glass pane, feeling the sun's rays penetrate her skin.

She sighed sorrowfully. Just when she started to really enjoy her work again, felt confident about her job, this happened. No contact with coworkers and students and no work to do at home.

If she had extra cash, she'd fly to Arizona to visit her family. A suspension without pay also meant no money. No money and no job for a week left her moping at home.

Her stomach rumbled. Absently, she rubbed her belly, although it continued to demand food. Time to cook, she decided, rising from the window seat and heading for the kitchen.

Jordan opened the refrigerator, examining its contents before removing a packet of chicken breasts, onions, celery, carrots, and mushrooms, placing them in the sink, and switching on the water. Maybe a stir-fry would take her mind off her problems and give her something positive to do.

The doorbell rang. Surprised, she dried her hands and headed for the door. In the living room, she glanced out the window, searching for a recognizable vehicle, but saw nothing.

Shrugging, she strolled down the hallway. At the apartment door, she checked the peephole. Smiling, she shook her head and opened the door. Her heart filled with happiness. "Mike! What are you doing here?"

"Hi." He gave her that smile that sent her pulse throbbing.

"How did you get my address?" she asked.

Mike waved a sheet in her face. "Fan out sheet."

Nodding, she said, "Oh yeah." She remembered receiving a fan out sheet with the addresses and telephone numbers of all the staff in case of emergency or school closure. "What brings you here?"

"You forgot something and I thought I'd bring it to you."

"What?"

"This." Grinning down at her, Mike whipped an item from behind his back, revealing the little dinosaur that he had lent her.

All of her sadness and self-pity dissipated with his small, but thoughtful gesture.

"Oh." She moaned, reaching for Mike and wrapping her arms around his neck. Unnamable sensations surged through her when he returned her gesture, wrapping his arms around her. Tongue-tied, she stammered over her words. "Th-Th-Thank you. This is so sweet of you."

He let out a sigh of contentment. His arms moved

around her small frame and held her close against him. "You're welcome. Can I come in?"

Slowly releasing him, she grabbed the green toy and opened the door wider. "Oh. I'm sorry. Sure. Come on in."

Jordan flipped on the hall light. Her eyes opened wide and her throat went dry. Mike looked incredible, dressed in black denims, a black T-shirt, and white Michael Jordan sneakers. Tall, in control, and completely handsome, he looked like one of those breath-stealing models in *Essence* magazine.

Jordan glanced down at her top and felt the sting of embarrassment as heat burned her cheeks. She wore an olive-green jogging suit that had seen better days. Bleach stains decorated the front of her top and the pants lay limply around her legs.

His hands rested at her waist, sending pleasure pumping through her body. He examined her intently, then asked, "What's wrong?"

She couldn't look at him. Instead, she focused on a light switch beyond his shoulder. "I'm embarrassed," Jordan whispered in a soft voice. "I don't deserve your friendship. I've been so ugly to you since the game and you've been great to me."

"Hey, I told you. First, I'm your friend."

"Thank you."

Mike waved a dismissing hand in the air, then wrapped an arm around her, heading down the hall to her living room. "All that baggage is over, done. We're going to forget it. Now my friend needs me. I plan to do everything in my power to get that suspension rescinded."

She needed his reassurance. Mike oozed confidence. He made her believe this situation just might work out in her favor.

Curious, he shoved his hands inside his pockets and checked out her apartment. Her place displayed a great deal of character. The hallway stretched into a long living room. Crème walls and blue carpeting made the room appear larger. A silver-blue, three-cushion tuxedo sofa rested against one wall. Shells patterned in mauve and white dotted the sofa's fabric. Two white Queen Anne chairs displayed the same shell pattern in blue and mauve. The chairs were strategically placed near the large bay window.

Mike examined several framed photos of the Grand Canyon and other picturesque locales decorating the walls. Family portraits graced the glass coffee and end tables.

"You don't have to check on me," Jordan said, flopping into one of the chairs. "I'm fine."

He sat on the sofa and stretched his legs out in front of him. The living room opened into a small dining room and he got a glimpse of the tiny kitchen beyond it. "I'm not a babysitter," he assured her.

"Why are you here?"

"I came to see my friend."

A warm, engaging smile spread across Jordan's face and she pointed to the kitchen. "I just started dinner. Would you like to stay?"

"Yes. Thank you. There's some stuff we need to discuss."

Standing, Jordan headed for the kitchen, determined to keep them both busy so that nothing stupid would come out of her mouth. "Come help me in the kitchen. Talk to me while I finish preparing dinner."

"Sure," he answered, following her. "What are we having?"

"Chicken stir-fry."

"Sweet," Mike said.

"Can you chop vegetables for me?"

"Sure." He turned on the faucet and reached for the liquid soap, washing and drying his hands.

She handed him a bowl and pointed to the vegetables waiting on the counter. Reaching for a pot, she added water and a dash of salt. "Is brown rice all right with you?"

"Yeah."

Jordan placed the pot over the range eye and turned on the jet. A flame sprang to life and she covered the water with a lid.

Mike grabbed a knife and washed the vegetables. As he chopped, he asked, "Did you notice anyone when you locked up the other night?"

She sighed. "I've told you before. I didn't see anyone."

"What about the custodian? Did you see him?" he asked, as the pungent aroma of onions nipped at his eyes, causing them to tear up.

"No, I didn't. Don't the cleaning people come in later?" she inquired as she washed, cleaned, and cubed the chicken.

"Sometimes." Mike tossed a handful of chopped vegetables into the bowl. "There are a few that show up before we leave for the day."

Facing him, she asked, "Why are you asking me this?"

With the knife in his hand he turned to her. "I've talked to Harold Crawford. Do you know him?"

"No." She shook her head, removed a wok from the rack, dribbled a bit of olive oil into the pan, and turned on the jet.

"He's the custodian assigned to our part of the building. I caught up with him today." He frowned. "Something's not right with him."

"Mike, don't the cleaning people have keys to all the

rooms?" she asked, measuring brown rice before adding it to the pot of boiling water.

"Yeah, they do."

"Are they suspects?"

"Yes."

"But it doesn't make any sense," she said, gnawing on her bottom lip. "Chemicals were taken. What would the custodian need with them?"

"I don't know. When I talked with Harold, he acted shifty. Nervous. Like he had something to hide. He's not to be trusted, Jordan." He raised a hand as if he were reaching for the answer. "Harold hit me wrong. I don't see him as a drug dealer, but there's definitely something going on."

Jordan tossed the chicken into the wok and used a wooden handle spoon to stir the sizzling poultry. "I would love for someone else to be responsible. All I know is I locked that door. After that point, I don't have an answer."

"I believe we have another suspect and I'm going to watch him. I have this feeling that Harold knows more than he's telling."

"I don't know him personally, but I've seen that guy. He doesn't strike me as the type to manufacture drugs. That would take a bit of knowledge about composition of chemicals and how to process them." She sprinkled spices, garlic, and Mrs. Dash over the chicken.

"You're right."

Jordan lifted a finger in Mike's direction. "Here's my problem with your scenario. School is a perfect location to sell drugs. But Harold isn't in the building when the kids are in class. When would he have a chance to do business?"

"Good point."

She opened the cupboard and removed dishes. "Come on, let's set the table. Dinner's almost ready."

Mike took dishes into the dining room and began to set the table. Jordan followed with water and wineglasses and a bottle of white Zinfandel.

"You drink wine, correct?" she asked.

"Mmm-hmm."

"Good." Jordan placed the corkscrew next to the bottle of wine. "Would you mind opening the bottle while I serve up the food?"

Minutes later, they sat down to dinner. Mike and Jordan completed the meal in silence.

Sighing contentedly, Mike pushed his near empty plate aside and picked up his glass of wine. "That was great, Jordan. Thanks for including me."

"Thank you. I'm glad you're here. Until you arrived, I was feeling pretty sorry for myself." She grinned. "I enjoyed having you for dinner. I guess you aren't the only one who hates to eat alone."

He reached across the table and squeezed her hand. "I loved being here. Plus, it gave me a chance to ask some more questions."

She sat, whirling the liquid in her glass. "You know, Mike, part of me agrees with you about Harold. But I'm not sure."

"It's okay if you don't agree with me. Harold is one of the avenues I'm pursuing. Don't worry. I'm going to find out."

"How?"

He took a sip of wine, then held Jordan's gaze with his own. "I'm going to stick with him and find out everything I can about how that man works."

"What do you expect to learn?"

"I don't know. The pieces aren't fitting together properly. I'm going to find out why."

She linked her fingers with his. "Be careful. We don't know enough about him or what he's capable of."

"Don't worry. I don't plan on becoming a statistic. All I want to do is find out what happened to those chemicals and who left the lab unlocked."

Chapter 13

I'm no James Bond, Mike silently admitted as he ducked behind the lab's door. He barely missed being seen by the subject in question.

Promising Jordan that he planned to do everything in his power to help her, Mike started a covert operation and surveillance to get the skinny on Harold Crawford. If he proved someone other than Jordan entered the lab after school hours, then she'd be off the hook.

Basically, there were two linked investigations. First, Mike needed to find out if Harold left the lab unlocked and to gather evidence to prove it. Second, he needed to discover who stole the chemicals and to pass on that information to the authorities.

I've got this feeling, there's more going on, Mike decided as he watched Harold shut and lock the math teacher's door. He pushed his cleaning cart down the hall, stopping to fumble with his radio headset before resuming work.

As Mike watched the custodian, his grandmother's image sprang to mind. He imagined her standing in front of him with one hand on her hip, strumming a finger in his face. Granny always said, "Baby, your instincts are the best guide that you'll ever have. They're better than all the other senses put together. Don't discount 'em."

And Mike never did. She'd been right. Throughout the years, his instincts had served him well and gotten him out of a lot of unexpected and unpleasant jams.

As he watched the older man, Mike's instincts cried that Harold failed to fit the profile of some big- or small-time drug dealer. Granted a school provided the perfect locale to establish a youthful client base. Mike refused to accept this scenario. It just didn't match the image he held of the custodian.

The cart's wheel scraped against the tile floor and pine cleaner lingered in the air as Harold continued down the hall to the main office. The older man opened the door and braced it with the cart, then went about his nightly tasks of emptying the wastepaper basket and dusting the furniture and countertops.

Quietly, Mike sprinted past the office, taking a quick peek. He settled in the copy room, listening to Harold's toneless rendition of Nat King Cole's "When I Fall in Love." The lyrics faded as Harold shuffled from the outer room to Chet's inner sanctum.

Pacing the floor, Mike checked his watch, flopping onto the stacked boxes of copy paper, content to wait for Harold to make his next move. Generally, he took approximately fifteen minutes to complete cleaning each room. Mike needed to vacate the copy area soon so that Harold didn't catch him.

Ten minutes later, Mike slipped across the hall to Ms. Hamilton's door. He quickly slid his key into the lock and entered the school counselor's office. He sighed. For the present, he felt safe.

There were times when being the basketball coach and athletic director came in handy. Chet gave him a master key in case he needed to contact parents after a game or received money that needed to be placed inside the safe in the principal's office.

Twenty minutes later, Mike waited anxiously for Harold to emerge from the office. He studied his watch, pacing the room. The door stood open, the lights were turned on, and the cleaning cart gave testament to his location. Harold had been in the principal's office for more than thirty minutes.

The faint strings of music floated through the air. What in the heck was that? Mike wondered. Had Harold turned on Chet's radio? Minutes later he heard a noise that reminded him of an airplane taking off.

Fifteen minutes later, the custodian closed and locked the door, then pushed his cart down the hall. Mike checked his watch. Harold had remained in the main office for close to an hour. What had he been doing?

Determined to find out, he crossed the corridor and used the master key to enter Chet's office. Everything appeared to be in its proper place. The room looked neat and clean while fresh trash bags lined the wastepaper baskets. What kept Harold in this room triple the time he'd spent in the other offices?

Mike's brows crinkled over his eyes as he examined the desk, searching for what had delayed Harold. The room looked fine, except the computer monitor and the printer were on. That was a big no-no.

He moved closer to the desk. Chet never left any equipment on. He preached energy conservation, going so far as to use the paging system to remind the faculty and staff to turn off all electrical equipment at the end of the school day. And he set an example by shutting down his office and switching off his computer.

Mike knew one way to figure it out. He moved to the desk and switched on the computer. The Microsoft Windows screen popped up and the tune confirmed what he suspected. There it was! The music he had heard earlier. Thinking back, he remembered a clicking sound that could have been the typing on a keyboard. Mike immediately tapped the log-in button, waiting for icons to configure into the appropriate order.

What had Harold been looking for? Mike popped his fingers when his eyes landed on the icon for Internet Explorer. Yes! That must be it. The custodian had been surfing the Net.

Nodding ruefully, he double-clicked on the icon. Internet Explorer loaded and Mike immediately went to History. Pleased with his progress, he felt a smile of satisfaction stealing away the edge of gloom that had controlled his emotions for the last couple of days.

There it is, he thought, tapping the screen. Harold had done an Internet search, and that sound he had heard earlier had been the printer.

Shutting down Chet's computer, Mike locked the office and headed for the lab. If his suspicions paid off and his luck held out, he'd be able to prove that Harold had entered the lab after Jordan, switched on the computer, and left the door unlocked after he finished surfing the Net.

The computer Internet history included a date/time stamp. That would achieve his goal and finally get Jordan out of this mess.

Excitement soared within him as he unlocked the lab and hurried to the computer. Mike pulled out a chair, sank into it, and booted up the machine.

His hopes rocketed when the log-in screen presented the stars that represented her password. "Bingo!" He clapped after following the same procedure he used on Chet's computer. Several entries were logged under the date and time that Jordan supposedly left the lab unlocked. The logged times were hours after the school day had ended. This should be enough proof to get the suspension rescinded.

Mike hit the Print Screen button, logged off the computer, and shut it down. He locked up the lab and rushed to the teachers' lounge to pick up his printout.

Satisfied, he folded the sheet and pocketed it and headed to the parking lot. Next, he needed to figure out who stole the chemicals and Jordan would be home free and her name completely cleared.

The next morning, Mike didn't have a chance to talk to Chet until his prep period. By the time he strolled into the office, he felt like a mass of nervous energy. He walked past Donna and stuck his head inside his boss's office.

"Chet, I need a minute of your time."

At hearing Mike's voice, Chet swiveled his chair in that direction. "Sure, come on in." He moved stacks of multicolored files from a chair to the floor and patted the cushion. "Have a seat."

"Debbie and Thurman may need to be in on this." He folded his arms across his chest. "But that can wait. I'd like to talk with you first."

"Is this about Jordan?" Chet asked, picking up a pencil and tapping it against the desk's surface.

"Yes. Jordan didn't leave the lab unlocked. She's not responsible for what happened with the chemicals—"

Chet sighed as if he'd gone over this stuff a million times and didn't plan to cruise the same territory. "Now, Mike, I understand that you're concerned for Jordan because you're her mentor. You feel responsible—"

"You don't understand," Mike interrupted.

"But she'll survive. This type of incident can not go

unpunished. It's a major problem to have chemicals missing. It's not pretty."

Mike nodded. "I understand all of that, but Jordan didn't do it. Here's proof." He removed the sheet of paper from his back pocket and handed it to Chet. "Last night I did a little snooping."

"Snooping against who?" Chet's brows drew together as he examined the sheet. "What is this?"

"It's the history for the Internet on the lab's computer." Mike pointed a finger at the date and time. "Look at the log-in times. They are well beyond when Jordan left the building. This proves that someone else entered the lab after her. The only people around that late in the day are the cleaning crew."

The principal dropped the sheet on his desk. He tented his fingers, reviewing the information. "How did you get this?"

"I asked around. Found out who was in the building that day. I even talked to the supervisor." A bit embarrassed, Mike scratched the side of his neck with a finger. "He told me who worked which sides of the building. When I talked to Harold, his explanations didn't click. He felt wrong. Something didn't add up, so I watched him."

"That's not appropriate behavior."

Mike pulled up a chair next to Chet and sat. "Maybe not. But it did get me what I needed."

"Oh, come on, Mike. Look at the sites he supposedly visited. Ameritrade. The *Wall Street Journal.*" Chet slapped the page with the back of his hand. "Do you really think our custodian would be interested in stuff like this?"

"Why not? Do you know him personally? Harold has a life outside of this building." Mike glared at Chet. "Do you socialize with him outside work hours?"

"No, but—"

"But nothing. You don't know any more about Harold than I do. Actually, I know more." Mike fell silent for several moments as he searched for a way to drive his point home. An idea hit him when his gaze landed on Chet's computer.

"Get on the Internet, Chet."

"Why?"

"Harold cleaned your office yesterday."

Chet shook his head. "Mike, this is crazy. He's here every school day."

"Just trust me. I think I can make my point using your computer."

I should have done this first, Mike thought as he waited for the programs to load.

Mike rose from his chair, leaned over his boss, and clicked on History. A pull-down menu displayed a variety of sites that had been visited within the last two weeks. He tapped the monitor with a finger, addressing the items on the list. "First of all, you weren't here at five thirty-eight p.m. But, just in case you were, did you visit E-trade? Or the stock exchange Web site? How about ING or Fidelity Investments?"

"No."

Nodding, Mike returned to his chair. "I waited outside your office while Harold cleaned last night. He takes approximately twenty minutes to clean each classroom. Yet it took him almost an hour to finish in here."

Chet's eyebrows climbed toward the ceiling. "Oh?"

Mike nodded. "Yeah. When he left, I looked around, trying to figure out what kept him for damn near an hour. Then it hit me. He'd used your computer."

"Wait a minute. Even if that was the case, how did he

log in? He's not an authorized user." Chet studied his computer screen.

"You are."

"What?"

"You have your computer set up so that the system automatically remembers your log-in and password. That's all Harold needed."

The principal ran a hand over the fine fuzz on his head. Conflicting emotions raced across his face. "Well, if that's the case, Jordan didn't do anything wrong."

"That's my point," Mike answered with a note of satisfaction in his voice. "She's innocent."

Chet grimaced. "I owe her an apology."

"You owe her more than that," Mike answered decisively. "She deserves back pay, rescinding the suspension, and a public apology."

"You're right. But there's still another problem."

"The chemicals, right?"

Chet nodded.

"I'm working on that. I think someone knows Harold's routine. They waited until he left the lab and then took what they wanted."

"Possibly."

"My gut tells me a student is involved. Harold doesn't strike me as the type who operates a drug business."

Chet waved the sheet at Mike. "A minute ago you revealed my own prejudices. Couldn't you be blind to your own?"

"Maybe. But it feels like a student to me. Give me a little time and I'll sort this out and I'll prove my case."

"Let me know what you find out right away."

"I will."

Chet glanced at his white wall clock. "I'll call Jordan with the good news. It's Friday. She won't be able to come back to work until Monday."

"Just so long as she makes it back." Mike backed out of the office. "Thanks, Chet. Do you want to tell Debbie what I found, or should I?"

Chet waved him away. "No. It's my job. I'll take care of things."

Mike left Chet's office with a sense of satisfaction. A great weight had been lifted from his chest. He'd done what he set out to do and got Jordan reinstated.

One down and one to go, Mike thought as he considered how best to flush out the thief. All of his instincts told him that their thief was a student, someone in the building who saw everything that went on and knew how to use each opportunity.

Strolling down the hall, Mike pursed his lips as he considered ways to smoke out their culprit. A sting operation might be his best approach. It might force this person out of the shadows and into the light.

Chapter 14

Friday night found Mike settled on his sofa in a charcoal jogging suit. After a long, stressful week of school, kids, and Jordan's investigation, he needed time to kick back and relax.

He planted his legs on the cherry-wood coffee table and crossed them at the ankles. Duke Ellington's "Take the A Train" punctuated the silence of Mike's Indian Village home through a Bose stereo system while he sipped his glass of burgundy merlot.

A gigantic sigh of contentment escaped Mike. He rested his head against the back of the sofa and smiled as Jordan's image took shape in his mind. Monday morning, she'd return to Pierson, strutting down the corridors as if she owned the place.

Now phase two of his plan needed his prompt attention. Romancing Jordan shared the top slot on his agenda with finding the person who had stolen those chemicals.

The doorbell rang, breaking into his thoughts. He dropped his legs to the floor, got off the sofa, and started across the room.

At the front door, he glanced through the peephole.

His eyes widened. Jordan! What brought her to his door? A rueful smile replaced his surprised expression. He knew.

A gush of fall wind blew through the foyer, depositing dead leaves on the marble floor when he opened the door. Giving himself precious moments to compose himself at this unexpected turn of events, he waved Jordan inside and closed and locked the entrance. With a quick step, he blocked the hallway leading to the living room.

"Jordan." He nodded at her, then asked in an even tone, "What can I do for you?"

She hesitated, observing him with uncertain eyes. His tone hadn't been particularly friendly.

"I—I—I wanted to thank you." Clearly at a loss, she stammered, reaching out a hand to touch him. Her hand halted before it made contact, fluttering indecisively in the air before dropping to her side.

His gut twisted into knots. He didn't want Jordan to come here gushing her thanks. When she came to him, Mike wanted her at his place because she needed and wanted him, not because she felt indebted.

"Mike, you did it. Chet called and told me that I'm back on the schedule for Monday."

His glance trailed along her body. In a split second his heart rate shot over a thousand. *Lord, give me strength.*

A skimpy black silk dress peeked through her coat opening. The garment hugged her thighs and left bare her shapely legs, while revealing a wonderful helping of soft brown skin at her neckline.

Mike drew in a ragged breath that felt like knives in his chest. "Don't worry about it," he said, leaning against the door frame.

A multitude of conflicting emotions flirted across her

face. "Well, I just wanted to let you know how much I appreciated you and what you did."

"I'm your mentor. It's my job to make sure you get through your first year with a minimum of problems," he answered in a tone that revealed nothing.

She stepped closer and placed her warm palm against the side of Mike's cheek. His eyes drifted shut as he leaned into Jordan's caress, savoring the delightful sensations her gentle touch created.

Opening his eyes, he examined the tense expression on her face, his heart sank. If only she truly wanted to be with him, then he would sweep her into his arms and never let her go.

After a moment Jordan's hand dropped and she moved closer. She wrapped her arms around his waist, hugging him. Jordan lifted her head, offering her mouth, and he accepted her gift.

Her lips moved over his and unconsciously he began to kiss her back, releasing all the emotions in his heart. A soft moan rose from deep in her throat, encouraging him to explore her essence more thoroughly. He drank deeply, memorizing the unique favor of Jordan as his flesh reacted to her closeness.

Mike began to shake, touched by the gentleness of her gesture, but frustrated by how little the kiss truly meant. Their kiss promised so much and yet it gave so little.

Drawing her closer, he felt a tremor course through her. His fingers caressed her throat, detecting traces of perspiration at the base of her neck. He wiped the liquid from her neck and gently pushed her away, presenting his damp fingers as evidence.

They weren't ready for the next step. The emotional connection that he longed for was absent.

"No." He panted, leaning his forehead against hers. "This isn't happening tonight."

"Why?" Jordan asked. Eyes clouded over with disbelief, she reached for him a second time. "I don't understand."

"That's for sure. Let me make things clear. I know that you don't want to be here," he muttered, drawing a wobbly hand over his hair. It hurt him to push those words from his lips. With all his heart, he wished she wanted to be here with him, but this visit involved guilt and gratitude.

"This is my way of thanking you," she stated in a small, puzzled voice.

"Yeah, I got that," Mike muttered, running his tongue across his lips. His stomach clenched as he savored her unique taste, wanting more and hating the fact that he must deny himself that fantastic pleasure."

"Maybe I should come in and we can talk some more." She swallowed loudly and glanced pointedly past him to the living room. "I mean, we'll be more comfortable inside."

Shaking his head, Mike caught her arm and kept her in the foyer. His emotions were in an uproar. On one hand, he wanted to drag her inside the house and take what she so blatantly offered. But he didn't want her if guilt and obligations were the only feelings that brought her to his door.

"No. You've said your thanks. I appreciate the gesture." He rolled his shoulders, relieving a tiny fusion of tension. "It's getting late. You need to be on your way."

Jordan's forehead crinkled into a frown and her voice held a confused quality. "Don't you want to . . . talk?"

"I don't want that kind of talk."

"I thought—I thought—" she stammered, worrying her bottom lip with her teeth.

"Let me lay my cards on the table. I want you. Now, tonight, tomorrow, and always. But you've got to want to be here, because you believe this is where you belong. I can't and won't take anything less."

"I do want to be here."

His voice dropped. "Jordan, I don't want your gratitude."

"This isn't about gratefulness," she answered quickly. Too quickly.

One eyebrow raised suggestively, Mike chose his next words carefully, and then aimed them like daggers. "Isn't it? Chet asked you to return to work Monday. Aren't you the least bit grateful?"

Like a reprimanded child Jordan stood silently before him, refusing to look at him.

"You know that I'm attracted to you and want to be with you. Can you honestly stand in front of me and say that Chet's call had absolutely nothing to do with your being here tonight?"

Jordan's gaze dropped and she fidgeted with the buttons on her coat.

Disappointment and pain warred for supremacy. "Here's the deal. When you're ready to come here because you want to be with me, then come back. You have an open invitation. Tonight, I'm not interested in what you're offering. Once you've resolved the situation in your mind, gotten over your moment of 'I need to pay him for helping me'"—Mike's voice dropped an octave—"then we can have an honest dialogue about our feelings and the future."

"I thought you would want to . . ." Her voice trailed off.

"Not today. And not like this."

"Oh."

He placed his hands on her shoulders and turned her to face him, using a finger under her chin to tilt her face up. "Don't get me wrong. There's a lot I do want from you. But not like this. Not this way."

"I'm so embarrassed," she muttered, turning away.
"Don't be."

"You probably think I do this kind of thing all the
time."

"Never crossed my mind." Mike smiled sadly. "Here's
some hypothetical questions. Say we enjoy tonight and
each other. Will you be here tomorrow morning? What
about dinner after work next week? Are you willing to
open yourself up to whatever comes next between us?"

A delicate shade of pink stained Jordan's cheeks
and she shifted away before he had an opportunity to
read the expression in her eyes. It didn't matter. He
knew how she felt. A pity party for one didn't appeal
to Mike. She could take this shindig elsewhere.

He whispered, soft and enticing, "Jordan, your heart
isn't in this. That's what I want."

Drawing on his emergency energy bank, Mike stepped
around her, unlocked and opened the front door, and
grabbed a jacket from the coatrack. He took her arm,
gently guiding her from the warmth of the house into
the cool evening air. "It's getting late, you need to get
home. I'll walk you to your car."

Jordan drove aimlessly along Jefferson Avenue. Why
hadn't he accepted what she had made available? She
saw how his eyes strayed when she unbuttoned her coat.
The atmosphere in the room grew thick with tension
as they discussed her unannounced visit.

Wearily, Jordan shook her head. *I need to think,* she
thought.

Turning into the parking lot connected to the International House of Pancakes, she slipped her car into
the first empty space. Jordan shut off the engine, got

out of the car, and crossed the pavement to the front doors of the restaurant.

IHOP on Jefferson presented a unique variation on the standard International House of Pancakes. Its décor gave the patrons a glimpse into Detroit's Motown heyday. Photographs of the Temptations, the Supremes, the Jackson Five, and the Queen of Soul, Aretha Franklin, graced the walls of the eatery while music from Motown greats filled the restaurant.

The Supremes' "Baby Love" greeted Jordan when she opened the door. Finding a booth at the back of the restaurant, she dropped onto the blue vinyl bench and ordered a hot chocolate. Drowning in the muck of self-pity, she covered her face with her hands.

She felt so stupid, forcing her way into Mike's home. After receiving the call from Chet, she'd wanted to see Mike and give him something special. A gift designed for him alone. After deciding on her present, Jordan got his address from the fan out sheet and did a quick MapQuest search for directions on the Internet. She'd rushed to his home determined to show him how much she appreciated his efforts on her behalf.

Sitting in Mike's driveway, Jordan questioned her crazy plan. Uncertainty crept down her spine as she made her way up the steps and onto the porch. Had she been wrong to try and offer him this gift? Unfortunately, or maybe fortunately, Mike had refused her, insisting on an emotional commitment.

Afraid to give him her heart, she left and started home. But she didn't feel quite ready to give in completely.

Jordan shut her eyes, seeing Mike's drawn features. She did a quick mental flashback over her time at Pierson and how he had changed her life.

Mike had been at her side since her first day, offering

support and affection. When her panic attacks rendered her useless in the classroom, he'd provided the perfect solution to get her back on track. She looked forward to his visits to her classroom each morning, sharing a cup of hot chocolate as they discussed their day.

When she got in trouble, he never stopped until the truth had been revealed and her job was safe. He'd shown himself to be a wonderful friend over and over and yet she hadn't done anything to show her gratitude. And that's what led her to his house tonight.

What did she really feel for Mike? He was one of the first thoughts she had in the morning and they spoke every evening before she went to bed. Yes, she cared deeply for him. No man had ever stood at her side the way Mike had.

Whenever Mike was near, she saw the love shining in his eyes. Although those emotions frightened her, she suspected that she would miss this feeling of being cared for if he disappeared from her life.

Jordan wanted everything Mike had to offer. More than wanted, she loved having him around. In fact, she loved him. If she was honest with herself, she needed him in her life.

What did she have to lose? Her heart, her soul. Hands shaking, Jordan lifted her mug and drained the hot chocolate.

How long did she plan to hide from life? Mike had taught her how to cope in the classroom. Now he offered an opportunity to have more, to have the love she'd always wanted. She needed to stop hiding and get on with life, take what Mike offered, and toss her worries aside.

Her heart skipped a beat and a smile formed on her lips. Standing, Jordan picked up her purse and the bill, then marched to the cashier. For the first time in a long time, she planned to seize the moment, take a leap of faith, and hope for the best.

Jordan climbed back into her car and started the engine. She drove down Jefferson back to Indian Village. If Mike wanted her, she was his.

Chapter 15

With a flash of fierce determination blaring from her eyes and fear in her heart, Jordan pulled into Mike's driveway, turned off the engine, and got out of the car.

For the second time in less than two hours she approached his front door. After ringing the doorbell, she waited, silently praying for inspiration. Her first visit had led to some pretty intense soul searching and a revelation that eventually led her back to Mike's house.

She loved Michael Walker. Had loved him from the day he brought her the little dinosaur to help calm her nerves.

Armed with her new resolve and wavering courage, Jordan returned to clear the air between them. If Mike didn't reject her before she had a chance to explain, she hoped to convince him that she was sincere in her feelings.

The door swung open and Mike loomed over her, large and disapprovingly. Well, she refused to allow his height to intimidate her.

His hand dropped from the doorknob to his side and he asked in a harsh tone, "What is it now, Jordan?"

Stunned, she swallowed past the huge lump lodged

in her throat, squared her shoulders, and gazed boldly back at him. "I need to talk with you about what happened earlier."

"Go ahead."

Jordan floundered, stammering, "C-c-can I——" She halted, drawing in a deep breath and letting it out slowly. She tried a second time. "This is personal. Can I at least come into the hallway?"

Mike opened the door wider and moved away. She stopped inside the entrance with the door open, allowing the damp, night air to flirt around her ankles. She was filled with worry; her hands fluttered around the neck of her sleeveless black dress before settling in the pockets of her trench coat.

"First, you were right. I did come here to thank you for helping me. I wanted to give you something special. Something only I could offer you and I know you wanted."

"And?" he prompted.

"I knew that you were attracted to me and so I figured you couldn't resist." Embarrassed, she blushed cherry red under the brown of her skin, studying a point beyond his shoulder. "Obviously, I made a mistake."

"You didn't make a mistake," came Mike's quiet but powerful statement.

Jordan's mouth parted in surprise. Had she heard him correctly? Her gaze switched from the floor to Mike. "What do you mean?"

He shrugged. "You heard me."

"I don't understand." Bewildered, she asked, "Why did you turn me away?"

"I told you. You're special, at least to me."

Those words warmed her heart, but didn't change the fact that she'd been brutally rejected earlier that evening.

"Jordan, trust me, there are willing women out in the streets. But," he said, cupping her cheek in his warm palm, "I chose you."

"And I'm choosing you," she said boldly. "But I need you to know that I'm not good at relationships. I've screwed up a lot, Mike. Do you honestly believe I can give you what you need?"

Mike's hand rested on her shoulders, stroking them, and he answered in a soft, husky whisper, "Yes. I don't have a doubt. All you have to do is love me. That's what I need. Stop shutting me out. Let things happen naturally between us. That's all I want. The rest will come."

She frowned. His reasoning sounded too easy to be true.

"I want to be part of your life and vice versa." He drew her into his arms and kissed her hair. "Now, tomorrow, and forever."

"Oh, Mike. I can't deny how you make me feel." Jordan gazed into his eyes, took his hand, entwining her fingers with his.

He brought her hand to his lips and kissed it.

"And I'm tired of pretending that what I feel doesn't matter, because that's a lie. I don't want to live a lie anymore. Mike, I care about you. I don't want to say the love word yet because it's still too new to me. But I want to see where this leads."

The warmth of his smile was infectious.

"There's something else," she muttered softly, afraid of his reaction.

"Tell me," Mike encouraged.

Jordan continued, fingering the gold chain at her neck, "I'm not sweet sixteen. Mileage comes with this particular model. If you can't handle it, now is the time to back out. Because once we cross this line, it's going to hurt both of us to go back to the way things were."

Mike stepped forward and took her into his arms. "I don't want to go back. I want us together. Just don't get scared. Promise me that you'll talk to me."

She hesitated, frightened by the sea of emotions that she'd hadn't felt in a very long time, if ever. Had she lost her mind, allowing this man into her life? He had the ability to destroy the balance she'd searched for since joining the staff of Pierson High School.

Opening her life to him carried the possibility of rejection, pain, and ridicule. If or when their relationship became public knowledge, she could almost hear the catty comments from her colleagues.

Running a shaky hand across her forehead, she turned slightly away from him. This was hard. Opening herself up this way made her feel more vulnerable than she'd ever been in her entire life. She loved Mike and wanted everything that he offered. It might not last, but she had to seize the opportunity and enjoy their time together.

"I will," Jordan answered.

Fear knotted Jordan's insides as she stood, paralyzed, in the center of Mike's living room. She loved Mike, she truly did, and wanted to be with him, but her old insecurities were choking all of her good intentions.

Silently, Mike crossed the living room floor and took her hand. Like a lamb being led to the slaughter, she followed him up the stairs to the second floor. They stopped at an ajar door. He led her through the entrance and into his bedroom.

Immediately, Jordan's gaze flew directly to the bed and she shivered slightly. She'd never been very good at sex. Always felt inadequate when it came to the art of making love. After several unsatisfying romances and misfires, Jordan decided to find solace in her career and leave love and relationships to others.

Now she was on the brink of another relationship and she was scared. More than scared, she was petrified that she'd mess up things and lose the man that had become so dear to her.

Gently, Mike cupped Jordan's face between his large hands, lowering his mouth to nibble on the edge of her bottom lip. Unconsciously, she eased closer and nibbled back as he stroked the spark of desire. She slipped her hands under his sweats, enjoying the feel of his muscles.

Mike deepened the kiss, allowing his tongue to slip between her lips, eager for a taste of her sweetness. He drank deeply. The kiss went on and on. It grew hotter and wetter, until she didn't know where he stopped and she began.

Time slowed and yet moved quickly as he removed her clothes with maddening unhurried movements. Her dress slid through his fingers, gliding to the floor with a soft *whoosh*.

Within minutes she stood before him in her midnight lace bra and panties. Her heart pounded against her breasts. What would he think of her? she wondered. Sheer fright swept through her and she folded her arms across her chest to shield herself from his view.

"Don't," he whispered quietly, pushing her arms away from her body. "I want to see all of you." The huskiness in his voice made her quiver in response.

"This is embarrassing," she admitted in a weak voice. "I don't want to disappoint you."

"There's no way that can happen," he answered. "You don't know how I've ached to be with you. Don't be embarrassed."

I can't help it, Jordan thought, wishing he'd turn off

the lights and let her slide under the covers. Although she maintained a regular regiment of exercise and diet, she still had the form of a thirty-eight-year-old woman.

He smiled. The reassuring twist of his lips reached his eyes and warmed her soul. "There's no way you could do that. I love everything about you."

"How could you think that?" Jordan asked, doing a mental comparison of herself with the young women closer to his age. "I'm old. I have wrinkles."

"Only in your mind. You see wrinkles, I see a woman with character, warmth, and beauty beyond anything I've known in my life." He gathered her into his arms, holding her snugly against him. "To me it makes you more precious and desirable. Don't hide yourself from me. I want all of you."

Tears pooled in Jordan's eyes and a knot rose in her throat. Mike always knew the perfect thing to do or say that made her feel wonderful. At this moment, she felt complete.

Mike swung her into the circle of his arms and marched to the bed, laying her in the center. He stood over the bed, removing his clothes. Jordan watched, admiring the sleek, muscular lines of the man she loved. He settled onto the mattress beside her.

He was gorgeous, smooth, dark, and handsome, and Jordan wanted to touch and taste him all over. Her hands roamed the hard planes of his chest and back. A loud guttural growl of pleasure left his lips.

"You are so beautiful," he whispered softly, drawing her against his hard frame as he ran a finger along the slope of her neck. He kneaded her breasts through the lace of her bra. Her nipples hardened to taut nubs waiting for his attention. Moving lower, Mike slipped her panties over her hips and off her body.

"So are you," she returned, sliding a hand over his belly, hovering mere inches from his shaft.

He flicked the clasp on the front of her bra and gasped when she was revealed to him. "God, you're everything I expected and more," he muttered reverently.

His lips created a trail of soft kisses down her neck and she found it nearly impossible to remain still. Returning his caresses, she stroked the tight muscles of his chest.

Desire flickered in the pit of her stomach, spreading through her veins. He worshipped her with his hands and mouth. Suckling her nipples, he learned the texture and taste of her breasts. She whimpered, craving more.

Jordan moved restlessly against him. Her hands caressed his broad shoulders and torso, moving lower. Jordan took his hardened flesh in her hand, stroking the smooth skin. Mike groaned, shutting his eyes as he savored the sensations. Adding an additional element, she nibbled on his bottom lip before deepening the kiss.

Mike rolled onto his side and retrieved a condom, tore the tiny tinfoil package open, and rolled the latex over his erection. He positioned himself between Jordan's legs at her entrance, then pushed into her wet, welcoming core.

Jordan moaned, loving the sensation of having him sheathed completely within her. Carefully he began to move, thrusting in and out at a strong, steady pace as he stroked her inner walls with his flesh. Jordan rose to match each thrust of his body, wanting and needing everything he had to give. Their pace increased to a frantic frenzy as he pumped into her until he began to tremble.

Panting, Jordan felt her orgasm start deep within her, building as Mike continued to make love to her. Her muscles tightened around him and he immediately flew over the edge, spilling his hot seed into her.

Hours later, Jordan lay cradled in Mike's arms. She snuggled closer, enjoying the warmth of his body and the earthy scent of sex that filled the room. It felt right to be here with him.

The comfort of darkness lent support to her remaining insecurities. "So," Jordan began, purring like a satisfied cat while circling his nipple with the tip of her fingernail, "was having sex with your teacher one of your fantasies?"

Mike pulled her tighter against his side and tenderly kissed her forehead. "No," he answered in a strong, confident voice, "but making love with Jordan Anderson has been my fantasy since the tenth grade."

She savored each word, hugging him. Even if it wasn't true, she loved hearing it.

"If I'm your fantasy," she said with a silky suggestive tone, "how did I rate?"

"A-plus," he growled into her ear, tracing the outline with the tip of his tongue. The deep, husky rumble and wet tongue sent ripples along her spine.

Jordan giggled, loving this man. "Thank you."

How did he do that? she wondered. He made her feel so special with such a simple phrase.

Without hesitation, she lifted her head and offered him her lips. Mike accepted her invitation, sampling the sweet nectar of her lips.

"You're welcome. But we need to conduct a series of tests to make certain that I haven't missed anything," Mike suggested, weaving his fingers through her hair.

"Sounds good to me."

They lay in the afterglow, enjoying the closeness.

Jordan contemplated how wonderful it would be together like this forever.

"Jordan?"

"Hmm?" she muttered back.

"Why?" he asked.

She knew what he wanted. "I told you earlier."

"Tell me again, Jordan. Make me understand."

"Mike, look at me."

"I am." He gently stroked her cheek, then smiled.
"And you're beautiful."

"No, I'm not. I'm a thirty-eight-year-old woman that
doesn't want to make a fool out of herself." She refused
to look at him, instead choosing to fidget with the
edge of the sheet that protected them against the cool
evening air.

"You can never be that."

"Spoken like a young man who never had to worry
about looking silly."

Chuckling, he asked, "What are you talking about?
You've pretty much reduced me to silliness. I've done
everything but stand on my head to get your attention for
months while you walked around me like I didn't exist."

Giggling, she held his gaze with her own. "Trust me,
no matter how I appeared, you're difficult to ignore."

"Good. I like that."

She muttered uncomfortably, "Seriously, what are we
going to do?"

"About what?" Mike asked, caressing her back with
light, tender strokes of his hands.

"I'm ten years older than you."

"So?"

"I'm not like the girls you probably date."

"No, you're not," he answered.

"You may be disappointed in who and what I am."

"I doubt that. Jordan, from the minute Debbie announced that you were joining the staff, I've been waiting for you, fantasizing about you. Not some young woman. You! With that lean, willowy body and smooth tea-colored skin. Believe me, if I wanted a relationship with someone my age, I'd have it. But you offer much more and I want everything that you're willing to give."

"I don't understand what you see in me." Jordan bit her lip. She didn't mean to sound so insecure or needy. There were times when she felt so baffled by the whole attraction thing it was as if she was walking barefoot on shifting sand.

Mike laughed out loud. The hearty sound filled the room. "You don't see it, do you?"

Confused, she answered, "See what?"

"What I see when I look at you. Jordan, you're a beautiful woman. But I'm drawn to so much more." He hugged her close and tasted her lips. "There are wonderful things about you. I can't believe that you don't see them. You're intelligent, caring, and loving and wonderfully passionate beyond belief."

Basking in the warmth of his compliment, she kissed his chest. Feeling more confident about their relationship, Jordan began to hope. Maybe things would work out for them. Maybe they had what it took to make their relationship last. She hoped so, because she'd just put everything on the line to be with him.

Chapter 16

The sultry voice of Ella Fitzgerald swirled through the room as Mike moved around his large country kitchen. He hummed softly, removing a black iron skillet from the hook on the baker's rack, then glanced in the direction of his houseguest, sitting at the kitchen table.

The smile on Mike's face grew broader. His eyes softened at the sight of Jordan, admiring the delightful picture she made, waiting patiently for her breakfast. Unaware of her effect on him, she sat in the chair cocooned in his white button-down shirt and nothing else, while she sipped a mug of green tea and read the *Detroit Free Press*.

She glanced from the paper, noticing the expression on Mike's face. Her eyes grew large and liquid. "What are you smiling at?"

"You."

Confused, she blinked, then shook her head. "Me! Why?"

Mike returned to the table, took her hand, and kissed the palm. "You have no idea how long I've wanted to see you like this, how beautiful you are, and how much I love having you here."

Jordan glanced down at the borrowed shirt, grinning back at him. "You wanted to see me like this?" she asked with a provocative sway of her shoulders. A trace of laughter filled her voice.

His gaze followed her movements, settling on the chocolate expanse of her neck before shifting lower. Her breasts moved freely and gracefully under the shirt and Mike's breath caught in his throat. Reluctantly, he spun away from this enticing view, fighting the urge to sweep her into his arms and return to his bedroom.

Facing Jordan, he lifted his eyebrows suggestively. "Actually, I'd like to see you dressed in nothing at all. You game?"

A flash of desire flared in her eyes. "First, I need nourishment to continue our bedroom aerobics. So feed me." She winked, sending him a smile filled with sensual promise. "Then we'll discuss the rest."

"So romantic," he bemoaned good-naturedly.

"What do you expect?" she teased. "Generally, I have to prepare my own meals. This is too good a treat to ignore and I plan to enjoy it."

Chuckling, Mike turned back to the stove. He sprayed the pan with a nonstick coating. "I see your point. One ham and cheese omelet coming up."

The grin returned to Mike's face. Happiness filled him. It felt wonderful to have Jordan in his house, in his bed, and in his kitchen on a Saturday morning. Finally, after months of struggling to persuade her to see him as more than a colleague or former student, she'd realized that she did have feelings for him and wanted to pursue their relationship.

The aromas of fresh green onions, cheddar cheese, and ham wafted throughout the kitchen. He glanced at Jordan and caught her sniffing the air appreciatively.

Hair flowing around her shoulders and her lips moist from his kisses, Jordan made his heart pound and his pulse jolt.

Mike moved to the refrigerator and opened the door. "Multigrain or wheat?"

"Wheat, please."

Nodding, Mike removed a loaf of wheat bread. He dropped two slices into the toaster and returned to the refrigerator for orange juice, butter, and jam.

"I hope you like strawberry jam. It's all I have," he explained, setting the items on the table.

"Hmm, strawberry is perfect."

"Good. Breakfast is almost ready," Mike announced, flipping the omelet.

The toast popped up and he buttered it, placing the plate of brown slices in front of her.

"I'm starving. Mike, do you mind if I munch on a slice?"

"No." He gazed her way. "Help yourself. I don't want you telling people that I wore you out and wouldn't feed you."

Jordan laughed as she reached for the jam, spreading a hearty portion on the slice of bread. Seconds later he heard an appreciative moan. "This is heavenly."

"I'm a connoisseur of toast making." He smiled at his own joke.

"Darn it!"

Mike glanced over his shoulder at Jordan. "What?"

Strawberry jam oozed down the front of the shirt Jordan wore. She held the front of the shirt away from her body as if it were wet.

He turned off the range.

She smirked. "You know, you can't take me anywhere. Sorry about the shirt."

"It's no biggie," Mike responded, scooping the

omelet from the pan and placing it on a plate. He returned to the table with the food in his hand.

She reached for a paper napkin, dabbing ineffectively at the stain.

"Wait," Mike ordered in an urgent tone, sliding the plate onto the table. He hurried to Jordan and removed the napkin from her hand.

Puzzled, Jordan crinkled her forehead as she gazed at him.

"I've got a better idea," he said, dropping to his knees in front of her.

"Oh?"

"Mmm-hmm," Mike muttered, leaning toward the strawberry jam. His tongue flicked out and licked at the red blob.

Flustered, Jordan gasped. Her body quivered as his eager tongue met soft skin concealed by cotton fabric. Delighted, she gripped his shoulders.

Mike's eyes found and held hers as he concentrated on removing every drop of jam from the shirt. With a long, slow stroke of his tongue, he wet the fabric, sliding up the garment and lingering over the brown nipple visible under the damp shirt.

On his next stroke, he suckled her erect nipple, rolling the nub between his teeth before sharply drawing on it. His hand crept under the hem of the fabric and inched its way up her beautiful body, caressing her skin. He cupped a breast in his large hand, toying with the tip while stroking her flesh, providing loving attention to both breasts.

Jordan leaned closer. Her tantalizing scent filled his nostrils as she ran her hand over Mike's hair. She cradled his head against her breast, encouraging his touch. As the sensations took control, her eyes fluttered shut. Sharp gasps punctuated the air as her body moved in harmony with the exotic dance of Mike's hand and tongue.

Mike was in heaven. Everything he did, he did for Jordan. He wanted to build a strong foundation of trust between them, boost her confidence in their relationship and most importantly in his commitment to her. He wanted Jordan to feel that she belonged at his home and they were a couple, a team.

He gazed at Jordan, captivated by the rapture on her face. Her eyes were closed. A fine film of perspiration dotted her forehead.

"See?" Mike stroked a finger over the damp spot that moments earlier had been covered with strawberry jam. He deftly unbuttoned the shirt and freed her breasts from its confines, leaning back on his haunches, he admired his handiwork. "All better."

Slowly, Jordan's eyes opened to narrow slits, revealing deep desire and the promise of satisfaction. "Thank you."

"You're welcome," Mike answered in a voice made husky with passion and love. His lips trailed openmouthed kisses over her body, tasting her flesh as he worked his way from her navel.

His hands spanned her small waist as he brought her closer, moving along her rib cage. He captured a breast in one hand, running his thumb back and forth against her nipple while kissing the top of the soft mounds. His tongue raked the hard, little bud, then he attached his lips firmly to her nipple.

Jordan arched her back, pressing her flesh eagerly against his lips.

He kissed the nub before suckling it.

Soft kisses were pressed against the side of her neck, along her jawline, before his lips settled against hers.

Mike closed his eyes as his lips brushed against

Jordan's. Before the first kiss ended, the second began. Jordan moaned against his lips as he felt a tingle make its way down his spine. "It's time we take this to another place."

He lifted her into his arms and strolled through the house, up the stairs, and to his bedroom. Gently, he placed her on the unmade bed and climbed in after her, facing her. He brushed his lips against hers. As he deepened the kiss, his fingers threaded through her loose hair.

"Let's try something different this time." Mike turned her on her side, spoon fashion, molding her soft curves to the contours of his body. Brushing the hair away from her neck, he kissed his way up from there, tasting the soft flesh quivering under his lips.

The heat of her excitement radiated from her body, heightening his desire.

Taking a moment to put on a condom, Mike thrust inside her from behind and wrapped his arms around her waist, keeping her glued to him, then slowly settling into a smooth, steady rhythm. His hands crept up her body, settling on her breasts, stroking her nipples as they moved together.

He withdrew, then plunged into her, moving faster and faster, driving deeper with each stroke. Her fingers ran over the smooth, warm skin of his thigh as their passion burned hot. She rocked her hips upward to meet his, welcoming each stroke of his hard shaft.

"I love you, Jordan," he whispered into her hair as he drove them higher and higher toward ecstasy. Pleasure mounted until he felt the first tentative quivering of her internal walls.

She cried out his name. Her body pulsed around him, holding him tightly within her own.

Mike gasped as she convulsed around him, marveling

at the sensations their lovemaking created. Her inner muscles tightened as he slipped over the edge. He pulled out and drove back into her once more, burying himself to the hilt within her quivering flesh. Seconds later, he exploded, spilling into her.

With his face buried in the side of her neck, he panted, riding the wave of his climax. He'd never experienced anything as powerful as this.

Recovering, he slipped from her warmth, limp and sated. After a while, Jordan shifted to face him, snuggling against his side. She wrapped her arms around his chest, wiggled her hips against his, saying, "Maybe you'll feed me lunch. But in the meantime, I'm looking forward to round two."

Chapter 17

Hours later, Mike entered his bedroom with a bed tray laden with food. The silver plasma-screen television mounted on the wall played Billie Holiday's "If You Were Mine" from one of the DirecTV music channels.

He placed the tray on the bedside table and approached the sleeping woman. Smiling, he replayed the hours they'd spent together. His lower anatomy began to swell and he immediately chastised himself for his lustful thoughts. Jordan hadn't eaten since sometime Friday afternoon.

His gaze slid over her naked form, spread across his bed. The chocolate-and-platinum-colored sheet was draped across her midsection. Her face was turned away from him, buried in the pillow, and her hands cradled her head. Her silky hair fanned over her cheek, flowing freely across her shoulders and naked back.

Perching on the edge of the mattress, Mike stroked his knuckles over her cheek, enjoying the warm skin. "Sweetheart," he whispered, caressing her back with a gentle stroking motion.

"Mmm?" she muttered, as her eyes fluttered open a fraction, then shut.

"Come on." He pushed her hair away from her face and eyes. "It's time to eat."

With her eyes still closed, she asked, "Eat?"

"Yeah. I couldn't salvage your breakfast, but I brought you a bowl of soup and a sandwich."

"Okay," she agreed, remaining on her stomach with her eyes closed.

"Wake up. We've got things to discuss."

Jordan flipped onto her back and stretched. His eyes strayed and focused on her naked breast. The enticing flesh was displayed in all of its magnificent beauty and Mike considered delaying their meal so that he might appease a different appetite. Gazing into her face, he realized how fragile she looked and decided that she needed nourishment.

He drew the sheet over her breast and stood, moving to the head of the bed to fluff her pillows. "Time to eat. The soup is hot."

Mike retrieved the bed tray and placed it over her lap. He sat next to her on the mattress, spooning up a mouthful of soup.

She opened her mouth, accepting a spoonful of vegetable soup. "Thanks. I really need this."

"You're welcome. Besides, I need you fully awake."

Frowning, she asked, "Why?"

"We've got to find out who took those chemicals."

She sighed, wiping her mouth on the cloth napkin, then picked up the sandwich and pulled a piece of lettuce from between the slices of bread and popped it in her mouth. "I told you I didn't see anything."

Mike planted a kiss on her hair. "I understand. But we have to figure this out. I don't believe Harold's responsible."

"Don't forget we have a repressed economy." She

picked up the spoon. "Money is a great incentive to steal."

"True." Mike folded his legs under him and sat Indian style. "Money is always a great enticement. But I still don't believe he's behind this."

"If it's not Harold, then who?"

Mike's tone remained determined. "That's what we're going to find out."

Jordan arched an eyebrow above a skeptical eye. "*We*, Kemo Sabe?"

Laughing, he insisted, "Yeah. You and me. We're a team and we can figure this out together."

"How?"

Mike brushed the soft locks of hair from her forehead with a tender finger. "I've been thinking."

"Uh-oh!"

"Hey, watch it." He narrowed his eyes and speared her with a warning glare. "Harold's not my image of a drug dealer. I can't imagine him in a lab, cooking chemicals. He doesn't have the knack or the expertise."

"True." Jordan held out her sandwich, offering Mike a bite. He took her offer, sinking his teeth into the wheat bread and chicken. "But that doesn't mean anything. If Harold's smart enough to cook his own drugs, he's also bright enough to create layers of employees to keep the police from turning an eye to him."

Swallowing the mouthful of sandwich, Mike said, "I know. It just doesn't feel right."

"There is another option. He may be recruiting students from the school." She rolled her eyes. "Creating his own posse."

"I thought of that. He doesn't have a lot of contact with the kids."

Jordan offered Mike a spoonful of soup. "Sure he does."

He wiped his mouth after swallowing the soup. "You're wrong. Listen, he arrives between three-thirty and four. Most of our kids have left the building for home."

"I disagree. After-school programs are in full force. Sports, tutoring, and clubs are going on for a couple of hours after he reports to work." Jordan popped the last of the sandwich into her mouth. "Some programs go on until after six."

"True! But our kids would run the opposite way if he approached them."

She sighed. "We're back to who?"

"Maybe we're missing the obvious. It could be a student."

Jordan let out a moan of pain and her face crunched up as if she'd tasted something awful. "I'd hate for that to be the case."

"If we think about this logically, it makes perfect sense. Who else knows about what goes on in our lab? This person has to be familiar with our procedures."

"You're right," Jordan agreed, reluctantly considering an additional point. "He or she must be comfortable with how to use a lab and have some knowledge of the chemicals and how they should be combined. We have a vague idea about who, but when and how still needs to be addressed."

"Think about this. All he needs to do is hang around after school. Wait for Harold to leave the room unattended. It would only take a minute to rip off the lab."

"What if it's not a him?" Jordan asked thoughtfully.

His lips pursed. "Doesn't matter. We've got to find whoever it is and shut them down." He studied her face for a moment. "What's on your mind?"

"Erin and Paradise. They're in my first-hour chem class. Neither girl is dumb."

Mike shook his head. "Sweetheart, they're a pain in

the butt and wild as they come. But I don't see them as drug dealers. I can't imagine them collectively being able to mix the proper proportions without blowing up a lab and themselves."

Jordan giggled, imagining Erin and Paradise blowing the roof off their parents' houses.

"I don't think they're behind this."

"You're probably right. How do we find our culprit?" she asked.

"Let's set 'em up."

"How?" she asked.

Mike lifted the tray from her lap and returned it to the bedside table. "You're my cosponsor for the Science Olympiad, correct?"

"Correct."

"Wednesday after school let's have our meeting in the lab," he explained, returning to the bed.

"And?"

He grinned. "Make sure the kids see the new shipment."

"I'm with you so far," she said. "Then what?"

"We stake out the lab after hours. Then," he popped his fingers, "we'll snag them."

"Sounds good, Mr. Secret Agent Man."

"It's James Bond the Second to you," he teased. "But, seriously, we're in sync here, correct? Remember, Monday we post flyers. Wednesday we'll have our meeting."

"Got it." Nodding, Jordan warned, "We need to be careful. If Debbie suspects anything we'll be in deep crap."

"I know. That's why we're going to work together. Jordan, we've got to keep this plan under wraps until we figure out who's behind it." Mike crawled into bed beside her and took her into his arms.

"So we've got a plan." She dragged her hand down Mike's body, caressing his male flesh.

Panting slightly, he kissed her lips. "That we do. But let's concentrate on us for a little while longer. You game?"

Stroking his chest, she answered, "Oh yeah."

A small part of Jordan feared returning to work Monday morning. After the time she'd spent with Mike, she suspected they would find it difficult to disguise their feelings or the change in their relationship.

Lying in his arms, Jordan mulled over whether she should try and talk to him about her concerns. "Mike," she said, hesitating, "there's something more we need to discuss."

The urgency in her voice must have reached Mike. He glanced down at her, asking, "What's up?"

She nibbled on her bottom lip. "I'd like to keep our business quiet."

Frowning, he asked, "What do you mean quiet? And what business?"

"Us. As in you and me together."

"Why?" he asked cautiously.

What do I tell him? Jordan wondered, opting for a part of the truth. Glancing away, she cleared her throat. "Call it my insecurities, but I don't want the people at work to know about us."

"Insecurities? About what?" Mike rubbed a warm hand up and down her spine.

"You name it and I've got problems with it. My age. Your age."

"Honey, please. Those are not problems. They're parts of our relationship. It's what makes us unique."

She shrugged. "Maybe. I don't know."

"I know. We're together now and I'm proud to be with you."

"I know." She laid a hand on his chest. "Please, give me some time to adjust. I'm not ready."

"Jordan, what are you asking me? You want me to pretend that I don't care about you? Act like I don't love you? Treat you like everyone else?" He shook his head. "I'm sorry, that's not possible. You are special to me and I can't hide my feelings."

How long will I be special to you? she wondered.

"What are you afraid of, Jordan?"

"Oh, Mike. I don't want people to think that I'm some silly older woman, getting her jollies off with a former student."

"Number one, you're not old. You're perfect. And two"—he grinned down at her—"that's just what you are doing. I mean, you're getting your jollies off with a former student." The shocked expression on her face touched him and he hastily added, "But I hope there's more. You may even love this former student and want to be with me for more than the sex."

"Mike—"

"Jordan—"

She silenced him with a finger to his lips. "No. Please let me talk first. You know how the gossip mill gets around at work. I don't want my personal life being discussed in the faculty lounge by people who don't know me."

"They won't."

"Right," Jordan drawled, rolling her eyes. "They would never do anything like that. No, no. Of course not."

Chuckling, he caressed her naked back, sending shivers of pleasure coursing through her veins. "Okay, you've got me on that one. Do you really care?"

"Yes."

Mike cradled Jordan's face between his hands. "Make me understand."

Jordan nibbled on her bottom lip, searching for a way to explain her fears. "I'm new to Pierson and I don't want people to think that I'm some horny woman looking for a good time with a young guy."

"Honey," he began, softening his voice to a persuasive purr, "I think you're overestimating the faculty's interest in our relationship."

She glared back at him.

"Sweetheart, I've told you that you're the most important thing in my life. What can I do to make you feel better about things? About us?"

"Give me time."

Mike sighed heavily, shaking his head. His jaw tightened. "How much time?"

Smiling encouragingly, Jordan answered, "Not long. A few weeks, maybe."

"And then?"

"Then I'll reveal things at my own pace. Okay?"

"I don't like it. But I have to admit everything happened pretty quickly between us," Mike conceded, but his voice carried a note of steel. "Maybe we both need a little time to adjust." He tenderly kissed her lips. "Let's keep things under wraps for a few weeks. After that, we'll go public."

This wasn't exactly what she had in mind, but their agreement gave her a window of time to adjust. This whole going public thing would blow over, if she kept Mike occupied, she thought.

Chapter 18

Wednesday afternoon, the bell rang, signaling the end of the school day. Jordan laughed, watching her students race into the hall as if this were the final day before summer vacation. The somber and reluctant manner they entered the classroom in was in direct contrast with the way they exited it. They always flew from the room as if she'd flashed a pair of vampire fangs.

Jordan locked up her room and strolled to the connecting door that led to the lab. Beethoven's Fifth Symphony greeted her as the pungent odor of sulfur stung her nose.

Entering the room, she found Mike surrounded by an array of canisters, bottles, and boxes. With a clipboard in his left hand and a pen in his right, he stood among the shipment, checking the supply order.

"Hi," she greeted, rubbing her nose.

His gaze slid over her like a soft caress, sending her pulse into a gallop. "Hi yourself."

Eager to be close to him, Jordan hurried across the room, stood near him, and placed a hand on Mike's arm. The muscles rippled under her fingers while she fought the urge to stroke his arm. Remembering her request to keep their relationship low-key, she reluctantly took a step back. Waving a hand at the bottles and cartons, she asked, "What's all this?"

"New supplies and chemicals for the lab." Mike unlocked the storage door and loaded several items into the cabinet. "Are you ready?"

"Yes. Ten kids signed up for our first meeting," she said.

"Good. I got five, possibly six."

Jordan moved to the door and unlocked it. "Did you put together an agenda for this meeting?"

Shaking his head, he said, "Don't need it."

"Okay, I'll follow your lead."

Mike smiled, crossed the room to hover near her. "Is that a promise?" he asked, taking a moment to glance around the room before leaning in to plant a warm, quick kiss on her responsive lips.

"Hey!" Surprised, she drew away, scanning the area to make sure no one saw them.

"Yesssss?" he drawled, grinning devilishly.

She gave him a stern look, wagging a finger at him. "We're at work. Be careful."

Gently, he grasped her hand, fondling her fingers. "I'm sorry, honey. You looked too adorable, I can't help myself."

The look she gave him spoke volumes.

He burst out laughing. "I'll behave. Honest." Releasing her hand, Mike used three fingers to create the Boy Scout sign.

"Were you a Boy Scout?" Jordan asked.

"No."

Laughing, she shook her head and playfully swatted his arm. "What am I going to do with you?"

"Love me," came Mike's instant response.

Jordan's eyes widened, but she remained silent. She

found it extremely difficult to commit herself completely to this relationship and allow her emotions to rule her. A small part of her refused to let go of the idea that Mike might not be ready for a long-term relationship with an older woman.

A part of her felt certain that she'd found the place where she belonged. But there were times when insecurities overwhelmed her. Was she making a terrible mistake that would eventually lead to a broken heart? She wished things were simpler. That she could throw her insecurities aside and just love Mike unconditionally.

Jordan used a shaky hand to push her hair from her eyes. None of that could be resolved today. This issue belonged on the back burner until she could devote more time to it.

The first batch of kids entered the lab. Pandemonium reigned as everyone found a seat, settled down, and got ready for the activity.

Completely unfazed by the commotion going on around him, Mike continued to store the items, shoving the last box in the cabinet. He fished inside his pockets. "Hmm, where did I put them?" he muttered, removing all the stuff from his pockets. "Ms. Anderson, did you bring your keys with you?"

Jordan pantomimed Mike's performance, searching her pockets. She shook her head. "Sorry. They must be in my desk drawer."

With a careless shrug Mike shut the door, returned his belongings to his pockets, and strolled to Jordan. "We'll lock up after the meeting."

Smiling back at him, she answered, "Okay. Let's get started."

Mike shoved his hands into the pockets of his trousers. Jordan heard the slight jingle of coins in his pockets as he moved between the rows of lab stations.

"Welcome to Science Olympiad. In case you don't know, I'm Mr. Walker." He pointed a finger in Jordan's direction. "And this is Ms. Anderson. She's my partner for this activity."

With a slight tilt of her head, Jordan acknowledged the group. She stood near the front of the room, running an assessing gaze over the students. Kids like Michelle, Derrick, and Takisha were great participants with an exceptional understanding of science. On the other hand, there were several students that never received grades above D-plus. Trevien Davis was one of those young men. He sat in the room, waiting patiently.

"The Science Olympiad will be held at Thurman High School, the first week in December. That gives us approximately six weeks to bone up so that we can compete against schools like Renaissance, Cass Tech, and King."

A student with thick glasses and a laptop computer raised his hand.

Mike pointed at the young man. "Yes? What's your name, son?"

"Brandon Hughes. What do we get if we win the competition?"

"I wish I could say money and glory. But you're only going to win glory," Jordan responded. "You'll get a write-up in the local papers and a trophy."

Nodding, Brandon said, "That'll work."

"Ms. Anderson, would you like to start?" Mike asked.

"Thank you. I'd like to do some simple games to determine your level of competence." Jordan picked up the red erasable marker, stepped to the whiteboard, and began to draw a hangman's noose, adding seven lines, an equal sign, then two additional spaces. "We're going to make this fun. This is an element from the periodic table. You need to give me the element name and atomic symbol. "

A girl with long dark braids stated confidently, "Man, this is going to be easy."

"Maybe. Maybe not. Each person will get one chance to come up with a letter. That will give everyone an opportunity to participate." Jordan twisted the hand on an old egg timer. "I'm going to give you five seconds, starting now."

"Do you think they bought it?" Jordan called over her shoulder, retrieving her keys from her desk drawer and returning to the lab. They locked the supply cabinet, then strolled into her classroom, securing the connecting door.

Mike perched on the edge of one of the desks, watching as Jordan gathered her belongings. "We did put on quite a performance. I mean, Denzel Washington and Halle Berry didn't compare."

Giggling, she said, "Yeah, but don't quit your day job."

"Hey! Watch that. I'm very sensitive." He pouted, laying a hand over his heart.

"Right! The only place you're sensitive is in bed." Her eyes slid over his body and settled below his beltline.

His breathing quickened and Jordan noted the sensual fire gaining momentum in his eyes. The husky quality of his voice became more pronounced as he fought to control his emotional and physical response. "Can we get back to the point, please?"

Jordan shrugged. A sense of power overwhelmed her at how quickly she got him all hot and bothered.

Mike cleared his throat and the fire began to rescind. He stepped closer, one eyebrow raised suggestively. "I recall some bed talk about being careful at work. Do you remember any of that?"

"*Moi?*" Her eyes widened innocently.

"Don't give me that innocent act. I've seen you in action. And personally, I can't wait to see you in action again." His hand slid along her spine, creating a series of sensations that made her legs as weak as boiled pasta noodles. "Save those thoughts for when we get home. Are you coming home with me?"

"Oh yeah." She smiled her most seductive smile. "Can't wait."

"Enough." He drew in a deep breath of air and refocused. "It's time to get back to the problem. Regardless of the quality of our performances, I think we made our point."

Jordan agreed, sliding the strap of her purse on her shoulder before picking up her briefcase. She started for the door with Mike on her heels. "What's next?"

"For the next few days we'll leave the lab and the supply cabinet unlocked."

Lifting her eyebrows, Jordan asked, "You'll stay close to the lab, correct?"

"Correct," Mike answered.

"I don't fancy another encounter with Debbie," Jordan admitted anxiously. "The last one stirred up a lot of problems. So let's keep close tabs on the supplies and not lose this shipment."

"I agree."

Silently, they stepped into the hallway, both focused on their own thoughts.

Jordan broke the silence with a question. "Mike, what did you think of our recruits?"

"There were some good ones. We may have a chance at winning the Science Olympiad."

She smiled. "That would be so great. But I must admit there were a few kids that I didn't expect to see."

"Like who?"

"Trevien Philips and Martel Adams. They are not the poster kids for science nerds."

Chuckling, Mike answered, "You're right. Trevien seemed to know his stuff today."

"I know. He surprised me. Trevien averages a D-plus in my class."

Mike grimaced. "What about the other guy?"

"Martel's not a bad kid." Jordan shrugged, scrunching her face up as she considered the student. "I'm just not sure why he chose to join this particular activity."

"Hmm." Mike scratched his ear. "Do you think he might be one of our thieves?"

"I don't know. It's possible."

Nodding, Mike said, "Maybe we should keep an eye on the pair. Check out their friends."

She agreed.

Mike studied her profile silently. "What's wrong?"

"I hate to think of Trevien stealing. And I don't think Martel is smart enough to be the mastermind behind a drug ring. We've talked about doing this and I know you're right. But I don't want to see one of my kids land in jail."

Mike rubbed her back reassuringly. "Sweetheart, we can't let these drugs end up with our students. Someone needs to take responsibility for that."

Frowning, Jordan answered in a worried tone, "I know. But they're kids. More times than not, they haven't got a clue what they're getting into."

"True. But more importantly, we've got to stop them before those drugs get distributed among our students. After we find them, we'll decide how best to help them. Okay?"

"Okay."

With one hand Mike removed her briefcase from her hand and settled the other on the small of her back, guiding her down the corridor toward the parking lot. Their footsteps echoed off the cavernous hallway. Exiting the building, he laced his fingers with hers.

"Hey!" Jordan muttered frantically, scanning the area for any signs of their coworkers. "What if someone is watching?"

"Let 'em."

She stopped on their way to her SUV. "You agreed to maintain a professional relationship at work."

"And I will." He sighed, lifting her hand to his lips. "Come on, Jordan. Look around you. The only cars in this parking lot are yours, mine, and the custodial staff's. It's almost six. If there's anyone in the building I'm certain that we're not their hot topic of discussion."

"I know. I just want to keep things quiet." She glanced at him.

His face tightened with disappointment. Guilt reared its ugly head as she looked at Mike. He didn't deserve this kind of treatment. He'd been nothing but loving to her since the day she arrived at Pierson.

A tight band of worry squeezed the air from her lungs. "Please understand." Their relationship and her career were too important to let the situation just happen. She needed to maintain some control over both areas of her life. Having the faculty and students know that she'd been sleeping with Mike would cause additional trouble that she just didn't have the strength to deal with.

She knew he wanted to make their relationship public. He felt honored to be with her and wanted the world to know. Jordan wasn't ready. She needed time to resolve her feelings.

A tiny voice in her head whispered, *when will you be ready?* She wished she had an answer. And it worried her that Mike might get tired of waiting.

Chapter 19

An air of excitement sizzled through Jordan as she exited the John C. Lodge Freeway, spilling onto Jefferson Avenue. She cruised past Hart's Plaza, admiring how the moon and stars were reflected off the Detroit River.

Giggling like a schoolgirl, she considered the evening ahead. Tonight, she and Mike were sharing their first official date. He had insisted they go out and get to know one another better.

Thrilled by Mike's invitation, Jordan agreed, although somewhat surprised by his choice of restaurant for their evening together. Fuddruckers didn't strike her as a romantic locale for a first official date.

Jordan shook her head, unable to ignore the irony of her and Mike's situation. His face lit up when he asked her out. It hadn't fazed him that up to this point they had completely skipped the dating process and gone straight to an intimate relationship.

They'd done everything backward. Yet he planned to move them through whatever process he believed necessary to make her as comfortable with him and their relationship as possible.

Returning her attention to the road, she glanced at

the steel and concrete fortress called the GM Renaissance Center. It loomed large and forbidding as she coasted toward Chene Avenue.

Stopped at a red light, Jordan observed a parade of young women strolling across Jefferson Avenue. An enthusiastic group of young men followed, talking loud, drawing the women's attention. The ladies slowed, allowing the men to catch up with them and pair up. The happy group entered Tom's Oyster Bar together.

With a smile on her lips, Jordan muttered, "Oh, young love." More like young lust, she amended, remembering a time when men reacted the same way to her.

The light switched to green and she resumed her drive along Jefferson Avenue. Reflecting on the group, she realized that Mike gazed at her in the same manner that those young men admired the women. In those moments, he eliminated all of her doubts and made her feel as if she were the most precious thing in the world.

Slowly, her smile faded as she admitted that her reservations regarding their relationship remained. Questions about how long that wonderful light of admiration would remain in Mike's eyes frightened her. When would his eyes start wandering to some sweet young thing without sagging breasts and flabby thighs?

After all, Mike was ten years her junior. She ran an agitated hand through her hair.

What if their relationship fizzled? Would they be able to remain professional following a breakup?

Desperately grasping for something positive, Jordan chastised herself, *Come on, girl. Are you trying to destroy your relationship before you've finished the first date? Give the man a chance to prove himself.* She shook off the feeling of gloom and doom, instead concentrating on arriving at the restaurant in one piece.

The white canopy covering Chene Park's Pavilion

appeared on the horizon and Jordan switched to the right lane. She turned south onto Chene Street, then whipped into the strip mall parking lot that housed Fuddruckers.

Jordan sailed into a vacant spot near the front door of the restaurant, then flipped down the visor, checking her makeup and hair in the mirror. Satisfied with her appearance, she left the car. She straightened the sculpted lace top under a waist-length coral jacket and matching midthigh skirt.

After locking up the SUV, she crossed the parking lot and entered Fuddruckers, halting inside the double doors to examine her surroundings. The aroma of sizzling beef and the grinding sounds of industrial-model blenders, plus Stevie Wonder's tunes, filled the air.

She grinned. It was indeed a burger joint.

Jordan skirted the edge of the takeout line and turned into the small dining area facing the west end of the restaurant. She searched for Mike's tall frame among the occupied tables and found him with his back to her, sitting at a table near the window. A warm glow engulfed her as she exhaled a whimper of anticipation and hurried across the hardwood floor.

"Hey," she whispered close to Mike's ear, placing a gentle hand on his shoulder. Instantly, he stood, running an appreciative eye over her outfit.

"You look incredible." The expression in his eyes certified his words and made her feel beautiful.

Reveling in his open admiration, Jordan did a little curtsey and said, "Thank you."

Now she took her time ogling him. Her breath caught in her throat as her eyes did a slow dance down his tall handsome frame. He looked fabulous.

Unconsciously, she ran her tongue across her lips. The man was a gorgeous specimen. Outfitted in a tan, long-sleeve sweater, a black T-shirt winked from the deep V neckline of the sweater. Midnight-colored trousers completed his attire.

Jordan slid onto the chair opposite him and removed her jacket. She smiled. "Hi."

"Hey yourself." He grinned back at her, entwining his fingers with hers. "Did you have a hard time finding the place?"

"Strip mall on Jefferson near Chene Park. I figured it out." She gave the restaurant a quick sweep. "Burger joint, hmm?"

"Yes, the best," Mike answered, placing a menu in front of her.

"Thank you," Jordan muttered, scanning the menu and quickly decided on a Motor City burger, fries, and a strawberry shake. "I know this is our date, but I'd like to ask a couple of questions about work. After that, I won't bring work up again this evening. I promise."

Mike groaned.

"Please," she begged.

Relenting, he said, "Go for it."

Grinning, she said, "Thanks. It's been more than a week. Have you learned anything new about Trevien?"

His expression turned serious and he shook his head. "No."

Frustrated, she scrunched up her face and asked, "Nothing? I expected something more by now."

Mike leaned back in his chair, waiting as their server placed a shake in front of her and a malt at his side. "Me too. I've been making it in to work around seven so that Debbie won't find the lab unlocked. Nothing's missing."

"Are you sure?"

"Unfortunately, yes." He picked up his banana malt and sipped it. "I put a little booby trap together so that I could tell if anyone touched the stuff in the cabinet."

"And has anyone?"

"No. Nothing's been touched. Everything is in the exact same order I stored them."

The server returned with their meals. Silently, she placed the food before the couple and left without a word.

Smothering his cheeseburger in ketchup and mustard, Mike said, "I've watched Trevien for the past week. That boy has been a model student. He doesn't stay for any of the other after-school activities." He picked up a French fry and dipped the tip in a mound of ketchup on his plate. "What about Martel?"

"Nothing," she admitted, slicing her Motor City burger in half. "I mean, normally he's got to have the last word on any and all conversations. But he's been a top-notch young man. Turns in every assignment on time, helps his fellow students. No back lip. He's been leaving after the end of the school day. Just like Trevien, we're the only after-school activity that he participates in."

"I'm at a loss," he admitted.

Jordan pursed her lips, considering the problem. "Maybe it's time to reevaluate our list and add some additional suspects." She shrugged. "What do you think?"

"Could be." He took a bite out of his cheeseburger, chewing as he considered her suggestion. "I don't have an answer for you."

"What about Harold? Have you ruled him out completely?"

"Yes. Chet finally got around to giving him a few unpaid days off for leaving the lab unlocked. The days you initially received," he emphasized.

"I can't say I want to see anyone in trouble. But he deserves the time off."

"Yeah. He's been away for about a week. He's not due

back until Monday. I'll keep an eye on him once he returns."

"I thought we'd have this all resolved by now." She tore a strip of lettuce from her burger and nibbled on it.

He reached across the table and stroked her hand, sending a sliver of pleasure up her arm. "Me too. All we can do is stay vigil to our plan. I know things will come together."

"I'm sure you're right."

Mike smiled at her, sending her pulse into orbit. "Now I don't want to talk any more about Harold, Trevien, or Pierson High School."

"What do you want?" she asked softly.

"I want to enjoy being with a beautiful woman on our first official date."

"Ohhh, that's so sweet," she muttered. "And so do I."

With a fake expression of shock, he teased, "You want to enjoy a date with a beautiful woman?"

"No, silly." Her expression turned serious. "Actually I want to enjoy this date with you."

Pleased, he squeezed her hand. "Good."

With that said, they settled down to finishing their meal, watching the crowd, and commenting on the variety of musical tunes floating through the restaurant. Thirty minutes later, Jordan pushed her plate aside and picked up her strawberry shake.

"How about a movie?" Mike asked.

"Fine. Do you have anything in particular in mind?"

He unfolded the entertainment section of the *Detroit Free Press* and said, "Let's check it out. What's your preference?"

An idea sent her spirit soaring. Jordan pointed a finger at her forehead. "I've got a better alternative. There's a Hollywood Video in the strip mall, correct?"

"Correct."

She smiled a slow, sensual smile that promised him so many things. "Why don't we pick up a couple of DVDs and head back to your place? We can get comfortable, relax, and watch the movies on your big-screen plasma television."

A responding smile curved Mike's full, sensual lips. A ripple of excitement swirled around her.

"I like it," Mike admitted, a husky edge creeping into his voice. "I'd love to spend the rest of the evening alone with you." His face fell. "But I promised you a date. And I want you to have that."

"It doesn't mean that we can't explore other areas of our relationship. Am I right?"

"You're so right."

"Good." Satisfied, she glanced around the restaurant. "Once I have dessert, we can go."

Mike grinned. "I tell you, older women are the best."

"That's me." Jordan tipped her shake in Mike's direction. "The best."

"Yes, you are."

The light from the television cast a romantic glow over Mike's bedroom. He removed the remote from the nightstand and switched the station from the eleven o'clock news to his favorite music channel. The saxophone of David Sanborn filled the room. "Hey, how long do you plan to stay in there?"

"I'll be out in a minute," Jordan promised.

Mike grinned, waiting for her to put in her appearance. He didn't care how long it took. He just wanted to tease her. However long it took, she would be well worth the wait. Although he wouldn't have to wait as long if she'd accepted his offer to help her bathe. After all, why not conserve energy and water? With a knowing smile, she'd declined his generous offer, then firmly closed the bathroom door in his face.

He didn't mind. Mike felt confident that there would be a time when they would share a shower. *All things in the proper time,* he thought. The most important thing was having Jordan in his home, bed, and life. The rest would work itself out in time.

The bathroom door opened and Jordan strolled into the bedroom. He gazed at her and his heart began to hammer in his chest.

Jordan looked beautiful. Fresh from her shower, her tantalizing fragrance floated through the air. Her hair flowed over her shoulders. As she made her way to the bed, he admired her smooth, tight thighs and shapely legs.

"That's my T-shirt," he said, hoping that he'd get lucky and end up as close to her as that garment.

"It sure is."

Playing along, he answered, "What do you plan to do with it?"

"Wear it."

"And what about me?" he asked.

"You seem okay to me. But maybe not. Do you want it back?" she asked with a sassy twist of her hips.

"Yeah."

"No problem." She pulled the cotton T-shirt over her head and tossed it toward the bed. He caught it, bringing the item to his face, inhaling her unique scent.

Desire shot through Mike like a rocket. His mouth went dry as he watched Jordan's nude form stroll to him. Her slim, willowy frame made his body grow hot while his male organ hardened.

She sauntered over to Mike and planted a knee on the edge of the mattress, leaning close to lightly brush her lips across his. His tongue slipped between her lips and found her tongue, tasting a hint of peppermint on her lips.

Moving in for a second kiss, she began a slow, thorough exploration with her hands, gliding them lovingly along his body. He let out a little moan and wrapped his arms around her neck, pulling her down to the bed next to him.

She ran her hands across his shoulders and stroked his broad chest. He gasped as Jordan pressed butterfly kisses over his chest. Every place tingled where she touched. It felt like sweet heaven and he never wanted it to end.

A fresh wave of desire shot though him when her fingertips drew a path from one taut nipple to the other. He groaned when she captured a pert nipple in her mouth and sucked. Soft, wet kisses created a path down his chest and over his belly.

Jordan's other hand was busy stroking his shaft. Her fingers caressed him from base to tip and back again. He shifted restlessly against the sheet, loving everything she was doing. Her hand touched the head of his flesh and she ran her thumb across the droplets of fluid collecting on the tip.

"Jordan! Oh, babe," Mike gasped.

The ache in his groin grew tighter and he reached across her, opening the nightstand drawer. He removed a small foil packct.

"Let me," Jordan said, removing the package from his hands. Using her teeth, she tore opened the item and removed the latex condom. She gave his erection a loving kiss, swirling her tongue around the sensitive head before quickly rolling the protective covering over his hardened flesh. Pushing herself up against his chest, she straddled his body, positioning herself above him.

Jordan lowered herself until Mike was sheathed

182   *Karen White-Owens*

within her warmth. Using slow, delicious movements she slid up and down his hardened flesh, making them both moan. Mike placed his hands on her hips, helping to establish a tempo that pleased them both. After a few minutes, she hit the perfect rhythm. He shut his eyes and let her control their lovemaking.

Mike panted, thrusting upward so he was completely encased in her wetness. "Oh, baby, that feels so good."

Jordan rode him, slowly at first, and then took him deep inside her. She increased her pace, rocking back and forth, and Mike felt the familiar tingling at the base of his spine. The sensation built, growing stronger and stronger, and he forgot everything but the feel of Jordan as she rubbed against him.

As his mind cleared, he heard Jordan cry out, then saw her collapse against his body. She buried her face in his shoulder. Mike wrapped his arms around her and kissed her neck. "Thank you," he muttered. "Thank you."

Jordan raised her head and smiled down at him. "You're welcome. Give me a few minutes and then we can practice some more."

Holding her closer, he said, "Sounds good to me."

Chapter 20

After a fantastic weekend with Mike, Monday morning Jordan pulled into her usual parking space at Pierson High. Happy to be back, she switched off the engine and grinned. Her body hummed as a feeling of peace and goodwill pulsed through her.

Mike was responsible for Jordan's good mood. After a weekend of pampering, romantic dates, and thrilling lovemaking she felt confident that she could handle anything Pierson and its administration dished out. Yes, indeed. She felt strong, rested, and happy.

Jordan's smile slowly faded. A weekend with Mike made her realize how much she'd missed having a relationship. Her insecurities cast the only shadow over an otherwise wonderful weekend. She massaged her forehead, feeling the dull throb of a headache behind her eyes.

Suddenly, the interior of her SUV felt too warm. Jordan scrambled from the car intent on finding Mike. She needed his reassuring presence to chase away her doubts.

Chilled by the cool November breeze swirling around her, she zipped up her black leather jacket to the throat. Her jade knee-length skirt and opal turtleneck sweater offered little protection against the wind as it sliced through her. Black pumps covered her feet and crunched against the pavement, kicking up small bits of gravel as she crossed the parking lot.

A blast of heat greeted Jordan as she hurried into the building and down the corridor. She nodded at her coworkers while unlocking her classroom.

Jordan entered and crossed the lab, pausing at the entrance that connected the lab to Mike's classroom. Voices were coming from his room. Reaching for the doorknob, she hesitated. Her forehead crinkled as she brought her ear against the wood surface.

She heard a female voice. Worried, she felt her pulse quickening. Could it be Debbie? Smothering a groan, Jordan waited. Had their department head found the lab unlocked and now stood on the other side of the door demanding an explanation?

This is stupid, she decided, reaching for the door handle. Ready to take her share of responsibility for any problems their scheme had caused, she turned the knob. But something stopped her. She remained absolutely motionless for a beat.

The voices got louder. Erin! Jordan bit her lip as jealousy spread through her veins.

Her eyes widened when she recognized the other voice. Shocked, she stiffened.

"Erin, you're mistaken. I'm not going to do it," Mike said.

"You don't understand. It's important. Please," Erin begged.

"No. I made my decision long ago and I don't plan to change it."

What decision and about what? Jordan wondered.

"What if I tell?" Erin challenged.

"Go ahead," Mike snapped back. He sounded almost bored by Erin's threat.

Okay, this was getting stranger by the moment. What did she have on Mike? What would she tell?

"You have nothing to tell."

"There's plenty. And it could make you look really bad. Remember the time in the locker room?"

Mike sighed. "Erin, I'm not going to do what you asked. Period. End of discussion. Do whatever you think you have to, because I'm not buying it."

That's enough, Jordan decided, opening the door. The pair turned. A hint of relief played across Mike's face when he saw her. He stood near his desk. His arms were folded across his chest and his legs were spread apart in an aggressive stance.

Offering the pair her brightest smile, she said, "Good morning."

Mike crossed the room, stopping next to Jordan. "Good morning, Ms. Anderson. How are you?"

"Fine. And you?"

"Okay. Erin dropped by to discuss something with me before class."

"Did she now?" Jordan muttered, turning to the young lady.

"Yes. But we're all done. And I'm sure she needs to get to class." He turned to the young woman and asked, "Don't you, Erin?"

Erin had the look of a slick panther, ready to pounce. Dressed in a tight little top that revealed more of her youthful flesh than it concealed, she completed her ensemble with a pair of equally tight jeans.

Her eyes flashed with angry heat, but Erin smiled. Tossing her head, she flounced out of the room with a curt "Bye."

Mike moved to Jordan's side. Together they watched the young woman leave.

Jordan's eyes widened. The word *booty-licious* in bold red letters covered the butt of Erin's second-skin jeans. *Amazing*, Jordan thought, shaking her head. *This young lady would do anything to draw attention to herself.*

The moment the door closed behind Erin, he let out a huge sigh of relief, then rubbed Jordan's arm. "Thanks for coming. I don't want to be caught alone with her."

"What happened?"

He ran a hand over his head. "Erin stood outside my door when I got in this morning. She insisted that she needed to talk with me."

"Mmm." Jordan nodded. "What did she want?"

"Same old thing," he answered in a troubled voice. "Put Jarell back on the basketball team."

Jordan stared at the closed door, trying to determine what Erin truly wanted. "That happened almost a month ago. Why is she still harping on it?" She tossed her hands in the air in a helpless gesture as her voice hardened. "I've said this before. Jarell is Paradise's boyfriend, not Erin's. I would expect Paradise to be in here begging you to forgive her boyfriend. Plus, I believe Jarell should plead his own case."

"You're right. I'd be willing to discuss things if, and this is a big if, Jarell would haul his pitiful butt in here and say he's sorry. He'd be on the team in a minute if he'd offer some signs of remorse about the way he behaved. Although I also believe he should apologize to the team. He let them down."

"What's keeping you from doing it now?"

"Because Jarell still doesn't understand how important it is to work as part of a team. I don't want his antics hogging the show. I want people working together to get the job done. Until he learns that, he's a liability, not an asset."

"It's a shame. He's a good player," she said remorsefully.

"Yes, he is. But Jarell's attitude is funky. It erodes the spirit of the team." He rubbed a hand up and down her arm. "By the way, thanks for coming in here. That girl makes me nervous."

Smiling back at him, she answered, "No problem."

Mike's voice dropped and turned husky. "Did you need something?"

Her body responded to the sensual note in Mike's voice, and her skin began to tingle. "Yes."

"What?"

"I needed to see you." She grinned, unable to suppress her feelings. "I wanted to tell you how much I enjoyed our weekend together."

His brown eyes sparkled with tenderness as they slowly glided over her, causing a sensual current to pass through Jordan. He drew in a deep breath and stroked her arm. "Not as much as I did."

Each look or gesture made her love him more. Smiling, she admitted, "Maybe, maybe not. All I can really say is that you made me very happy. Thank you."

His eyebrows did a suggestive double lift. "Thank you."

Jordan giggled.

Mike leaned forward and captured her lips. His large hands cradled her face and held it as he deepened the kiss. Unable to resist, she sucked the tip of his tongue into her mouth. Itching to get closer, Jordan wrapped her arms around his neck and rubbed against him.

They clung together, enjoying the feel of their entwined bodies and mingled breath. Mike's fingers slid into her hair while her hands caressed the well-defined muscles of his back.

Slowly moving away, Mike warned, "We've got to stop." A husky note lingered in his tone.

"Mm-hm," she agreed, running her tongue across his bottom lip. He shuddered against her.

"Okay, that's it," he announced, brushing a gentle kiss across her forehead, then stepped away. "See you at lunch."

"Lunch? Where are we going?"

"Teachers' lounge," he explained, straightening his tie and adjusting his belt. "Remember, it's Teachers' Appreciation Day. See you at noon."

Jordan strolled through the lab to her classroom. There was a great deal that hadn't been said between them. No matter how innocent the encounter, she felt uneasy finding Erin with Mike.

Jordan paused outside the teachers' lounge and composed herself. Normally, she avoided the lounge as much as humanly possible. The negative energy surrounding that place could ruin a good mood quicker than a mother-in-law's first visit to a newlywed couple.

Pierson's teachers' lounge consisted of several rooms. A traditional kitchen with a range, microwave oven, refrigerator, and sink completed one portion. A connecting room featured several long tables used by the staff, a sofa, and a computer and printer. The third and last section of the lounge housed rows of black metal file cabinets filled with student records, holiday decorations, and a restroom.

Jordan entered the room, immediately searching for Mike's reassuring presence. Chet, Thurman, and all the department heads were present, including Debbie.

They stood at one end of the table in a sort of receiving line, greeting the teachers and staff. Jordan waited in line as her fellow coworkers worked their way around the table filled with pizza, tossed salad, chicken wingdings, cheesy bread, chocolate chip cookies, and lemon pound cake.

Mike entered, zeroing in on Jordan. He headed straight for her. "Excuse me," he muttered to the person behind Jordan as he pushed his way between them.

"How was your morning?" Jordan asked, turning slightly to gaze in his direction.

"Great."

"Hi, Mike, Jordan," greeted George.

"Hey, man. How are you?" Mike responded, shaking hands with his colleague.

"George, how's calculus going?" Jordan asked.

He sighed heavily, running a hand through his thick, straight hair. "Slow. The kids are not getting stuff as quickly as I would like."

"I hear you," Mike said. "It's frustrating."

Jordan studied George as he and Mike conversed. The rotund, Hispanic math teacher wore his raven-black hair to his shoulders. A round face framed intelligent dark eyes. His weather-beaten skin looked as if he'd spent too many hours worshipping the sun.

Leaving the two men, she scooted around the table, filling her plate with pizza and salad. Jordan stood, debating whether she should add a slice of lemon cake or cookies to her lunch, when George dropped his bomb. "Hey, man, I meant to ask you earlier. How did you guys like Fuddruckers? The burgers are the best, although there are too many teenagers in that place for me and the service could be better."

Startled, Jordan stopped the knife midway through

the cake. A soft gasp escaped her. *Ohmigod,* Jordan whined silently. She and Mike were toast.

Her gaze moved around the room, gauging the impact of his question on her colleagues. Everyone seemed involved in their own conversations and missed George's question. She let out a shaky breath. Her eyes focused on Debbie.

Debbie had heard them. Instantly, Debbie's gaze swung to the three teachers. Her expression turned glacier. Jordan's heart pounded in her chest. Her worst nightmare had become a reality. Their secret was out.

Mike's brown eyes searched her face, reaching for her thoughts. Skirting the issue, he inquired cautiously, "When were you at Fuddruckers?"

"Friday night." Oblivious of what he was revealing, George babbled on, "I came into the restaurant to pick up a takeout order and saw you guys having dinner. I meant to come by and say hello, but the staff got my orders screwed up and I needed to speak to the manager."

Mike nodded. "Do you live near there?"

"Yes. My wife and I live on Lafayette. So it's an enjoyable and generally quick place to eat. But I always have to check my order." George plucked a slice of cheesy bread from the tray and munched on it as he warned, "Don't forget to do that."

"I won't."

Mike slid into the chair next to Jordan and whispered close to her, "No one seems to have caught on to George's rambling. I think we're safe."

"You're wrong."

Forehead wrinkled into a mask of confusion, he asked, "What makes you say that?"

"Look at Debbie," Jordan whispered frantically, gripping her slice of pizza so tight that her fingers were painted in pizza sauce. "She heard and she's got that sour expression on her face."

"Calm down. It'll work out. Don't get upset."

"Debbie doesn't like me. All she wants is for me to give her a reason to get me out of here." Jordan wiped her hands on her paper napkin. "We better be super careful from now on."

Mike's hand slipped under the table and squeezed her hand. "I hear you and you're right. We'll discuss this later."

Chapter 21

Jordan glanced at her wristwatch, then kicked up her pace. There were only a few minutes left to her prep period. She turned in to the copy room and went to her mailbox, searching for telephone messages.

Her brows furrowed over curious eyes as she removed an envelope with *Anthony Pierson High School* embossed in the left-hand corner. She ripped it open, removed a single sheet of paper, and read it.

Gasping, Jordan turned sharply on her heels and marched down the hallway to Mike's room. After a sharp rap on the door, she poked her head into his classroom, scanning the room.

"Got a minute?" she asked.

"Yeah," Mike responded, moving away from the whiteboard and capping his black marker.

"Sorry to bother you, but I need a little advice."

"Sure." He waved her into the room. His gaze swept over her. "What's going on?"

"This!" Jordan crossed the room and thrust the letter at him. "I found it in my mailbox today."

Mike took the letter and skimmed it. After a moment

he gave her a reassuring smile and a quick hug. "Honey, this is nothing."

"Nothing!" She stared at him as if he'd just declared his allegiance to North Korea or Cuba. "You think it's nothing?"

"Yeah. You know how instructional observations go. I'm sure you've had those before." Giving her a knowing look, he added, "And I'm certain you've done a few as assistant principal."

"Yes, I have," she admitted, pacing the room.

"Then you know the drill. Don't worry about it," Mike said, handing the sheet back to her. "At Pierson, everyone gets at least one observation each year. Depending on how well your first observation goes, you might get a second one."

As she unconsciously twisted a lock of hair around her finger, a shadow of alarm spread across her face. "I am worried. This is pretty early in the school year for an observation. I've only been at Pierson for a few months."

Mike stepped into her path, halting her. He ran a comforting hand up and down Jordan's arm while his voice had an infinitely compassionate tone. "Honey, it'll be okay. Why are you so upset?"

Jordan's face went grim. "Maybe the administration doesn't think my work is up to standard. Or it could be Debbie trying to find a way to get rid of me."

With extreme patience, he asked, "Why do you think Debbie is behind this?"

She waved the letter at him. "That woman's been giving me the evil eye ever since George mentioned seeing us at Fuddruckers."

Uncaring, he shrugged. "So what?"

"What about the incident with the lab?" Jordan asked.

"Debbie hasn't said anything to me."

She snorted. "Yeah, but Debbie likes you."

"What makes you think that she doesn't like you?"

Shocked that he would have to ask her that question, Jordan glared back at him. Men were so blind at times.

"Hello," she drawled, softly smacking him on the head. "Debbie hates me. If I didn't know better I would swear that she was jealous of our relationship."

Looking a bit shamefaced, Mike admitted in a soft voice, "You're not wrong."

Turning back to him, she asked, "What do you mean?"

He sighed. "Debbie just went through a bad divorce."

"Really? How do you know?"

"We were close a while back."

A spark of jealousy quickly turned into a forest fire. Jordan sauntered over to where he stood. "How close?"

"Not that kind of close. We were friends. She used to talk to me, Jordan," he answered, returning to his desk. "Her husband and I played ball together a couple of times a month. Debbie fixed me up with her younger sister."

"Really?"

"Yeah. We double-dated a few times. Things didn't work out."

"And now?" she asked.

"Nothing. Clay moved to St. Louis to be near his family. I haven't heard from him since the divorce."

"What about Debbie? Do you think she's envious of our relationship? Or is she upset because of her sister?"

Mike bowed his head slightly. "Maybe both."

"Why are you telling me this?" Jordan studied him for a beat. Something more was going on here. Something that he felt reluctant to express.

"Because I think you should go easy on her. She's

hurting and I don't think she has an outlet to talk things out."

Shaking her head, she muttered, "I don't know. I don't know." A thought hit her. "Mike, has Debbie asked you anything about us?"

"No. Nothing," he answered. "Did you expect her to?"

"I'm not sure. What do you think we should do?"

His head snapped back. "Do? There's nothing to do."

"I mean about us. If Debbie asks you, what will you tell her?"

"I don't know. Number one, I don't want to lie. Number two, I can't hide my feelings for you," Mike admitted. His voice dropped an octave, sending shivers up and down her arms. "It's pretty difficult for me to pretend that we're just colleagues. And it's getting more difficult each day."

She understood how he felt. There were days when she found it almost impossible to control her eagerness to be near him. It didn't matter whether they'd just parted. She found herself searching for him from the moment she entered the building.

Examining his earnest features, she wondered, what did he truly feel for her? Did he love her? That question really frightened and thrilled her. Frightened because it meant that she would have to admit her feelings and talk about committed relationships, and thrilled because her feelings were so strong and true.

Whenever Mike came near her, he couldn't keep his hands to himself. Who was she fooling? She enjoyed everything he did and always begged for more.

But things were getting out of hand. First George and now other staff members were giving them suspicious glances, making assumptions about their relationship.

How were they supposed to maintain any level of privacy if everyone could see through their paper-thin facade?

"What have you told staff and faculty?" Jordan asked.

"Not much."

She touched his hand. "What does that mean?"

Anger burned hot in the depths of his eyes. "It means that I don't answer them. Are you satisfied?"

His anger surprised her. She stroked his arm, feeling the muscles jerk responsively under her fingers. "Mike, what's wrong?"

"I hate this. I feel like a fraud," he hissed between clenched teeth. "I don't like lying!"

"I'm sorry." His pain hurt her and intensified her frustration. "I need a little more time, then we'll be open with everyone. I promise."

"We've been through this. You don't want people knowing about me. Jordan, are you ashamed of being with me?"

Her eyes widened and she tossed her arms around Mike, holding him close. "No, no, no. Of course not. We talked about this last week. This relationship is new and very precious to me and I need time to adjust. I don't want to blow it."

Confusion warred with Mike's need for honesty. He shook his head, untangled himself from her, and studied her broodingly. "Yes, we did talk. But I didn't understand then and I don't understand now."

Jordan gnawed on her bottom lip, gauging the changing expressions on Mike's face. How do you tell your lover that you expect him to leave you for someone younger, prettier?

"I haven't had a relationship in a very long time," she admitted, measuring each word for the correct effect. "We've only been together a short while. Let's enjoy each other before we let the rest of the world in."

"When will you be ready?"

"Soon," she answered.

"Are you sure? Can we put a date on it?"

Laughing nervously, she twisted a lock of hair around her finger. "You can't put a date on something this important."

"Yes, you can. Let's say two weeks," he suggested, moving around his desk. "We'll keep things quiet for the next two weeks, then we'll tell anyone who asks. Fair enough?"

Flabbergasted, she moved her lips, but no words came out. This was not what she had planned. She didn't want anyone to know about them, ever.

At the end of his lunch period, Mike made a trip to the cafeteria to return his empty tray. He seldom went to the student lunchroom, but today the cook had prepared catfish, fries, and coleslaw. He weaved between the students and lunch tables as he started out the exit.

As he slipped through the doors, he noticed Terry Mann and Martel Adams talking inconspicuously in low tones at the rear of the room. Something about them grabbed Mike's attention. He backtracked, moved out of their frame of vision, and stepped into the shadows.

Martel topped their current list of suspects, although Terry's name had never come up. Terry's status as one of Pierson's premier students made him the kind of high achiever most teachers wished they had the ability to clone.

Mike didn't recall Martel and Terry being friends. He needed to discuss this with Jordan to determine what this particular pairing meant.

Their body language seemed so different from what they generally displayed that he found himself mesmerized. Terry leaned into Martel, speaking in low tones, using slow, easy hand gestures.

And Martel responded accordingly. He nodded while systemically scanning the area, keeping anyone from getting close as they discussed the items on their personal agenda. With a hand in his pocket, Terry also examined the cafeteria crowd. Not wanting to be seen, Mike stepped behind a group of students while keeping an eye on the pair.

Terry reached in his pocket and withdrew a roll of cash. Laughter bubbled up inside Mike and it took everything in him not to laugh out loud. This was playing out like a scene from one of those hip-hop gangster movies. Terry peeled off several bills and handed them to Martel, then slipped out of the cafeteria door. Martel shoved the bills inside his pocket and headed in the opposite direction.

Mike sped out of the cafeteria. He needed to get Jordan's take on what he had just observed.

Phyllis Hyman's voice filled the room when he opened Jordan's door. Her lovely voice softly accompanied the songstress. She turned and gave him one of her brilliant smiles. Responding, he completely forgot why he'd returned to her classroom.

"Hi. I thought you were going back to your room," she said, grading a stack of papers.

Refocusing on recent events, Mike responded, "I saw something that I wanted to discuss with you."

Frowning, Jordan gathered the homework into a pile and gave him her full attention. "Oh? What?" she asked in a cautious tone.

"I saw Martel Adams huddled in a corner with Terry Mann."

"Our Martel from Science Olympiad?" she asked, reaching for a paper clip from her desk drawer.

Mike nodded.

"Interesting."

"More than interesting," Mike continued. He could feel excitement building inside him. He tapped it down. "Money exchanged hands. Big bills!"

Her eyes grew large. "Really?"

Grinning back at her, he said, "Yeah. Really!"

"Maybe we've found our thief," Jordan said.

"Maybe."

"I've always felt Martel had an agenda of his own when he joined Science Olympiad," Jordan confessed.

"Don't forget Terry," Mike reminded her. "He may be involved in this."

Immediately, Jordan came to Terry's defense. "I think you're wrong. He's a good student."

"Maybe. But we can't ignore the exchange of money." He noted the sadness that entered her eyes. "Honey, if Terry's involved we have to report him."

"I know," she answered remorsefully.

"What's the problem?" he asked.

"Terry has been a good student for me. One of the best. I hate to see his future torched this way."

He moved across the room and stopped next to her desk. He took her hand, caressing the soft skin. "We have to accept that he might be."

She nodded sorrowfully. After a moment, she recovered and asked, "What's next? Should we take our suspicions to Chet?"

Mike sat on the edge of one of the desks. "I don't think we have enough info to go to Chet. I mean, what will we say? I saw money exchange hands. If Terry is as smart as I think he is, he'll come up with a good lie."

"Here's a question." Jordan snapped off the CD player. "What was Terry paying Martel for? Could it be information? Maybe about the lab?"

"That's a thought. Especially since he's part of the Science Olympiad team."

Jordan's sigh of frustration filled the room. "So we're no further ahead."

"I wouldn't say that," Mike contradicted, ticking things off with his fingers. "We have suspects. People we can watch to make the wrong move. We're not just shooting blanks and hoping we'll catch someone. We can direct our efforts at a person."

"True. What do you suggest we do next?" She sat on the edge of the desk next to him, facing the front of the classroom.

He ran his hand back and forth across his chin. "We can do a couple of things. First, watch Terry and Martel. Something is going on between them and we need to find out what it is."

"Mike, does Terry or Martel drive to school?" Jordan asked.

"Drive?" He shrugged. "I don't know. Why?"

"Well, if either young man owns a car that is totally inappropriate for his age and income, we'll have more ammunition for our case. That's another indication that they may be involved in something illegal."

"Good point. Martel wears all the trendy, expensive gear." Mike shoved his hands into the pockets of his Dockers and paced across the front of the classroom, evaluating all that they had learned so far.

Jordan stepped into his path. "I think we should watch the lab and at our next Science Olympiad meeting make sure everyone knows that we don't lock the cabinet."

Mike nodded.

"But I also think we need to let Chet know what's going on. If something goes wrong, we'll have our butt covered."

"Yeah," he agreed. "But there's Debbie. She's another

issue that could put a halt to everything we're trying to learn."

"You're right. Debbie would. And she'd have a point." Jordan shrugged. "By doing this, we're putting the lab in jeopardy a second time. Besides, we don't know what type of liability the school has. I don't want to be responsible for putting the school at risk."

"I know. I've been thinking about that."

She placed a hand on Mike's shoulder. "We need to be very careful."

Looking into Jordan's eyes, he nodded. "You're right. And we will."

"Good."

Her hand dropped away from his shoulder and she returned to her desk. Picking up a pencil and notepad, she said, "Here's the plan. Check out Martel and Terry's cars. Make sure Martel sees the open cabinet with the chemicals in it—"

"Wait," Mike said, stopping her. "I just thought of something. If Terry and Martel are selling Pleasure, they're selling it to the students here. We need to try and keep an eye on them to see if they sell anything during the school day or on school grounds. It won't matter if we catch them in the lab."

"That's a good point."

He blew out a hot puff of air. "This has turned into something much more than I originally expected."

"That's for sure."

He skirted around the edge of the desk, leaned down, and kissed her. Enjoying the texture and taste of her lips, he allowed his fingers to thread through her hair. The kiss concluded much too quickly and everything in him cried out for more.

"Talk to you later," he promised, strolling out the door.

Chapter 22

I'm a science teacher, not James Bond, Mike thought as he kept a discreet distance from Terry Mann. He was such a good kid and student, Mike found it difficult to believe that this young man was involved in something that could destroy so many lives. On the other hand, he didn't believe Martel Adams had the skill to cook the drugs. He would need someone to help him.

After talking with Jordan, they had agreed that Mike would try to determine what Terry and Martel were up to and if they were responsible for taking the chemicals from the lab and manufacturing Pleasure. When school concluded for the day, Mike began trailing Terry, waited outside the computer lab where Terry worked, teaching local senior citizens how to use computers and complete searches on the Internet.

After working two hours in the lab, Terry went to the library and checked out books before heading to the gym. During all of Terry's activities, no one approached him.

If Mike hadn't seen Terry and Martel together earlier, he'd find it hard to believe the young man would be involved with something illegal. He didn't seem like the type of kid to risk his future for quick cash.

As Mike stood in the doorway of his athletic director's office, he kept a watchful eye on the young man as he sat on the bleachers in the gym, watching the basketball team practice for Thursday's game. Like with any red-blooded teenager, Terry's gaze wandered to the other end of the gym where Jordan and her cheerleaders were rehearsing.

After practice ended, the team left the court and Terry grabbed his book bag and headed into the main hallway. Mike jogged across the polished wood floor and slipped out the doors. Hurrying after Terry, he turned the corner, then quickly ducked back into the shadows when he noticed a student waiting near a row of electric-blue lockers.

Preoccupied with a bag of barbecue potato chips, the student hadn't noticed Mike. Mike's eyes grew large and his pulse increased. He ducked inside the doorway of one of the classrooms and waited. It was Martel Adams.

Terry halted at his locker. "Hey," he greeted, spinning the black-face dial on the combination lock. After three turns, he jerked the round base and the lock opened.

Martel grunted, turning the bag up to his mouth to finish off the chips. He balled up the bag and tossed it toward the trash bin. Missing, he shrugged, picked up the empty bag, and made a second attempt. This brought him close to Terry. "What's up?"

"Nothing much. What's going on with you?" Terry answered, shoving books onto the top shelf.

"Waiting on my ride."

Satisfaction spread through Mike's veins. Martel and Terry being together was not an indication that they were up to something. But the two young men were so different that it seemed unlikely that they would be seen together twice in one day.

He'd been right. There was something going on between the two.

Martel did a swift sweep of the hallway with his eyes, and then his voice dropped too low for Mike to hear what he was saying. He unzipped his book bag and pulled the edges apart, moving closer so that the locker door blocked Mike's view.

I can't see what's going on. I'm going to walk by them. Maybe I'll catch them doing something wrong, Mike decided.

He stepped out of the doorway and shoved his hands in his pockets. He strolled down the hall, whistling as he approached the pair. Martel quickly stuffed a small plastic bag in his pocket and zipped his book bag.

"Hey, Mr. Walker," Terry said, indiscreetly pushing the metal door shut.

"Hi." Mike stopped next to the duo. "It's almost seven. We'll be shutting down the building in a little bit. Do you need to call home?"

Martel slung his book bag over his shoulder and started for the door. "No, I'm straight."

"I'm waiting on my dad," Terry said, shutting his door and snapping the lock in place. He headed to the front door, and Mike followed. "Dad should be out there any minute. You have a good evening, Mr. Walker. See ya."

Mike watched the pair go out the front doors and split, heading in opposite directions. First thing tomorrow morning, he would tell Chet and Thurman about his suspicions and what he had learned.

He didn't have much to go on. Just a hunch, an exchange of money, and that plastic bag that Martel stuffed into his pocket. But administration didn't have to have a reason to do a locker check.

* * *

Jordan and Mike stood aside as Chet and Jefferson Thurman opened Martel Adams's locker. The brown, labeled bottles and white boxes of dry chemicals were roughly concealed by Martel's leather jacket and his Air Force One sneakers planted on top of the jacket. Jefferson confiscated the chemicals and asked, "What do you want me to do with this?"

Giving the items a final disparaging glance, Chet answered, "We need to check the other kid's locker. Let's see what we find and then we'll take everything back to my office."

Silently, the little group headed down the opposite corridor. They stopped at a navy blue metal locker. Using the master key, Chet unlocked the door and rummaged through the young man's belongings. One of the textbooks fell from the shelf, spilling turquoise pills from a plastic bag.

Mike glanced at Jordan with a look of surprise on his face. He retrieved the book and flipped through the pages, halting at a spot where someone had carved out a section of the book and replaced it with a plastic ziplock bag. Chuckling, Mike examined the handiwork, mumbling, "Inventive."

A roll of cash spilled from a blue Timberland boot. Chet shook his head, scooping up the bills and counting them. "What is this kid doing with this kind of cash?"

"You know why he's got so much money," Jefferson answered with a deadpan expression on his face. Jordan glanced at the former policeman. His poker-faced expression revealed nothing.

Bile burned the back of her throat. Each time she started to regain her confidence, she hit a roadblock. Like today, she felt betrayed by her students. A young man so devious he stole school property to make money while endangering the lives of his fellow students.

She bit down hard on her bottom lip. This disappointed her. She wanted to believe in these kids and help them become honest, productive citizens.

Filled with sorrow, Jordan laid her head against Mike's shoulder. She hated this, fretting over what she knew would follow. Her stomach cramped painfully as she watched Chet count the money and place it in an envelope.

Shaking his head, Chet collected the items and shut the locker. "Jefferson, we need to talk to these young men."

Mike clasped Jordan's hand and squeezed it reassuringly. "It's going to be okay, sweetheart." He offered her an encouraging smile, whispering, "I know this hurts you, but think about the harm these drugs could do if they made it to the streets or to our kids. We had to get Pleasure out of the building and off the streets."

"I know," Jordan answered in a soft, barely audible voice. Mike studied her closely, taking in her defeated expression. Her faith in the students had been severely rocked by this turn of events.

"Pierson will be a safer place for our students," Mike reminded her. He was trying to ease her disappointment. "That's important."

"I know," she muttered a second time, following Chet and Jefferson.

Stepping into the main office, Chet halted at Donna's desk. "Please call Martel Adams and Terry Mann to my office. Get Martel first. I'll let you know when I'm ready for the other young man."

"Should they bring their belongings?" Donna asked, eyeing the collection of items.

Nodding, Chet continued into his office. The

entourage followed, waiting along the fringes of the
room for Martel to arrive.

Chet placed the confiscated items on his desk, drew
a white cotton handkerchief from his trouser pocket,
and wiped his forehead. He sighed heavily and dropped
into his chair.

Sorting through the stuff on his desk, Chet muttered
disparagingly, "This is not the kind of thing I want in
our school. Jefferson, what's your recommendation?"

Jefferson ran a hand across his chin as he contemplated Chet's question. "We need to call the police."

"Hold on. Don't we call parents first?" Jordan asked,
concerned about the students' rights.

"Yes," Jefferson answered, examining the labels on
the bottles. "But we need to talk to the students first."

Martel tapped on the door, then sauntered into the
room with his hand stuck in the back pockets of his
jeans. His eyes were watchful and cautious as he took
a gander at the room's occupants.

Dressed in baggy-leg denims that hung under his
butt, expensive sneakers, and a Pistons jersey, Martel
looked like an average teen. He wore large bushy pigtails on each side of his head and a long silver chain
dangled from his left ear while a diamond stud winked
from his right. Under all that gear, Martel was a handsome young man.

He stopped in his tracks when his gaze landed on the
chemicals, designer drugs, and money prominently displayed on Chet's desk. His mask fell into place, guarded
and cool, waiting silently.

"Mr. Adams, come in." Chet stood and ushered Martel
into the room and shut the door behind the young
man, waving a hand at the conference table. "Why
don't you have a seat?"

Martel complied, sinking into one of the chairs at the conference table and swept the group with his eyes.

"Well, I think you have some idea why you were called to my office." Chet moved around the table with a yellow legal pad and pen in his hands. "Why don't you tell me what you know about this?" He waved a hand at the stuff on his desk.

The young man remained quiet.

"Son," the principal prompted, "several weeks ago these chemicals were taken from chemistry lab fifteen. Do you know anything about it?"

"I heard something 'bout it." Martel shrugged. "Why you call *me* in here?"

"Well, we found those items in your locker. One of our teachers watched you take this stuff from the lab. So we checked your locker."

The young man's gaze darted over the four adults as he worked out what to say. "Who told you that you can go in my locker without asking me?"

"You did know that this was in your locker?" Jefferson asked, pushing away from the wall to stand near the conference table.

"I don't know nothing about that crap."

"Can you tell me how these items found their way into your locker?" Chet probed further.

"I don't know," Martel answered belligerently.

Chet sighed. "Well, unless you can give me a good reason, I'm going to inform your parents, then turn this matter over to the authorities."

Martel's eyes seemed to pop out of their sockets. He jumped to his feet, searching for a quick exit. "This ain't my fault."

"I never said that. But the fact remains that you had stolen school property in your possession," Jefferson said. He stood behind the young man. "Unless you have a very good explanation, the police must be notified."

Mike stepped in, hovering near the principal's desk. "Martel, I watched you. I saw you shove Pleasure in your pocket."

"You're wrong, Mr. Walker." Martel shook his head and backed away from the adults. "You've got me mixed up with somebody else."

Mike shook his head. "No, I don't."

Martel appeared to be thinking hard and fast. He took another step away from the group of educators, fidgeting with one of his pigtails. Perched on the balls of his feet, he looked as if he was ready to bolt from the room. An edge of desperation crept into his voice. "No, man, you've got me wrong. I'm out of here."

Chet stepped between Mike and Martel. He placed a hand on the student's shoulders. "Son, you can't leave. We have to sort this out."

"But I didn't do nothing," Martel protested, shaking off Chet's hand.

Jefferson stepped into his path, blocking his exit. "Mr. Adams, I'm sorry. We can't let you leave."

"Get off me, man. This ain't right."

"Mr. Thurman, it doesn't look as if this young man plans to cooperate. Why don't you take him to your office?"

"No problem." Jefferson kept a firm hand on Martel, escorting the young man out a back door that connected his office to Chet's.

The principal went to his door. "Donna, please call the other student."

Five minutes later, a tap on the door drew everyone's attention. Donna stuck her head inside the room. "I have the other student in my office. Are you ready for him?"

Chet nodded.

Terry entered. In contrast to Martel, Terry looked like a bookworm. He wore a navy blue sweatshirt embossed with the University of Michigan logo in bold gold letters, blue jeans, and Michael Jordan sneakers. Unlike Martel, he wore his hair cut close to his heart-shaped face.

Terry had shown himself to be an intelligent kid with a great deal of potential. How had a student with such a bright and wonderful future in front of him gotten into this situation? Why had he chosen this path? How did you reach children when the lure of money and power played such a large role in their lives? The whole sorry mess weighed heavily on Jordan. She closed her eyes, shutting out this disturbing picture.

He waved at the group. "Hi."

"Terry, come have a seat."

Following Chet's request, Terry slipped into the chair that Martel had vacated and glanced at the adults. "What did I do?"

"Well, we have questions about some items we found in your locker."

Terry took his time, considering the situation. "My locker? What did you find?"

"Money and Pleasure."

"Pleasure? What's that?"

"It's a designer drug that someone has been manufacturing using school property."

"It's not mine."

"How did it find its way into your locker, Terry?"

He shrugged. "Don't know. What I do know is it's not mine, Mr. Bartholomew."

"Maybe you should take a second look."

Terry shook his head, leaning back in the chair. "I

don't need to. It's not my stuff and I don't know how it got in my locker."

Chet's tone became more insistent. "Do you know anything about it?"

Calmly, Terry pursed his lips and shook his head slowly as if he were truly considering the question. "No."

The principal touched the money and drugs. His voice had an air of sorrow. "By law, I have to turn everything over to the police once I've contacted your parents. Is there anything you want or need to tell us?"

Terry shook his head. "No. Nothing."

Chet ran a hand over his head. "Are you certain? It would help you if you cooperate with us."

"I'm sorry, Mr. Bartholomew," Terry answered. "I don't know what you want me to say."

"What about the money? Where did it come from? How about the pills? Did you make them?"

Terry shifted more comfortably in his chair and crossed his arms over his chest, speaking as if he were talking to a not so bright child. "What money? Whose pills?"

Defeated, Chet tossed his hands in the air. "All right. I tried. We'll let the police handle things from this point. Please remain in my office. Mr. Thurman will be down here to get you."

Jordan couldn't stand it another moment. She touched Terry's shoulder. "This is not a game. Your future in on the line here. Mr. Bartholemew is trying to help you. Tell him everything. Terry, don't throw away your future."

Confidently, he grinned, offering Jordan an open, I've-got-it-covered expression. "I'm sorry. I don't have anything to add, Ms. Anderson."

Mike moved closer and touched her arm. "Ms.

Anderson, don't. He's already planned how he's going to handle this situation. You can't change his mind."

She turned to Mike with tears in her eyes. "He's a good kid with a great future in front of him. I can't let him throw away his life this way. Not without trying to make him understand."

Mike leaned close and whispered, "Honey, he has to want your help. Terry's not a fool. This is his way of getting out of things."

He wrapped an arm around her shoulders. "Come on. There's not much else we can do right now. It's up to Terry to decide where he wants his life to go."

"Mike's right." Chet gave Terry a quick once-over. "This young man has made his decision. It's up to the police now. Why don't you get back to your classes?"

"Chet, if you need us, you know where we can be reached."

Dejected, Jordan halted in the main office and asked, "What do you think will happen to them?"

He shook his head. "I don't know for sure. They'll be expelled. The police will handle things after that. They're juveniles, so they may get out of this with probation. It's hard to say at this point. They won't return to Pierson."

As teachers they should be able to help Martel and Terry, guide them and keep them safe. In her heart, she felt like she had failed the pair.

As they left Chet's office, the police entered. Minutes later, they exited the building with Martel and Terry in handcuffs.

Chapter 23

Mike roared into the school parking lot, scrambled out of the driver's seat, and locked his Mustang. He drew in a deep breath as he contemplated the day ahead, then strolled purposefully through Pierson's employee entrance. Today might prove to be one of the most difficult days of the school year for Jordan. He wanted to be at her side offering support and encouragement.

As he marched to her classroom, his thoughts were propelled backward to the previous evening. He had stood in the center of Jordan's living room, waiting helplessly as she vacillated from confident to a bundle of worried nerves. She ranted about the upcoming observation, how Debbie hated her and might use her position as department head to further her personal vendetta.

After several unsuccessful attempts to soothe the woman he loved, Mike admitted defeat and gave up. Eventually, he'd returned to his own place, providing her with time to reflect on the situation and calm down.

Sighing heavily, he moved along the empty and dimly lighted corridor. School didn't begin for thirty minutes and the building had an eerie quality without the usual ruckus and antics of the students and faculty. Outside

Jordan's door, Mike halted. A Styrofoam cup of hot chocolate filled his left hand while he readjusted his pastel-colored tie with the right.

Mike slipped through the classroom door and immediately zeroed in on Jordan. She stood near the rear of the room, straightening a poster.

At the sound of the door opening, Jordan turned, welcoming him with the brightest, warmest smile he'd ever encountered. He stopped, captivated. It touched his heart in a place only Jordan could.

His whole body quivered in response to the smile on her lips. It took his collective willpower to tap down the growing need to take her into his arms and kiss her silly.

Refocusing on the day ahead, he studied Jordan. She looked beautiful, professionally dressed in a black knit dress with a matching jacket and black pumps. Gold jewelry accentuated her outfit.

"Hey," he greeted, drinking in her smile.

"Good morning." She strolled across the room to where he stood and pointed at the cup. "Is that for me?"

"Yeah." Feeling like an idiot, Mike handed her the cup.

"Ohhh! How sweet. Thank you." She ran a lightly manicured finger along his cheek, drawing circles as she stroked his skin.

Her gentle touch kicked his pulse into hyperdrive. He took her hand, turned the palm up, and kissed the center. "You're welcome. How are you this morning?"

"Good. Ready." Jordan removed the lid from the cup and sipped cautiously.

Mike's gaze slid over her, noting the air of confidence that surrounded her like a magical aura. Surprised, he lifted his eyebrows.

Pride welled inside him. The panic and confusion she'd displayed yesterday were conspicuously absent.

"What happened?" he asked.

Jordan shrugged, returning to her desk, explaining between sips of hot chocolate, "After you left I felt so guilty and helpless. Truly, I felt like a victim. That's not me anymore. I'm not a victim and I'm not going to act like one. I love my career and I don't plan to let anyone take it away from me."

Bowing his head, he smiled. "That's my girl. I'm glad you finally figured that out."

Jordan added, "I need to apologize to you."

"Apologize? For what?"

"Being such a turkey yesterday. You were trying to help me, comfort me, and I acted like a spoiled brat."

"It's okay," he said.

"No, it's not," she disagreed.

He moved across the room and touched her arm. "Then forget it, I have. We help each other. That's what people who care about one another do. So what are you going to do?"

"What I always do. Teach."

"All right!"

Jordan reached under the desk and snapped on the CD player. The stimulating composition of Beethoven filled the room. She stood in front of him with her arms folded across her chest. "When the last school year ended, I believed my teaching career was finished. I felt so disillusioned. The kids and their parents made me question my career choice. Honestly, I still have some reservations. But I love my job and I need to refocus on what's important, and I have."

"I'm proud of you," Mike stated, reaching her in several long strides. He wrapped an arm around her shoulders and pulled her tight against his side.

Remaining in his embrace, she continued, "The fear of being attacked paralyzed me. With your help,

I worked hard to put those feelings behind me." She stepped out of his arms. Determination sparkled from her brown eyes. "And it's going to stay that way."

Inhaling Jordan's gentle fragrance, Mike ran his fingers through her loose hair. In that moment, he'd never been more proud. She'd come a long way from the panic-stricken woman he encountered in August and had resolved many of the issues that had plagued her. Now Jordan stood before him confident and in control.

"No one is going to take away what I've worked so hard to accomplish," she promised. "Nobody."

"What have you got planned for today?"

"Same thing I scheduled before I knew about the observation," she replied.

"I'm proud of you," Mike said. The beginning of a smile curved his full lips. "Do you need anything from me?"

Jordan gave him another brilliant smile. "Just your support. I'll always need you. But I think I've got this covered."

Mike opened his mouth to add something, but shut it when a knock on the door interrupted him. Debbie and Chet strolled into the room.

"Good morning," Mike and Jordan chimed together.

"Howdy. Mike, I didn't expect to see you here," Chet said.

Wordlessly, Debbie stood next to Chet and gave them a curt nod of acknowledgment before marching to the back of the classroom. Her face scrunched up like a dried raisin. Her lips were pinched shut as if they were held together with clothespins. She sat, examining the classroom, and checked items off her list.

Mike shoved his hands into his trouser pockets, explaining, "I'm Jordan's mentor. I wanted to be certain she was prepared for her meeting with you."

Chet waved a dismissing hand in Mike's direction. "This is nothing," he proclaimed. "Jordan won't even notice that we're in the room."

Mike turned away, smiling as he shook his head. *Spoken like a person who's totally oblivious to the tension swirling around the room.*

The principal opened his portfolio and produced a pen. He strolled around the space, making note of the class rules posted for the students and the room's décor.

Jordan headed across the room and stood in the entrance. "If you guys don't mind, the bell is going to ring. I need to be in the hall. Excuse me."

Chet waved her away, continuing to inspect the classroom.

For the next five minutes, Jordan maintained her post in the hall as her first-period class entered the room. After the tardy bell rang, she returned to her desk. "Take your seats." She waited as her students moved around the room and slipped into their desks. "First, you need to know that we have guests today. I expect you to show them every courtesy."

Mike started toward the lab door. He halted for a moment, curious to see how she would handle her class.

"Okay, settle down," she said in a strong, authoritative voice. "We've got lots to accomplish today. I want you guys to be able to reiterate the atomic symbol when I give you the element. And to help you remember, we're going to play a game of 'Who Wants to Be a Millionaire?' By the way, you get two lifelines in this game." She opened a gold box and removed a stack of white index cards. "Eugene, the first question is yours."

Mike shut the door quietly behind him. He hurried to the opposite door and stepped inside his classroom. *She'll be fine,* he thought confidently as he began his day.

Chapter 24

A week after her observation, Jordan sat opposite Debbie and Chet, waiting impatiently for the results. United, the principal and the department head sat huddled together behind Debbie's desk, whispering in soft tones far too low for Jordan to hear.

I feel like one of the kids waiting to be reprimanded by the dean of students, she thought. Discreetly, she fingered the folded edge of her bone-colored turtleneck.

Signaling Chet with a nod of her head, Debbie straightened, eyeing Jordan with a closed, unreadable expression painted on her dark brown face. "We're ready to begin."

Suddenly, the chair felt like hardened cement under Jordan's bottom. She squirmed, searching for a more comfortable spot, but found none. Her pulse shot out of control, pumping so fast that she felt as if she might fly from the adrenaline rush as a lone bead of perspiration made a maddeningly slow descent down the back of her neck.

This was it. If the observation turned out badly, she needed to remain professional and open to Chet's and Debbie's suggestions. The students—and how best to educate them—rated above any personal issues she might have with her supervisors.

"Well," Chet began, shuffling the observation documents into neat piles before distributing them.

Accepting her copy, Jordan quickly skimmed the page, seeking any derogatory remarks. Chet cut into her thoughts before she finished a quarter of the first page.

"We're going to make this as painless as possible, Jordan. Debbie and I worked on your evaluation together." He smiled encouragingly. "We'd like to run down the list of items and spend some time discussing the ones that made an impression on us."

Frowning, Jordan silently questioned, *painless for whom? What the heck does Chet mean by that phrase? And what kind of impression? Good? Bad?*

He ran a hand over the soft peach fuzz on his head. "First, Pierson's instructor observation is broken into three major categories. Classroom instruction, student-classroom management, and professional responsibilities."

Jordan nodded, drawing in a shaky breath as she examined the faces of her supervisors. She gained nothing from their expressions and found herself hoping for the best, but mentally preparing for the worst.

At this point Debbie took over, using the sharpened point of her pencil to direct Jordan's attention to the appropriate sections. "First, we need to define our rating scale. As you can see, we use a one-to-five scale with one being the lowest score you can receive and five representing excellence."

Jordan scooted to the edge of her chair. She leaned close, taking a moment to skim the items as the department head referred to them.

Debbie tapped the point of the pencil on the rating they gave her for each item. "After talking with Chet, we agreed that you were exceptionally prepared for your class. Your students were enthusiastically engaged in learning. The assignment you gave your students provided prompt and appropriate feedback so that your students knew exactly where they stood."

Chet cleared his throat, adding, "For classroom instruction you received four and a half and you received the same rating for the student-classroom management section. Good job. We were greatly impressed. But we expected no less from a seasoned teacher."

Pleased, Jordan smiled as the tight band squeezing her heart loosened a notch. So far every comment made perfect sense. Sighing, she sank into the chair's soft leather. Her confidence grew as she listened to Chet.

Eyes sparkling, he gazed expectantly at Jordan. "You impressed me with the creativity you exhibited during our visit. Your students display a lively competitive nature about the material. Considering the use of such an interactive instructional tool, you maintained tight control over the activity." He gave her a broad smile of approval and his voice filled with admiration. "Personally, I thought your 'Who Wants to Be a Millionaire?' game using chemistry terms was brilliant. You should consider patenting that idea. It's a great product."

"Thank you. I'll keep that in mind," Jordan answered softly.

"No," he countered, tipping his head in her direction. "Thank you. We need instructors willing to go the extra distance to help educate our students. As an administrator, I'm happy to have you as one of my staff members." He turned to Debbie. "Do you have anything to add?"

"Yes," Debbie answered, flipping to the next section. "I'd like to draw your attention to the professional responsibilities portion of the observation."

Jordan scanned the sheet, noting several lower scores. She arched her eyebrow, silently requesting an explanation.

Debbie's eyes widened when she interpreted Jordan's expression. "Many of your scores were very high. But I felt that you need to improve in several areas."

Here we go, Jordan thought. *Time to stick it to me.*

"I'm sure you are aware that as a professional you need to stay abreast of current trends in education. Pierson allocates resources for professional development to enhance your teaching skills. I'd like you to consider taking advantage of those resources by attending some local conferences and workshops that can complement your teaching style."

I can do that, Jordan decided, accepting Debbie's request in the spirit she believed it had been given. Jordan silently resolved to surf the Net for a few appropriate classes. "I'd like that."

"Good. Also, I'd like to see your lesson plans for substitute teachers. We should have those on file in the main office."

"All right."

Chet glanced at his watch, then stood. "Excuse me, ladies. I'm sorry to leave during your evaluation, Jordan. But I've got another meeting. Debbie will finish up here." He inched around the desk and patted Jordan's shoulder before making his way to the door. "Jordan, we're happy to have you. Keep up the good work."

"Thank you and I will," she promised.

When the door closed behind him, Jordan felt the chilly shift in the room's temperature. Turning to Debbie, Jordan noticed an obvious but subtle change in her demeanor. The artificial smile displayed during Chet's presence had been replaced by blatant dislike.

Frightened, Jordan shied away from the emotions Debbie had kept in check until now.

What had she possibly done to cause this woman to dislike her? Maybe the proper time had come to learn the truth, since there were only the two of them in the room.

"There are some things that I want to add." Debbie's tone hit Jordan like chips of ice that were cold and painful. "Understand that the things we're going to discuss will not be placed on your observation. This is between you and me."

"All right," Jordan answered, wondering how much mud Debbie intended to sling.

"The incident with the lab—"

"We proved that I wasn't responsible for leaving the lab open—"

"Yes, Mike did. But . . . I want to reemphasize that you must be more responsible. Make sure everything is put away. We lost chemicals and equipment that day. That can't happen again. Understand?"

"I agree, it shouldn't happen again." Jordan linked her hands together. "The lab was locked when I left the building. No matter what you say, those are the facts and I'm not responsible for what happened. Point your finger at Harold."

Debbie's eyes glittered with anger.

"Is there more?" Jordan asked, starting to rise.

"I have one additional item to address," Debbie stated in a tone laced with contempt.

Jordan's eyebrows crawled upward. "Oh?"

"I plan to reassign you to a new mentor."

"Reassign? Why? Mike and I work well together."

"He's gotten too involved with you."

Stunned, Jordan shot back, "Where did you get that idea? We work together."

Debbie drew in a breath and let it out slowly, taking her time over her next comment. "His responsibilities included helping you acclimate to our Pierson family. But he seems to be holding your hand through each and every crisis."

Shocked, Jordan gasped. Debbie had dropped her professional facade and landed a verbal punch that had Jordan struggling to regain control. *Calm down, Jordan. You need to take a step back and evaluate the situation.*

"Stand on your own two feet," Debbie continued, flipping through the observation and landing on the final page. "I don't want to see Mike propping you up anymore. We hired you to teach and that's what I expect you to do."

"And that's exactly what I've been doing," Jordan reasoned, fighting to keep her voice even. "I don't think you're being fair. The situations that have come up were hardly daily occurrences. Why are you so against my friendship with Mike?"

Debbie leaned back in her chair and folded her arms across her chest. "If he was just your mentor, I wouldn't have a problem."

"What are you really saying here?" Jordan demanded.

"All right." Debbie tossed the pencil on the desk and glared at Jordan. "If you want to know, I'm saying that I don't approve of office romances."

"Debbie, you can disapprove all you'd like. But the truth is you can't stop Mike and me from being friends."

"No, I can't. I don't have a problem with friends." She twirled a blond braid around her finger. "But we both know that you and Mike are more than friends."

Jordan held her tongue. She didn't want to increase Debbie's arsenal of information.

Debbie chuckled nastily. "Do you think I'm blind? It's obvious that you two are more than friends."

Jordan felt cold and hot all at once. A bead of perspiration slid down her neck as she shifted in her chair.

She wasn't going to live the rest of her life like this. It was time for her to take charge of her life and stop letting these panic attacks rule. Drawing in a deep breath of air, she folded her arms across her chest, taking control. "Is there a clause in the handbook that prohibits fraternization between coworkers?"

"No."

"Then it's none of your business," Jordan snapped.

"Office romances always end badly. People get hurt. The extreme friction between the ex-lovers generally causes tension among the other staff members and the students. I don't want that kind of thing here. Kids react to that kind of tension."

"I repeat, it's none of your business. Mike and I are professionals, Debbie. We also know how to control ourselves while we're at work. You don't have anything to worry about."

Debbie rolled her eyes. "And let's not forget the other issues."

"What do you mean?" Jordan asked cautiously.

"Oh, come on. Don't play dumb with me, Jordan."

"I don't know what you're talking about."

"Okay." Debbie shrugged, obviously enjoying this little repartee. "You are entirely too old for Mike. What are you doing with this kid? He doesn't need a mother. Mike belongs with some young lady his own age."

There it was. The reason she hated Jordan. Finally, Debbie had revealed what had been on her mind and in her heart for months. Debbie's words hit their mark and fueled Jordan's insecurities. She was hurt and embarrassed.

"Again, this is none of your business." Struggling to

remain civil, Jordan added, "I'm not going to dignify any of this with a comment. But what goes on between Mike and me has nothing to do with you. Unless we are behaving inappropriately in the classroom, or on school property, you have nothing to say about our relationship. I suggest you learn to live with it. You're entitled to your opinion."

"Fine. But if any of this reaches our students," she warned, "expect to hear from me."

Jordan rose from her chair, looming over the older woman, and said in a firm voice, "I think we're about done here."

"Almost." She removed a pen from her desk and handed it to Jordan. "I need you to look over everything, then sign the form, indicating that you've reviewed the observation. If you feel that you need to add any comments, put your initials next to the item, then write your rebuttal on the back."

Jordan scribbled her name on the last page of the observation, eager to get out of this crazy woman's office. She dropped the pen on the desk and escaped without another word.

Jordan headed straight for Mike's classroom. She was furious. Debbie had no right to interfere in her relationship with Mike.

She rapped once on the door before slipping inside the room. Mike sat at his desk, grading a stack of papers.

He glanced up, smiling broadly. "Hey. How did it go?"

She grimaced, moving across the room to take the chair next to his desk, and sighed. "The observation went well. I got a four and a half overall."

"Good." Mike jumped from his chair and pulled Jordan from hers, hugging her. "I told you that it would all work out."

Smiling sadly, she answered, "Yeah. You did."

Mike stepped away from her, eyeing her closely. The broad smile dimmed a bit. "There's more. What happened?"

She shrugged, but remained silent.

"Come on. Spill it."

Her head dropped to his chest. "Oh, Mike. Everything went great until Chet left for another meeting. Debbie turned into a she-beast the minute Chet stepped out of the room. She told me that she doesn't believe in office romances and that you don't need a mother—"

"What?"

Jordan nodded. "Yeah. She believes our relationship will cause all manner of drama in the office."

He rubbed her arm. "First of all, what we do outside the school is none of her business. As long as we maintain our professionalism at Pierson, nothing can be said or done about our relationship."

"I agree."

"Second, if I get hurt, I'm an adult. I can handle it. I figure, whenever you get involved with someone there's always the chance that the relationship won't work. All we can do is give it our best."

"I'm still with you." Jordan flopped down in the chair. "Debbie seems to feel that she needs to protect you from the big, bad older woman."

Annoyance flashed from his eyes. Mike folded his arms across his chest. "I don't need protection. I'm a grown man and I can handle my business. And I'm not looking for a mother."

"I believe you. Maybe you should tell Debbie." Jordan

glanced at Mike. "She has a very proprietary attitude about you."

"Jordan, that's the baggage from Clay, Debbie's ex. Did I tell you that she met him at Pierson? Well, there's more. I didn't mention to you what happened to cause them to break up."

Interested in any information that could help her understand this woman, Jordan demanded, "Tell me now."

"Clay treated her badly. He flirted and bedded several of the women on the staff and got involved with some students."

Sighing heavily, she shut her eyes against the images. "That's terrible."

"Yeah, it was. That's not all. One of the teachers got loud and obnoxious with Debbie. It caused a real stir in the school. Everyone saw them, including kids and parents. That's when Debbie became this hard-ass woman that refuses to take any crap from staff or students."

Nibbling on her bottom lip, she considered how embarrassing that situation must have been. "No wonder she doesn't want the drama."

"No, she doesn't. She's seen it all," Mike agreed.

Turning in her chair to look at him, Jordan asked, "I can understand Debbie's reasoning. She doesn't want a repeat with us."

"True. But we're not going to end up that way."

She grunted. "How can you be so sure?"

"We're committed to each other. I think that's what caused the drama between Clay and Debbie. They weren't committed to their relationship."

"That could be. Maybe we should listen to what she's saying."

"No. Eventually, I want people to know that we're a couple. I'm happy and proud to be with you. Jordan, you're a big part of my life and I want to show you off and be able to say that you're with me. I want to share everything with you."

"Thank you." His words were beautiful, but going public really frightened her. She was afraid that the relationship wouldn't last and that she would be left with nothing. She didn't want people laughing at or pitying her.

"This is our place of work and we need to act accordingly. We should be careful while we're here, agreed?"

She nodded. "Agreed."

"I'd kiss you, but we're professionals and at work." Smiling back at her, he said, "There's time for that later. Now that the dreaded observation is done, how about a celebration dinner?"

"Sounds good to me," Jordan answered, allowing Mike to pull her from her chair.

"Dinner at Mario's," he said, leading her to the door.

"Oh, Italian. I'm all for it."

Mike grinned. "Meet me at my place around six."

"Will do."

Chapter 25

After weeks filled with tension and stress, Jordan planned to spend her weekend relaxing at her apartment. Shortly after 10:00 a.m., Mike arrived on her doorstep with a completely different agenda for them.

Without consciously agreeing to it, she found herself dressing warmly and following him out the door. A half hour later, they arrived on the streets of Detroit's Eastern Market.

The temperature hovered near thirty degrees and a chill invaded her body as they stood under the green covering, sheltering the vendors. Wind whipped across Jordan's cheeks, adding a rose flush to her skin while they waited for a farmer to bag up their bananas.

Dressed in a peach sweater, black jeans, and a matching suede jacket, Jordan strolled hand in hand with Mike down Russell Street past a block of fruit and vegetable vendors and a sprinkle of small restaurants. She stopped, leaned close to Mike, and gave him a quick kiss on the lips.

Grinning down at her, Mike asked, "Not that I'm complaining, but why did you do that?"

"It's a thank-you for dragging me out of the house."

She stroked his cheek with her fingertips. "This is great. I'm so glad you brought me here."

Mike hugged her close. "My pleasure, sweetheart." With his arm securely on her shoulder, he steered her down the street, negotiating the landscape through the Saturday morning crowd.

"So much has happened over the last couple of weeks, we haven't had a chance to go out and enjoy ourselves. That's my plan for us for today." He brought her hand to his lips. "Have fun and buy groceries."

Jordan giggled, playfully jabbing him in the side with her elbow. "Always thinking about your stomach."

"No, not really." He did a suggestive double lift of his eyebrows. "There's an organ a little lower that needs constant Jordan attention."

She blushed, unable to get the image of them entwined on his bed or that particular organ out of her mind. "Oh, you."

"That's me."

Entering the pavilion, they stopped at the first vendor. "Here you are." Jordan plucked a grape from the bunch and popped it into his mouth.

"Mmm, good." Mike gathered a bunch of red grapes, examining them before making a purchase. They moved to the next vendor. "You know, fruit is good, but we need to consider dinner. While you were getting dressed, I peeked in your refrigerator. There's not much in there. What are you planning to feed me?"

Brushing an irate lock of hair from her eyes, Jordan answered, "Excellent question. And it needs an excellent answer." She glanced around them, focusing in on a spot on the opposite end of the market. "Before we head home, let's go by the Gratiot Market and Hirt's to pick up some spices." Taking his hand, she moved to the next vendor, examining the vegetables. She selected a half dozen yellow squashes, then added tomatoes and fresh green beans. "I can add a salad along with these veggies for dinner if you want."

"Salad is good. What about some protein? Chicken or a steak would work for me." Mike's forehead crinkled as he concentrated. "Oh, maybe a fillet of salmon or trout."

"You know, I have a George Foreman grill. We could pick up a couple of New York strips from the Gratiot Market," she suggested. "Steak tastes delicious from the grill."

Nodding, Mike removed the brown paper bag filled with vegetables from her hands and placed them in the blue woven sack he carried at his side. "Sounds perfect." He punctuated his sentence with a kiss. "Steak and vegetables or trout and vegetables, even chicken and vegetables would work for me." He tasted her lips a second time. "What's for dessert?"

With a mock expression of surprise on her face, she answered, "Well, me, of course."

"Of course." Chuckling, he wrapped her in his embrace. Jordan enjoyed the warmth of his touch, feeling safer than she had in a long time. Sometimes he was just too appealing to resist.

"Mike, is that you? And Ms. Anderson?" interrupted a voice from Pierson.

Jordan froze, paralyzed. Why hadn't she kept her rear end at home?

Mike loosened his hold on her, but kept his arm around her, glancing over her head. "Hi, Donna."

"Hey," she answered, eyes filled with mischief. "Boy, I never expected to see you two together."

Jordan turned in Mike's arms. "Hi."

Donna manned the main office efficiently, although she held the trophy for biggest gossip at Pierson. Jordan felt certain that Donna would spread this bit of news all over the school campus by the time she arrived at work Monday morning.

"What's going on?" Donna asked. Her gaze shifted from Mike to Jordan and back again.

"Nothing much," he answered, lifting his woven bag. "Buying stuff for dinner."

She nodded. "Mike, you live near here, don't you?"

"Yes. In Indian Village. What brings you out here?"

"Shopping. Same as you." Donna lifted her bag of groceries. "I wanted to get a head start on my holiday grocery list."

"Good idea," Mike said.

"Boy, you guys look awfully cute." Donna's voice held a hint of surprise. "How long have you been together?"

Pulling Jordan closer, Mike remarked on the statement, but ignored the question. "Thanks."

Taking the hint, Donna glanced past them. "I see my husband has just found his way out of the coffee shop. I better get down there. You guys have a good weekend and I'll see you on Monday."

"You too." Mike waved as Donna moved on.

Jordan unlocked her door and hurried through the apartment to the kitchen. Mike followed at a slower pace, locking the door after them before making his way through the apartment with their groceries. He entered the kitchen, depositing their Eastern Market bags on the counter.

The silence seeped into the room like fog, thick and deadly. He knew an explosion was going to happen, he just didn't know when.

Jordan and Mike worked side by side, washing and storing the produce in the refrigerator and dividing the fruit between the bowl on the dining room table and the refrigerator's crisper. After several additional minutes of taut silence, Jordan whipped around to face Mike. "What are we going to do?"

"About what?" he asked, leaving the kitchen with fruit in his hands.

An expression of irritation flashed across her face. "Donna!"

Mike shrugged, stopped in the center of her dining room, watching Jordan closely. "Nothing. There's nothing we can do."

Her jaw clenched and her fingers tightened around the knife's wooden handle. "I'm serious."

"I know you are," he answered. He arranged the bananas, apples, and grapes in the aqua fruit bowl.

Jordan let out a loud audible sigh, gnawing on her bottom lip. "What if Donna tells everyone about us? What are we going to do?"

Returning to the kitchen, Mike said, "I repeat, there's nothing we can do."

He didn't like their personal business being spread across the school any more than Jordan. Gossip could be so mean and destructive. But he understood and accepted that things were out of their hands. The simple truth remained that when Donna caught them kissing like teenagers, they had opened themselves up to public scrutiny.

And like Jordan he didn't want their relationship to become the new gossip piece for his colleagues, because it could be embarrassing and intrusive. However, like everything at Pierson, they could get over this and move on.

Until the next bit of gossip pushed them out of the limelight, the next few days were going to be difficult. He felt bad for Jordan. All they could do was ride out the wave of curious coworkers and students in a dignified fashion.

She pushed up the sleeves of her sweater, turned on the water, dropped the squash in the sink, and washed them, placing them on a paper towel on the countertop.

"It's not a problem unless we make it one," Mike prophesied, returning to the kitchen and placing his hands on Jordan's shoulders. He massaged her tense flesh through her wool sweater, speaking in a soft, encouraging tone. "Eventually, it had to come out. Someone would have seen us and that would have been that. Actually, that's exactly what happened. It's time for us to come clean. Besides, we planned to tell people in a couple of weeks anyway. Donna beat us to it."

"That's easy for you to say." Jordan shook off his hand, turned to the countertop, and removed the pan spray from the cupboard. Lifting the Foreman grill's white top, she sprayed the surface, then plugged the grill into the wall socket.

"What do you mean?"

"You're a man. A young man. No one's going to laugh at you," Jordan scoffed, removing a knife from the drawer and slicing the squash diagonally. "I'm the one people will laugh at. I'm the one that will look like a fool. Not you."

Silently, he studied her. Jordan's expression didn't hold well for this discussion. But something in him wouldn't allow him to let this topic drop. He needed to know why she believed people would laugh at her.

Blood pumped faster and harder in his chest. What did she mean she'd look like a fool? And why did it matter?

Mike leaned against the wall. "Why should that be an issue? You're not a fool. And why bother worrying about it? Besides, what difference does it make what people think?"

"These are our colleagues. The people that we work with." Exasperated, she raised her voice as she waved the knife in her hand through the air. "Mike, look at us. We're not the traditional couple. I'm ten years older than you. You are one of my former students. Don't you think we look a little different to people? Our colleagues especially? And we haven't even talked about how the students will react."

"Sweetheart, there's nothing we can do. We've done nothing wrong."

Jordan opened her mouth, ready to say more.

"This was one of the reasons I wanted things out in the open. There's no gossip when the truth is presented in an honest way," Mike explained. "To me, the truth is the easiest and best way to handle a situation this dicey. If anyone asks, there's no reason to deny that we're seeing each other."

"I don't want my business on front street for everyone to take shots at, Mike."

"Neither do I. Unfortunately, sweetheart, we've passed the stage of what you or I want. I'm sorry. It doesn't matter, our business is out in the open."

Frustrated, Jordan turned away. "You don't understand."

"I understand. Remember, we were going to tell everyone anyway, right?"

"Come on, Mike. This has been difficult enough for me without adding that bigmouthed Donna to the mix."

"You didn't answer my question. I repeat, didn't we agree to tell people anyway?"

"Yeah," she answered reluctantly.

Mike shook his head and lifted a hand, halting her.

"The important thing is how we handle the situation. How we present ourselves. Monday morning we can walk into the building with our heads held high and ignore the gossip, because it's going to happen either way, or we can act as if we've done something awful."

She shook her head and turned to the counter, staring out the small window over the sink. "I don't know."

"What don't you know?" He wrapped his arms around her and drew her body against his. "We know that Donna is a gossip. Trust me, right now she's got the school's fan out sheet and is telling anyone on the list that happens to be at home. I'm sorry. That's the way things are."

"I'm not ready for this, Mike," she confessed quietly.

He pulled her closer. "Sweetheart, it's okay. We'll work through this together. I'll be with you, helping you." Gently kissing her forehead, he turned her to the refrigerator. "Come on, let's get dinner ready, okay?"

She nodded.

"Where's that trout?"

Jordan stepped from Mike's embrace and headed to the refrigerator. She removed a package wrapped in white paper and took it to the sink.

Waiting for the grill to reach the proper temperature, he couldn't shake the unsettling feeling gnawing at his gut. Although Jordan seemed calm, the situation had not been resolved.

Mike loved and respected Jordan and he liked the idea of being a couple. Even though it was difficult, he tried to understand her misgivings about them. He believed that she was becoming more comfortable with them as a couple. But if they stayed together, eventually someone would see them together and they would have to say something.

He prayed this incident didn't cause a major setback

in their relationship. And he silently hoped the staff at Pierson would give them a break and allow the situation to die a quick and quiet death. Truthfully, he didn't expect it to be an easy Monday.

Chapter 26

Gray clouds hovered overhead, matching Jordan's mood as she pulled into Pierson's parking lot. With a heavy heart and a great deal of trepidation she sat in her SUV waiting for inspiration to provide a solution to the current mess she found herself facing.

Why had she agreed to go to the Eastern Market with Mike? she bemoaned. This situation wouldn't exist if she'd kept her butt at home.

Instead, Donna had caught them kissing. The secretary had probably hurried home to spread the word that Mike and Jordan were involved. Jordan really hated being placed in this position.

She sat a moment in the parking lot, composing herself. As she switched off the engine, she'd caught sight of Mike's car zooming down the street. As quickly as possible, she gathered her belongings, exited her SUV, and deliberately ignored the roar of his Mustang as he flew into his favorite parking lot.

Jordan marched across the parking lot, triggered the auto alarm to her car, and entered the building through the teachers' entrance. The halls were empty of students and she fervently prayed that she'd make it to her classroom without crossing paths with other Pierson staff.

Behind her a door slammed shut with a bang, followed by swift footsteps. Seconds later, Mike's strong, clear voice echoed throughout the cavernous corridor, halting her. "Ms. Anderson, hold on a minute."

Sighing, Jordan shut her eyes and reached for calm. She'd hoped to avoid incidents like this. She and Mike needed to avoid any situation that would add to the gossip.

Today, she planned to disappear into her classroom and come out at the end of the day, remaining as low-key as possible. Avoid all social gatherings where the faculty hung out.

Facing him, she waited. He jogged up to her, drawing alongside her with his briefcase in one hand.

As he approached her, the heat from Mike's body reached out to her. His gaze skimmed her soft curves and he uttered a greeting in that bedroom voice that always achieved a response from her. "Good morning. How are you?"

Tiny ripples of sensations surged through Jordan as she responded to him. She clamped down her emotions and returned in a clear, professional voice, "Good morning."

Mike fell into step beside her. "Didn't you see me pull in?"

Jordan nodded.

His forehead wrinkled with puzzlement. "Why didn't you wait?"

She shrugged, wanting to prevent an explosion. "I don't want people to see us together."

"Why?"

She tossed him a look that questioned his sanity.

"This is going to be a day from hell without adding fuel to the fire. I want to pretend things are normal."

Mike laughed softly. "Sweetheart, nothing is going to be normal today. That's why we need to present a united front."

She glanced up and down the empty hall. "I don't want people to catch us in a position that provides a hint of intimacy between us."

"Why?"

"Come on, Mike." Annoyed, Jordan started down the hall. "Get real."

"No. Tell me," he demanded, grabbing her arm and whipping her around to face him.

"If she hasn't already, Donna is going to tell everyone in the building about seeing us at the market."

"I know, sweetheart. I know. We already talked about this."

"Everybody will know about us."

He shrugged. "We'll be fine as long as we don't get involved with the gossip and stick to the facts."

Exasperated, she shook her head and blew out a hot puff of air. "Mike, we'll be the talk of the building."

"Probably. But only until the next bit of good gossip turns up." He reached out and stroked her arm.

Instantly, she scrambled out of his way, scanning the halls. "Don't."

"Don't what?" His voice dropped an octave, taking on a dangerous quality.

"Please, people can see us."

He laughed. The harsh, uncompromising sound chilled her. "People have already seen us, starting with George and Donna. You might as well get ready for it."

"I can't."

"What are you afraid of?"

"I'm not ready for people to know about us."

"Why?"

"It's my business. And I don't want people gossiping about me behind my back."

"Sweetheart, we're out of options. The cat is definitely out of the bag. All we can do is present a united front and help each other over the difficult parts of the day."

Jordan shut her eyes, massaging her forehead with the tips of her fingers. "I just wish we had been more careful. Then we wouldn't be in this mess."

"Look, we talked about this Saturday. We've got to ride out the storm. In a day or two we'll be old news."

"I know."

Mike glanced down at her. "Jordan, are you ashamed to be with me? Is this why you're so upset?"

She didn't deny it, choosing instead to remain silent.

An annoyed frown creased Mike's forehead. "I'm good enough for your bed, but not good enough to be seen with you. Is that what you're saying?"

Again, she remained silent.

His eyes narrowed while his voice dropped to an accusatory whisper. "I hope you realize that we would have had to come clean at some point. There's no way we could hide forever."

"It's easy for you to say."

He drew away from her. "Jordan, what do you mean?"

Bent on making him understand, Jordan raised a hand, then dropped it to her side. Mike linked their hands.

"Mike," she whined, "we can't draw attention to ourselves. People will start talking."

"News flash, baby, they already know about us. If Donna hasn't spread the word throughout the building, it would have come out in a couple of weeks anyway. Remember, we agreed to tell people."

"Maybe we need to talk about this later," she

suggested, suddenly afraid that this conversation would cause new problems.

"Maybe we should." He sighed and stuck his free hand in his pocket. "I need time to think."

"Okay, guys. Your projects are looking good. Keep at it," Jordan complimented, moving between the rows of the lab. She glanced Mike's way, expecting him to add his praise.

He stood on the edge of the class, quiet and distant. He'd been that way most of the afternoon. She thought he'd calm down after their discussion this morning. But it didn't look as if he had.

Hoping to draw him out, she asked, "Mr. Walker, do you have anything you'd like to add?"

Mike shook his head.

She licked her dry lips and returned her attention to her students before saying, "Remember, Science Olympiad will be in another month. Keep working on your projects. And we'll meet again next week. If you have any problems, contact Mr. Walker or myself. We're here late two nights a week for tutoring."

Jordan stood at her door as the students made their way out of the room, hurried down the hall and out the front doors. She waited, making certain that each student had a way home before returning to her classroom.

As she slipped through the door, she found Mike silently straightening the room and putting away equipment and books that they'd used during the meeting. He glanced her way at the sound of the door opening, then returned to his task.

Uncertain what to say or do, she said, "We had a good meeting today, don't you think?"

He nodded, darting in between the rows of lab stations as he continued to put the room in order.

Strolling across the room to where he stood, she added, "When we started this project, I felt certain that I was out of my depth. But I've been having a lot of fun with the kids. They have pretty good ideas."

"Hmm," Mike muttered, glancing around to be certain that the room was in order. As he passed her on his way to the door, she touched his arm. Sidestepping her with a quick move, he turned to face her.

"Mike," Jordan began in a voice filled with puzzlement and hurt. "What's wrong?"

He snorted. "Nothing. I'm just following your *orders*. You don't want anyone to see us together. Although everyone knows we're together."

Her lips moved but no words came out. Finally, she found her voice and said, "I—I—I." Stopping, she tried to compose herself. "There's no one here but you and me. I don't think we have to be so formal when we're alone."

Mike scratched his ear. He added in a skeptical tone, "Really?"

Moving closer, she said, "Come on, Mike. Don't be that way."

For the first time since this morning, he looked at her. Shocked, Jordan took a step backward.

"I didn't like what happened this morning," he explained.

"I'm sorry. I just wanted to protect us by keeping the gossip down to a minimum."

"Mmm," Mike muttered with a slight nod of his head. "Let me tell you how I see things," he offered, moving away from her. He stopped at the teachers' workstation and leaned against the desk, folding his arms across his chest. "You're ashamed of being involved with me."

"No, no," Jordan quickly denied. "I'm not. I like to keep my private life, well, private. I worked in schools where the rumor mill caused so many problems. I don't want to be part of the same kind of rumor mill here at Pierson."

"It's too late for all of that. Whether people found out about us today or next year, they're going to gossip. It's human nature. What I don't like is the way you've behaved. You acted as if we, you and me, don't exist." He stood and began to pace the room. "I love you."

Cringing inside, she answered, "And I care about you." She knew this wouldn't be enough, but she didn't plan to say the words just yet. She needed more time. Saying "I love you" made her feel vulnerable and she wasn't ready for that.

Mike squeezed his eyes shut as if he were in pain, then opened them. A bleak expression filled his brown eyes and tore at her heart. "I'm glad you *care.* This is your way of telling me that you're not sure about us? That you're still not ready to say the words and make the total commitment?"

Jordan knew instinctively that she'd made a mistake. "Mike," she began, uncertain what to say.

"No, stop. I don't want to hear any more."

"I want to explain, please," she begged.

"I can't take your explanations right now." He ran his hand over his face, then said very softly, "I think we need a little time apart."

"What!" The expression on his face frightened her. Her stomach clenched into knots. Had she gone too far or pushed him away too many times?

Measuring his words, he said, "I can't help feeling that you're always looking for a way out without truly committing yourself."

Hurrying to assure him, she touched his arm, "No, really. It's not that."

Mike continued as if she hadn't spoken. "You've got issues that I can't help you with. And there's one question that you need to answer. Are you willing to take the plunge with me? Jump into this relationship and accept everything that it entails? I mentioned to you before that there is good and ugly in every relationship. This one is no exception."

Fear, tight and uncompromising, crept up her spine. Had she pushed him too far?

"I don't want someone that holds a part of herself away from me. I want everything, just as I've given you all of me."

He moved around the room, returning equipment to the shelves and locking the cabinets. "You've got to be willing to take the risk, because that's where the joy comes from."

"Mike, don't. Please."

He stopped, turned to face her. "Can you tell me what's really bothering you?"

In an act of total defiance, she threw at him, "Same thing that's always bothered me. Younger women. Old cows who gossip and laugh at me. I don't want you leaving me behind and everyone looking at me with pitying eyes as you enjoy yourself with the next sweet young thing."

His voice rose. "Have I ever given you a reason to believe that I wanted someone else?"

She couldn't lie. "No. But things change," she muttered. Unable to maintain eye contact, she stared out the window.

He sighed and ran a hand over his face. "I thought we got past some of this. You've been hiding those feelings and never thought you should share them with me?" He shook his head. "Unbelievable."

"I'm almost forty years old." Lowering her voice, she admitted, "I'm afraid."

"Of what?" he shouted.

"Losing you."

"I'm not going anywhere."

"That's what you say."

"That's what I mean. Jordan, what you're really saying is you don't trust me."

"It's not you. It's the women."

"Then why are you worried about some imaginary woman that I'm going to leave you for? Believe me, there'll always be women." His voice softened to a gentle purr, "But I love you."

"For now."

"Hell, that's all we've got." He hunched his shoulders. "Tomorrow isn't promised to any of us. Honey, you want clear guarantees and there aren't any. All I can promise is that I love you."

"I don't know. I'm scared."

"I'm scared too. Loving someone can be painful, messy, and dirty. You open yourself up for possible heartache." He shook his head. "On the flip side, there's so much love and joy and happiness that it makes being in love and caring for someone else worthwhile. I'm not saying it's easy or that we won't have problems, but if we work together there is so much for us to experience together."

"Mike, please. Try to understand how I feel. This relationship hasn't been easy for me."

He sighed heavily, moving to the door that led to his classroom. "Maybe we do need that time apart. Give you some time to come to terms with us and decide what you really want and need. Because, right now, I'm not feeling you. I'll see you tomorrow." Mike slipped from the lab and into his room.

The door closed with a final click that chilled her.

Chapter 27

Long after Jordan left the building, Mike remained at Pierson. He needed time to compose himself before attempting the drive home.

It hurt to think that he might lose Jordan. He loved her and wanted her in his life for all times. But they couldn't go on like this. She had to learn to trust him or they didn't have a chance of surviving. Plus, she needed to develop more faith in herself.

Mike found little appeal in returning to an empty house. Instead, he opted for a drink at a local bar. After locking up the lab and his classroom, he slid his arms into his leather jacket and left the building.

The day had faded into the softer hues of evening as he strolled through the parking lot to his Mustang. Climbing inside, he turned the key in the ignition. Hesitating, he debated where to go for his drink. Finally, he steered the car toward Eight Mile Road.

Detroit's Baseline Road featured a variety of unsavory bars highlighting adult entertainment. Before Jordan had entered his current life phase, he might have indulged in a few hours of harmless flirtation, but not anymore. This evening, his interest zeroed in on how much Absolut vodka he could legally consume without wrecking his car as he drove home.

Several blocks east of Evergreen on Eight Mile, Mike pulled into the Big D's Sports Bar parking lot. Chuckling, he shook his head. On a scale of one to ten, today sucked big time. He needed time to come up with a plan to put Jordan and himself back on track.

His decision made, Mike grabbed his jacket from the backseat of the car and strolled inside. Once he entered the building, he stood in the doorway, giving himself a minute to adjust to the darkened environment. He took a quick glance around him, finding the standard barflies who frequented places like this.

Strolling to the bar, he slid onto a stool and ordered a triple Absolut, no ice. Aretha Franklin's strong voice belted out a classic as he tapped out a different tune on the wood surface. Waiting patiently for his drink to arrive, he noticed a woman at the opposite end of the bar.

The redhead stood, picked up her drink, and ambled along the bar. She glided onto the seat to his right.

Sighing heavily, Mike watched her. He didn't need a pickup. He wanted a place to drink and try to put his life back together.

"Hi," she greeted, taking a sip from her glass of red wine.

Politely nodding back at her, Mike redirected his attention to the bartender. Reaching for his drink, he paid the man and ignored the woman, hoping she'd get the hint and move on. He didn't want to hurt her feelings, but he wanted to be alone to think about his troubles and work out a solution.

No such luck, the woman pushed her hand in his direction. "I'm Valerie. Val to my friends."

Ignoring her outstretched hand, he pointed at his chest. "Mike."

Val picked up her drink and sipped. "You don't look very happy. Want to talk about it?"

Slowly, he examined her, noting the round face, short red hair, and willing smile. His eyes glided over Val's slim frame, displaying a generous portion of flesh. *Pretty* described her.

Val's attention soothed his wounded ego. His gaze slowly slid down the length of her body, as he contemplated her. He could take what Val so blatantly offered and no one would be the wiser.

What would it accomplish? *Nothing*, the voice in his head whispered. He would destroy everything he wanted to build with Jordan and betray her fragile trust. Plus, add validity to all of her fears.

Jordan believed this type of woman would come between us, Mike thought. On the heels of that revelation, Mike realized other women carried no appeal for him. Wearily, his thoughts returned to Jordan. The woman he loved. Sadness settled inside his heart. Why couldn't Jordan understand that she was the only woman for him? He wanted only her. But she had to learn to trust him and understand that she mattered more than anything else in his life.

He shook his head and picked up his drink, taking a long swallow. "Thanks anyway. I'm fine."

"Yes, you are." Val stroked a long manicured finger along his arm, creating a zigzag path to his hand. "But I can show you better than I can tell you," she whispered close to his ear in a husky voice, adding provocatively, "I'm a pro at first aid."

"Oh?"

"Mmm-hmm." She ran her tongue across her wet

lips, drawing his attention to the particular orifice. "Especially mouth-to-mouth."

He felt absolutely nothing for this woman. Her movements and gestures were meant to entice, but they left him cold, unaffected.

"Can't I convince you to let me help you?" She intertwined her fingers with his. "I'm a good listener."

Mike untangled his hand from hers, swung around on the stool, and stood. "No, thanks," he answered, strolling to a small table and sinking onto the wooden chair.

From the beginning, he understood that Jordan had a problem with their ages. A situation that he believed had become less important as they grew closer. Unfortunately, he'd misjudged her fears and now they were at an impasse that he didn't know how to get beyond.

Sex represented only a part of their relationship. They shared a prior history, careers, and lifestyles. He felt a connection with her that he'd never felt with any other woman.

He loved her. But love obviously wasn't enough.

No relationship could survive for very long without trust. Trust played a major part in any relationship, but for Mike and Jordan it was paramount. Their age difference and their career choices made it essential for them to be able to go about their lives without worrying about what their partner might be doing.

One of his grandmother's phrases popped into his head. Anything worth having required a willingness to work hard and make sacrifices. This included fighting and conquering Jordan's demons. But how?

Mike swallowed the last of his vodka and stood. He picked up his jacket, slung it over his shoulder, and moved across the bar and out the door.

First, he'd give Jordan a little time and distance to

decompress. Once she spent time thinking about her future, they could talk again and hash out the intricate details of their relationship.

Pleased with this plan, he unlocked his car and got in it, roared out of the parking lot, heading downtown. Home didn't seem so lonely now that he had a plan to persuade Jordan to remain in his life.

Chapter 28

Jordan sighed sadly, glancing at the empty chair that Mike normally occupied during their lunch period. She really missed him and the time they spent together. Sharing their breaks and prep periods was one of the things she looked forward to.

She'd hurt Mike; Jordan knew that. Disappointed him with her fears and distrust. No amount of talking had produced a resolution and Mike had suggested they spend some time apart to decide if they truly belonged together. Jordan had racked her brain, searching for some form of compromise that would appease them both.

Shutting her eyes, she imaged Mike's handsome face. She loved him with all her heart, really loved him, but she believed whatever happened between them should remain between them.

Jordan sighed a second time, swallowing the last of her hot chocolate. Her brows knitted together when she glanced out the window.

A police car had just pulled up to the front of the building. Leaning closer to get a better look, she wondered, *Did something happen to one of the students?*

Standing, she discarded the remains of her smoked turkey sandwich and took a quick check of the time. There were fifteen minutes left to her lunch period. *I'll just wander by the main office to see what I can see,* she decided, crossing the room and locking the door behind her.

Casually strolling down the hall, she nearly collided with Kevin Mallard when he barreled from his classroom. Sidestepping her, he caught her arm and steadied her. "Sorry about that."

"No problem," she answered, continuing down the corridor.

"Where are you on your way to?"

"The office."

"So am I. Did you see the police car out front?" he asked, falling into step beside her.

Eyes sparkling, Jordan nodded. "Yes. I thought I'd make an innocent stroll by the office to see what's going on."

Chuckling, Kevin agreed. "Me too. Great minds think alike. Do you mind if I tag along?"

"Not at all."

They slowed their steps as they approached the main office, glancing through the large glass pane. Donna was working at her desk. The pair gazed past her to Chet's closed door. Unconsciously, Jordan grabbed Kevin's arm and whispered, "There's the police." Her eyes widened and her fingernails dug into the soft skin of his arm. "Kevin, isn't that Harold?"

Surprised, he stopped, prying her claws from his arm. Rubbing the red flesh, he took a second, closer look at the people in the office. "Yeah! What would he have to say to the police?"

Frowning, she tried to read the expression on Harold's face, but failed at this distance. "I don't know."

"I haven't seen much of Harold since that whole science lab thing," Kevin said.

"It freaked me out to learn that he'd made a lot of money on the stock market and was checking his investments on the Internet."

"Yeah. Who would have thought?" Kevin grabbed her arm and pulled her along with him. "Hold on. Let's get to the copy room and then give them a minute. We'll walk by like we're on our way back to our classrooms. We might be able to see more."

Nodding, she agreed. "Sounds good."

They strolled past the office as nonchalantly as possible. The moment they were out of Donna's range of vision they scurried into the copy room. Red and white boxes of Office Depot's copy paper sat stacked against the wall. Gray rows of mailboxes held memos, books, and pamphlets.

With a question in her eyes, Jordan glanced at Kevin. "What do you think is going on?"

Shaking his head, he tossed a hand in the air, whispering in a conspiratory tone, "I don't know. The only time the police show up is when something criminal has happened. I can tell you this much, if the police are involved it's something huge. Really huge."

Jordan twisted a lock of hair around her finger, pacing the small space as she pondered the lunch period events. What could have brought the police to the school? Drugs, fights, weapons were the things that sent administrators into a panic and had them scrambling for the authorities. Fights were out. The students had been dismissed at noon for the staff's professional development program.

She turned to Kevin. "Now what?"

"Come on, Jordan. Where's your creativity?" He took her arm and started for the door. "Let's wait

a minute and then we'll head back in the opposite direction."

"Hold on, hold on." She hurried to the mailboxes,
dragging him along with her. "Here's my prop. This way
we won't look so foolish if we do the stuff we normally
do. You know, like pick up our mail."

"You're right," he muttered, reaching over her head
to retrieve his mail. He gave the memos and letters a
cursory glance as he sifted through the pile before folding the stuff in half. "Ready?"

She nodded.

They started back down the hall and found Mike at
the door to the main office. "Hey," he greeted.

"Hey, buddy," Kevin said with a salute of his hand.

Mike turned to Jordan with a stiff uncompromising
expression on his face. "How are you?"

Filled with conflicting emotions, she couldn't maintain eye contact with him. "Fine," she muttered, studying the pattern in the floor tiles.

Kevin pointed a finger at the door to the main office.
"Hey, man, do you know what's happening in Chet's
office?"

Mike shook his head. "No. Donna just called me
down here."

"Did she say why?" Jordan asked.

"No." He scratched his ear. "I was surprised too."

"Why?"

"When I got down here I saw the police car."

"Hmm." Kevin ran a finger back and forth across his
chin. "You saw Harold, right?"

"Yeah, I did." Shrugging, Mike opened the door.
"The only way I'm going to learn what's going on is to
see what Chet wants." He gave them a halfhearted
wave good-bye. "See ya."

"Check you later," Kevin muttered.

"I don't have a good feeling about this meeting," Jordan confessed, watching Mike knock on the principal's door. "I'm going to stick around and see what I can find out. You go on."

"Nah. I think I'll wait with you."

Perched at an angle, she gazed through the window watching Chet and Mike. Kevin stood directly behind her. She didn't need to know sign language or be able to read lips to know that this was a bad situation. Mike shook his head, disagreeing with the cop, then began to talk fast.

Moments later, the officers escorted Mike out of the office and toward the main entrance.

Jordan ran behind him, asking, "What's going on here? Where are you taking him?"

"To the station, ma'am."

"Why? Is he being charged with a crime?"

One of the policemen turned to her, a spark of sympathy visible in his eyes. "I'm sorry, ma'am. We can't tell you that."

"Can I come along?" she asked.

"You can drive yourself. But we can't take you in the squad car."

Uncertain, she stood in the center of the corridor, watching as the police shuffled Mike out of the building. The policemen loaded him into the backseat of the car.

How had this happened? Who was responsible? Turning away, she made a silent promise to him. She would get to the bottom of this mess. Mike needed her. Nothing short of death was going to keep her from him. She planned to be at his side, supporting him.

Determination glittered like gold from her eyes when she turned on her heels and started back to the main office. She had questions. Jordan felt certain that Chet had all the answers.

Chapter 29

Jordan stormed past Kevin and into the main office. Her mind swirled with questions. What had Mike gotten himself into? And what would it take to get him out of this mess?

Jordan marched to Chet's closed door and knocked. She stabbed her thumb toward the shut door. "Is he available?"

Donna was engrossed in her work, but her head snapped up. Quickly, she rose, scrambled around the edge of her desk, and stood in front of the principal's closed door. "Umm, let me check." She hurried inside and shut the door behind her.

Through the glass windowpane, Jordan watched the interplay between Chet and Donna. After a moment the secretary returned and ushered Jordan inside.

"Chet, I need to talk with you," she began. *Keep your cool, Jordan. Don't blow your top. It won't help Mike or you.*

The principal swirled around in his chair to meet her gaze. "Good afternoon, Jordan. How are you?"

His calm, friendly greeting diverted her tirade, sending her mind into a befuddled spin. "I'm good," she muttered politely, stuffing her hands inside the pockets of her slacks.

Shaking her head, Jordan thought, *what am I thinking?* "Actually, I'm not," she corrected. "I need to know what's going on with Mike."

Chet stood and led her to the conference table, offering her a seat. "Obviously, you saw him leave with the police."

"Ah, yeah," she answered sarcastically. "But I'd describe it as being escorted out in handcuffs."

Sighing, he nodded, then speared her with a sharp, assessing gleam in his tired brown eyes. His voice carried an ominous but gentle quality that increased her anxiety. "I know you and Mike are close and this can't be easy for you."

"Just tell me, Chet."

"Well, I'm planning to explain this during our in-service meeting this afternoon. Unfortunately, the police took Mike in for questioning and I think you deserve to hear the details from me."

"Chet!" she exclaimed, balling her hand into a fist.

He glanced at her from across the table. "Yes?"

"Why? What is going on?"

"Attempted rape."

"What?" Shocked, she gasped and fell against the back of the chair, sending it crashing against the wall.

No! her mind shouted. She shivered as if someone had turned off the heat in the building and her head pounded unmercifully. This couldn't be happening. Chet was mistaken.

With the force of a hurricane, her fear resurfaced and almost choked the breath from her. *No!* her brain shouted. Mike would never do something like this. Jordan refused to accept Chet's explanation, so she desperately tried to find a logical reason to explain this dilemma.

She stood slowly and planted her hands on the conference room table, leaning over Chet. "This doesn't make any sense. Mike would never do anything like that."

As those words left her lips, she realized how true they were and how much she believed them. Whatever had happened with this girl or student, Mike didn't rape her.

"I would have said the same thing until a few hours ago."

Moving away from Chet, she examined his face before asking, "What changed your mind?"

"We have a witness."

She smirked softly. A knowing glint entered her eyes and she asked, "Harold Crawford?"

Surprise registered on Chet's face. His eyebrows arched questioningly. "How do you know about him?"

Shrugging, she answered sadly, "I was at my desk when the police pulled up. I decided to take a little stroll past your office to investigate. I saw Harold through the window."

He nodded.

"So tell me. Who's the victim?"

"Erin Hill."

With her eyes wide, Jordan's head snapped back as if he'd slapped her. "You're kidding me, right?"

Chet shook his head.

"And you believed her?"

"As I said before, we have a witness." He captured and held her gaze with his own, then stated in a firm, definitive tone, "Even if we didn't, I would have to investigate and contact the police."

"No." Jordan shook her head, rejecting the idea.

"This isn't right. That girl will lie on her way into heaven. Or hell, since that's where she really belongs. Erin's a troublemaker, through and through, and you know this. I'm not telling you anything that you haven't encountered since she's been at Pierson." Exasperated, she tossed her hands in the air. "How can you believe her?"

Chet sank heavily into his chair and answered in a soft, regretful tone, "Normally, I would agree with you. But Harold's account matched her story. Let's be honest, those two are not friends. His account puts them in the room together. If Paradise had come to me with Harold's story, I would have investigated because it's my job, but I would question her motives."

Jordan crossed the office and stood in front of her principal. "Chet, you have two people with questionable motives. And Harold may be lying."

He rose from his chair and placed his hands on her shoulders, offering in a gentle, compelling tone, "Jordan, I see where you're going with this. But you can stop right here. This could destroy Mike's career, not to mention the fact that he could end up in prison for years. Don't you think I'd do a thorough investigation of any claim of this magnitude? I've been a principal for more than twenty-five years. I don't take accusations of rape or attempted rape lightly. It's my job to investigate. And the law states that I must pass the information on to the police."

"I'm sorry, Chet. I understand that you're only doing your job." She patted his arm, studying the pattern in the floor tile. "But this is Harold and Erin we're talking about, an employee with a grudge against Mike and a troublemaker. There are far too many coincidences for me to roll over and play dead. I don't believe it."

"Maybe you don't know him as well as you think you do."

She shook her head. "No. You're wrong. Mike would never be involved in something like this."

Chet let out a long, audible breath. "I'm sorry to say, it's possible."

"So you believe Harold?"

"Yes."

"You're not the least bit suspicious of his little confession?" Jordan questioned.

"I would if he came to me."

Confused, she knitted her brows together. "I don't understand. What do you mean?"

"I went to the custodial supervisor to see if anyone had arrived early today. We checked the time cards and found that Harold worked the morning shift. When we questioned him, he hesitated to give me any info. He didn't offer up this info freely. I had to promise him that he wouldn't get into trouble. Besides, Harold normally works the afternoon shift. His supervisor changed his schedule at the last minute."

"And what he said made sense?"

"Perfect sense. I can't ignore that kind of information. Doesn't matter who provided it. I have to check it out and protect our students."

Agitated, she ran a hand over her face. "What exactly did Harold say?"

"There was a note in his box about a spill near the lab. Since the incident with the unlocked door, he always responds quickly to any request. Erin came running out of the room in hysterics. Her face was bloody and her clothes were ripped and torn away from her body. Harold tried to stop her, but she ran from him. When he stuck his head in the classroom, he saw Mike standing in the center of the room."

"This doesn't prove a thing. How could you call the police for this?"

Chet blew out a hot puff of air. "There's more."

"Like what?"

"Harold also said this wasn't the first time he's seen them together. Plus, he heard her cries for him to stop, to leave her alone."

Jordan felt faint and thought that she might pass out. She leaned against the wall for support as her heart pumped at lightning speed through her veins.

Mike wouldn't do this. No matter what others said. He wouldn't touch Erin. He wasn't the kind of man to take advantage of a student.

Dejected, Jordan crossed the room and opened the door. Straddling the entrance, she muttered, "Thank you for your time." She left the main office and started down the hallway to her classroom.

Jordan returned to her classroom and sat at her desk, staring blankly at nothing. Holding a tight rein on her emotions, she glanced at the clock, needing a few minutes to compose herself.

She shut her eyes, covering her face with her hand as she fought back tears. How had she and Mike landed at this point? Her heart shredded to pieces and Mike accused of rape. This wasn't the relationship she had envisioned when she surrendered her heart to him.

In everything Mike did for her, she felt his love. He would never get involved with someone like Erin. Her traitorous mind reminded her that on two separate occasions she'd found Erin and Mike together in what some would consider a compromising position.

Granted, Mike offered reasonable explanations for

each encounter and she'd accepted his account without hesitation.

Honestly, if she looked back on the occasions when Erin had put in an appearance when they were together, Mike always displayed the most conservative behavior. He never allowed Erin to do anything inappropriate. Nor did he.

Mike displayed a caring and helpful nature to all his students. And now that caring nature threatened to cost him his career and freedom. Although he didn't provide loans or excuse bad behavior, he demanded respect from the kids and listened without prejudice when they needed someone to confide in.

For the second time in less than an hour, Mike's upset and worried face flashed through her mind. He didn't have the appearance or attitude of a person who knew he'd been caught in the act of doing something wrong.

When she had landed in trouble he refused to give up on her until he learned the truth. He'd defended her to Chet and Debbie, even camped out at the school until he uncovered the culprit behind the lab incident. Didn't he deserve the same consideration from her?

Agitated, she drummed her fingers against her desktop. Mike didn't have anyone to support him. No family or close friends willing to roll up their sleeves and dig through the dirt to find the truth. Jordan represented the closest thing he had to a family.

Maybe it was time to put their problems on hold while they worked together to get to the truth. His future was on the line. If convicted of attempted rape, Mike could get years in prison.

What could she do to help? Her thoughts focused on Erin.

Returning to her desk, she pulled a pad of paper

from under a pile of student assignments and wrote Erin's name at the top of the page. From the start of the term, Erin had caused *mucho* problems.

On more than one occasion, she'd engineered disruption in Jordan's classroom and the cheerleading squad. The girl thrived on conflict and manipulation. Her claim of attempted rape connected directly to something she wanted from Mike. But what?

Jordan intended to find out. She had no intentions of allowing Mike to be shipped off to prison because of Erin. She loved him and he deserved her support.

Purposefully, she moved across her room and headed out the door. She hurried down the hall and slipped into Kevin's room, talking with him for several minutes.

With a plan in place, she returned to her classroom, certain that she had done the right thing. After the professional development program ended today, she'd put her plan in action. Mike deserved and needed her help and she planned to stand by him.

Chapter 30

Squirming uncomfortably on the hard wooden bench, Jordan waited silently for Mike to be released. Wind flirted around her ankles as she sat near the main entrance.

Convinced of Mike's innocence, Jordan and Kevin had hatched a plan to rescue him. At the end of the school day, they had met and hustled over to the police station.

She glanced around, taking in the unfamiliar sights and sounds of the daily activity of the police precinct. Frightened, she shrank away as an officer strolled through the precinct leading a man in handcuffs to the lockup. The prisoner focused on her as his gaze stripped her naked.

Kevin lingered protectively at her side. Glancing down at her, he noticed her constant fidgeting, reached between them, and covered her hand with his. "It's going to be okay."

"I know." She waved her free hand with a sweeping motion encompassing the complete scenario. "I'm just antsy about this whole business."

"Me too," he admitted in a low tone.

Fidgeting, Jordan wrapped the strap of her purse around her fingers. What a nightmare.

Putting that problem aside, Jordan concentrated on another. Would Mike allow her to help him? Could they get past their present problems to work together? She hoped so, because regardless of how he felt about her and the way things ended between them, she planned to stick with him until his name was cleared.

Mike emerged from one of the interrogation rooms. Jordan rushed to him, throwing her arms around him and holding him close. Kevin followed, moving near superspeed.

He leaned into the embrace, but quickly recovered and moved away. Confused, she glanced into his face. His eyes were so dull, devoid of the sparkle that generally accompanied his bright, fun personality.

Her heart hammered against her rib cage. *Oh my God,* she thought. *What happened to you?*

"Mike," she muttered, cupping his cheek. "Are you okay?"

Nodding, he dislodged her hand and turned to Kevin. The two men shook hands, then embraced.

"Man, we were worried about you," Kevin said.

"Thanks for picking me up. Both of you," Mike said, giving the precinct a final sweep with his eyes. He shoved his arms into his jacket and started for the door. "Come on. I want to get as far away from this place as possible."

Kevin glanced around the station. "I hear you."

Outside the building, Mike halted at the top of the stairs, drawing fresh air into his lungs. He glanced around the parking lot and asked, "Who's driving?"

"I am," Jordan volunteered.

"I need my car," Mike stated.

"We know. It's still at Pierson," she explained,

disarming the alarm on her SUV. "We'll swing by the school so that you can pick up your car. After that we need to find some place private and sit down and talk. Together, we can figure out how to get you out of this mess. Is my place okay with you guys?"

"Sounds good," Kevin responded

Mike sat silent in the passenger seat. He turned to Jordan. "I didn't expect you to come."

She licked her lips and ran her hand through her hair before answering softly, "I came because you needed my help. What's between us doesn't matter at this moment. Erin lied and I want to help you prove it."

Hours later, Jordan unlocked her apartment door and led the two men into the living room. Kevin deposited the large pizza on her dining room table while she went into the kitchen for plates, cutlery, and napkins. Mike followed, taking glasses from the cupboard and removing Coke and ice from the fridge.

Once everyone got comfortable, they opened the box, allowing the heavenly aromas of garlic, tomatoes, shrimp, crabmeat, and cheese to fill the room. They spoke of inconsequential things as they ate their meal, ignoring the real reason they were assembled together.

Kevin drained his glass and sighed contently. "That hit the spot."

Mike dropped a piece of pizza crust on his plate and agreed. "It certainly did. There's nothing like Pizza Papalis deep dish to get your juices going."

Kevin cleared his throat and rubbed his nose. "Okay, now that we've filled our guts it's time to talk." He turned to his friend. "Mike, what's your take on everything that's happened?"

He shrugged. "You saw me before I went into Chet's

office. I was as surprised as anyone when the police told me I needed to come down to the station."

"What about Erin?"

"What about her?"

Jordan tossed out the next question. "Tell us what happened. Maybe we can come up with a reason for her to do this."

Mike shrugged. "I was in my classroom at the board. She knocked. My back was to the door. I was working on an assignment. When I turned around, she was all bloody and pulling at her clothes." He paused, then continued, "I tried to stop her, but she started to scream and yell for me to leave her alone."

"What happened next?" Kevin asked.

"After that she ran out of the room."

"Did you report this to Chet?" Jordan asked.

"I meant to," he admitted, shaking his head. "The bell rang. Kids started coming into the classroom and before I knew it the day got away from me."

Jordan leaned closer. "Chet told me that Harold admitted seeing you and Erin together a few times. That you guys always looked very intimate."

"Well, we're not," Mike shot back. "Whatever she's telling people, it's not true."

"I'm not judging you. I'm trying to understand what's going on." Kevin stroked his chin. "We're no closer to understanding her motives. Or why she made this allegation."

"No, we're not," Mike answered, running a tired hand across the tight cords of his neck. "This whole rape thing came out of nowhere. I don't have a clue as to what this girl is thinking."

"Maybe it's not about thinking. It's about something she wants or needs. Do you know what that might be?" Kevin asked.

Sorrowfully, Mike shook his head.

"Well, obviously, she's pissed at you about some-thing," Jordan said, getting up from the table to remove the dirty dishes. She scooped up the leftover pizza. In the kitchen, she wrapped the slices and shoved them in the refrigerator.

Jordan crushed the empty pizza box into the trash, then rinsed dishes before stacking them in the sink. From the kitchen doorway, she said, "We have to figure out what it is and prove it to the police and Chet. That's the only way we're going to clear up this mess before it takes another turn."

"Jordan's right," Kevin agreed, tilting his head in her direction. "Let's start with the obvious. Did you flunk her or something?"

Mike laughed. The harsh and unpleasant sound grated on her nerves. "I don't have her this term. Erin is Jordan's problem."

Kevin raised his hands in an act of surrender and chewed on his bottom lip. "I'm going to apologize for this in advance," he stated, picking up his glass and shak-ing the ice cubes into his mouth. "I don't want to get in your business, but I have to throw this scenario out for us to consider. Could Erin be jealous of the relation-ship between you and Jordan? I mean, it was all over the school last week that you and Jordan are a couple. Could that have sparked a vendetta of some sort?"

Embarrassed, Jordan felt her cheeks burning red hot as she returned to the kitchen. She removed a second two-liter bottle of Coke from the refrigerator.

Mike blew out a puff of air and shrugged. "Who knows? She's a teenager and their minds are wired dif-ferently."

Jordan moved back into the dining room, placing the Coke in the middle of the table. "That's true, but don't blow off the idea. It makes sense. If I can't have you, no one will. You-betrayed-me sort of thing."

Mike reached for the bottle and refilled his glass. "I always considered Erin dangerous, so I put as much space between us as possible."

That's not completely true, Jordan thought.

Her gaze shifted from Mike to Kevin and back again. Should she correct him? Prompt him to discuss what had happened during his brief periods alone with Erin. Making a quick decision and acting on her thought, she asked, "What about the time at the game? Or when Erin cornered you in your classroom? She could be planning to use those incidents against you. We need to think like Erin, so that we can anticipate her next move."

Shocked, Kevin speared his friend with a condemning look. "What times? Buddy, you need to come clean. Because if you don't, you better believe that Erin will have it all organized if you get charged with rape."

"There's nothing to tell. At the game with the Jersey Bulldogs, Erin followed me into the locker room. I went in there to make sure we didn't have any stragglers. End of situation."

"And your classroom?" Kevin probed.

"Same thing. Nothing more."

"I'll take your word on it," Kevin said. "We've got to figure it out. And we have to do it before you get charged with anything. Right now it sounds like her case is pretty light."

Jordan said, "True, but we don't know what else Erin is telling the police. She's not above getting her friends to lie for her."

"Speaking of friends, what about Erin's friend, Mike?" Kevin questioned.

"Paradise?" Jordan asked.

Kevin pointed a finger in Jordan's direction. "And her boyfriend. He might know what's going on. The three of them always hang out together."

"Actually," Mike agreed, contemplatively, "I think they plot together too."

Kevin nodded, weighing the merits of Mike's suggestion. "You're right. Paradise always knows what Erin is up to."

"Let's divide and conquer. I'll talk to Paradise." Jordan pointed a finger at her chest, then turned to Kevin. "You talk to Jarell. If you can gain his trust, he might slip up and tell us what Erin has in store for Mike. One thing I know for sure, if there's a plan, Paradise and Jarell know about it, even if they aren't involved," she said.

"This can't be our only approach to the situation. If Erin, Paradise, and Jarell planned this we have to expect they will stick together," Mike said.

"You're right," Jordan answered. "But I believe that we still need to talk to them before moving on. There's a possibility that we can trip them up, make them say something they don't mean to. Let's shake that tree first, and if nothing comes from that, then we'll go to plan B, whatever that is."

Kevin clapped his hands, then rubbed them together. "Now we've got our own plan." He rose from the table and started for the door. "I've got to get home. Before I get to bed tonight, I've got to finish marking my tenth-graders' exams. Plus, I want to think about how to approach Jarell."

"I hear you." Mike rose from the table and walked his friend to the door. Jordan followed closely behind the pair. They stopped at the front door and Kevin turned to Jordan.

"Thanks for dinner. We're going to take care of this."

She wrapped her arms around Kevin and gave him a huge hug. "We'll get this resolved."

"I'm with you on that," Kevin agreed. "Mike, if I need you, where can I find you? Here or at home?"

Jordan and Mike exchanged uncomfortable looks, then quickly turned away. Mike cleared his throat and shoved his hands inside the pockets of his trousers, choosing his words carefully. Before he could say a word, Jordan answered, "Either place."

He stepped forward and slapped Kevin on the back, then pulled his friend close, capturing him in a big bear hug. "Man, thanks for being there for me."

"Don't worry about it. We've got to get you out of this mess."

Mike released the other man and Kevin slipped out the door. "Talk to you tomorrow."

"Well," Jordan said, moving down the hall toward her living room, "you're probably ready to get going yourself. Let me grab some pizza for you to take with you."

He followed at a slower pace, standing in the doorway as she puttered around her kitchen. His steady gaze made Jordan nervous and she found that she was all thumbs, dropping the package of Saran Wrap and losing her grip on the pizza.

"Why did you help me?" Mike asked softly.

"You didn't do this," she explained, unable to meet his gaze.

"How do you know? If I recall correctly, you expected me to ride into the sunset with some sweet honey."

She turned to face him. "Look, we've got our problems, there's no doubt about that. But I don't believe you are capable of rape. You're much too smart for that."

Mike moved into the kitchen, stood directly in front

of her, took the Saran Wrap from her hands, and placed it on the counter. "A few days ago you believed I was capable of anything. What changed your mind?"

"I said a lot of things that weren't very nice," she admitted in a soft voice. "Most were fueled by anger and fear. And I'm sorry. You didn't deserve those things."

"No, I didn't."

"Mike, whatever problems we have, I want to help you." She touched his hand. "When I needed help, you didn't hesitate to do whatever had to be done to save my job. I want to do the same for you."

His eyebrows rose. "Even though I may be looking for my next conquest? You still want to help me?"

"Yes."

His lips pursed. "What about us?"

She nibbled on her bottom lip. "Look, this is not the conversation I want to have now. We need to concentrate on clearing your name and getting you back on the job. After we've done that, then we can sort out the ugly details of our relationship."

Sighing, he ran a hand over his head. "You're right."

"Thank you. So we're in agreement. Let's postpone anything to do with us, as a couple, until you're reinstated."

"Agreed."

Chapter 31

Jordan drummed her fingers against her desktop, waiting for Kevin to arrive for their meeting. After three days of dogging Paradise and getting nowhere, Jordan tossed up her hands in frustration. Maybe Kevin had a suggestion or two that would help crack Paradise's armor.

Fifteen minutes after the final bell rang Kevin rapped on her door, then entered the classroom.

"How was your day?"

"It's getting tough," Kevin said heavily.

"How so?" she asked.

"There's only two weeks before Thanksgiving break and the kids are restless."

"They are," Jordan agreed, deciding that it was best to approach this situation directly. "Have you found out anything?"

He shook his head. Disappointment marred his features. "Nothing."

"Don't feel bad," she offered. "I didn't get anything either."

"I cornered Jarell in the locker room. Jordan, he acted as if he were brain-dead."

"Paradise laughed in my face and strutted from the room with all the 'tude in her teenage heart. I wanted to *strangle* her," she whispered fiercely, curling her fingers into claws. "We half expected them to act this way. So it wasn't a surprise. I was hoping to rattle her a little bit and maybe get a clue or two."

He uncurled her fingers, smoothing them out. "I know. It's frustrating, that's all."

"Mike's counting on us. At the very least his reputation could be destroyed, and at the most he might end up in prison if we don't figure this thing out, Kevin."

"That's not going to happen," he stated fiercely.

"We need more than Mike's good looks to get him out of this mess. Right now, Erin's got the upper hand and that girl plays for keeps." Jordan tapped her finger against her lips. "When you confronted Jarell, what did he say, exactly?"

Forehead wrinkling, Kevin tilted his head back and gazed at the ceiling, recalling the incident. "Jarell told me that he'd been expecting me to corner him. Then he said, 'I don't know nothin' so get off me.'"

Jordan speared Kevin with a thoughtful glance. "If he didn't know anything, why was he expecting you?"

"He said something about knowing that Mike and I are buds." His eyebrows shot to the roof. "Jarell laughed, then said something about Mike being caught with his pants down."

Her eyes opened wide. "Did he now! How would he know that unless someone told him? The students had a half day, they weren't privy to that information. The police came long after school ended."

Kevin chuckled. "That's right."

She smiled. "I think your buddy knows exactly what's going on. But he's not going to give up any info. Maybe we can squeeze him."

"What about Paradise?"

Jordan snorted. "What do you think? She blew me off."

"Did you get a sense of anything? Or feel that she might have more information that she's giving up?"

"I always believe Paradise knows more than she tells." Jordan flopped into her chair at her desk. "The dynamic duo are entirely too close for Paradise not to be in on the plan. That's the one thing that I do know. Girlfriends love to talk. And teenage girlfriends tell each other everything whether it's about homework, the new girl in class, or a cute guy. They can't keep a secret."

Shrugging, Kevin asked, "What do we do next?"

She raised a hand in the air and let it drop into her lap. "I need to think a bit and come up with another plan."

"How about approaching Erin?" Kevin asked, scratching the side of his neck. "Try to appeal to her conscience?"

She ran her tongue across her dry lips. "I'd be all for it, if I believed she had one. Plus, I don't want to aggravate her. She might tell Chet that we're harassing her. God knows we don't want her going to the police with more ammunition."

Nodding, he agreed. "You're right. Do you think she'd do that?"

"Kevin," she began slowly, measuring each word, "Erin just put Mike in the middle of an investigation for attempted rape. I think she's capable of just about anything. If all else fails, we can do the James Bond thing, split up the surveillance and try to catch Erin, Paradise, or Jarell in a lie. That's the only way I can see us getting to the truth. Now that she's gotten Mike in trouble, she'll never tell the truth willingly, at least not to an adult."

"I agree with that," Kevin said. "We're back to what to do next."

An idea popped into Jordan's head. She turned to Kevin eagerly and asked, "Have you talked to Harold?"

Kevin shook his head.

"Maybe we're going about this the wrong way. Harold's statement backed up Erin's accusation. We should try to discredit him. Or get details on the information he claims to have."

Kevin nodded, nibbling on his bottom lip. "That's not a bad idea."

"Thank you."

"The bad blood between Mike and Harold makes his statement questionable."

"And if that doesn't work we can try Mike's approach."

He groaned. "You don't give up, do you?"

Jordan grinned. "Nope."

"I don't know," he said reluctantly. "I'm not really into spending my free time checking on Harold."

"Trust me, I understand. But this worked before. I think it'll work again."

"If needed. I'll give it a shot."

"Good." She held his gaze with her own. "We can't let Mike down. This is his reputation and career we're fighting for."

With a heavy heart, Jordan slowly climbed the stairs to Mike's house. She halted, mentally rehearsing her prepared speech.

Before her fist made contact with his wood door, it opened. Surprised, she stared. "Hi." *Great,* she thought. *He was waiting for me.*

"Hey," he responded, stepping away from the door to allow her to enter his home. "Come on in."

"Thanks." As she stepped inside and removed her leather jacket, the warmth of the house engulfed her.

"How'd your day go?" he asked.

"Okay."

Jordan examined Mike's face, sensing a shift in his mood. A dark edge had replaced his normally cheery disposition.

He led her away from the foyer and into the warmth of his living room. Billie Holiday's sultry voice filled the air, singing, "God Bless the Child." The melancholy piece symbolized his growing despair.

"Have a seat." Mike waved a hand at the sofa before dropping onto its cushion.

Jordan slid into the position next to him, tucking her small clutch bag to her side. She drew in a breath, stalling for time while trying to find a way to soften the blow of disappointment.

"Let's get to the meat and potatoes of your visit." He swallowed hard, then asked, "Anything good from Jarell or Paradise?"

Jordan nibbled on her bottom lip. She'd hoped to have a few minutes more to compose her thoughts before plunging into this discussion. Honestly, what could she expect from Mike? He had every reason to be worried and concerned. His career and future were hanging by a thread.

"No," she answered, fidgeting with the clasp on her purse. "Jarell flatly refused to talk to Kevin, and Paradise blew me off like a bad hair day."

Although she didn't notice a visible change in his face or tone, on some subconscious level his disappointment touched her heart.

She plunged ahead, wanting to reassure him. "We're

not finished. Kevin and I plan to take a different approach to the dynamic duo."

"Good. I'm glad," he muttered.

Eager to reassure him, she scooted closer. "Listen, we're going to talk to Harold and see what he knows. Find out how he happened by your classroom that morning. Then Kevin and I plan to shadow Jarell, Erin, and Paradise and try to learn something from their conversations. We might open a door that way."

Mike shrugged. "Maybe."

Determined to lighten his mood, she placed her hand on his jean-clad thigh and said, "Mike, I promise we'll get through this. I won't allow Erin to steal Pierson's star basketball coach and best science teacher."

The first genuine smile tugged at Mike's lips. He grinned back at Jordan, asking, "I thought you were the best?"

"Generally, I am. But you've got seniority and the kids know you better. Next year, I'll run you out of town."

"I don't think there'll be a next year." He reached for the newspaper on the coffee table and flipped through it until he found the classified section of the Sunday *Detroit News/Free Press*.

Silently, she sat while Mike worked his way through the first page of the classified section. "What ya doin'?"

"Looking for a job," came his immediate response.

Dreading his response, she questioned, "What do you mean?"

"At the rate my life is going down the toilet, I won't be at Pierson next year, or next week for that matter."

Stunned, she felt her heart skip a beat at the harsh speculation on his future. Jordan decided to ignore his comment, choosing instead to steer the conversation in a different direction. She tried to keep the surprise from her voice as she reminded him, "You already have a job."

The paper rattled as he lowered it to his lap and studied her. "Not anymore. I'm suspended, remember?"

"Yeah. But that's only temporary," she answered. "As soon as Kevin and I get to the truth, you'll be reinstated and things will be fine. Don't give up. Pierson needs you and so do I."

"Thanks. I appreciate the effort." Mike smiled sadly back at her. He squeezed her hand, then lifted the paper to continue his perusal of job listings. "Unless you can figure out why Erin is crucifying me, my career in education is cooked. Actually, when the police escorted me from the building my career accelerated to well done. It's almost at the third-degree-burn phase."

Using a finger, Jordan lowered the paper and cupped his cheek, forcing him to look at her. "What's really going on here?"

Sighing, Mike glanced away. His shoulders slumped and he spoke in a voice devoid of the sparkle she'd come to expect. "I'm questioning my career and what I'm doing with my life. All I ever wanted to do was be a good teacher. I tried to help kids become responsible, caring adults that make good choices. Now I'm fighting to stay out of jail and salvage my career. That's not the way I envisioned my role as a teacher when I graduated from college."

Jordan put all the tenderness and encouragement she felt into her words and said, "You're not going to jail. I won't let you. We're going to beat this and you will get everything back."

"Jordan Anderson, high school chemistry teacher, cheerleading coach, and crusader for the falsely accused." He laughed, giving her a quick hug. "Where did all that fire come from?"

Embarrassed, she shrugged. "It came from you."

"When you came to Pierson, you could barely talk. Now you're telling me what you're not going to allow." Chuckling, he ran his knuckles across her cheek. "Amazing!"

"You helped me focus. I got my act together and did the job that I've always loved. Now it's time for me to return that favor."

Studying a spot on the opposite side of the room, he answered, "I don't think it's going to happen for me. This is the beginning of the end."

"Mike, I don't think I would have survived a week at Pierson without your support and encouragement. Don't give up."

"You don't get it, do you, Jordan?" he asked, folding the newspaper and laying it on the end table. "I'm beyond help. Even if everything works out, I don't think I plan to continue to teach. I'll finish out the school year, but that's it. I'm done with education and that part of my life."

She sat in shocked silence. There had to be something she missed. How could he make a statement like that? The students adored him and responded well to his teaching methods and skills. Mike, the rock, the man who walked her through the toughest school year of her fourteen-year career, had decided to quit? No way.

"Hey, how about something to drink? I have Coke and Seven-Up. Or tea? Lipton or herbal? I have green tea if that's your preference." He rose and started for the kitchen. "Would you like to stay for dinner? Nothing fancy. Beef stew."

She examined Mike as if he'd just been replaced by a body snatcher. When had this person replaced her

dear love, Michael Walker? This wasn't the Mike that
Jordan knew and loved. Her Mike loved his job and the
life that he had established. This man acted defeated,
lost, and confused.

She watched him leave the room, feeling a deep
sense of loss. What would it take to convince him that
things would get better—that they still had time to pull
his life together?

Chapter 32

Kira Scott exited the stall, crossed the lavatory floor, and dropped her backpack on the floor next to the sink. Sighing, she switched on the hot water. Testing the temperature with one finger, she blended cold water with hot before sticking her hands under the faucet.

Her stomach rumbled as she washed and dried her hands. Maybe skipping lunch hadn't been the best idea, but she hated spending time in the cafeteria with the seniors, especially Erin and Paradise. Those two were the biggest skeezers in the school and Kira had had more than enough of them for today.

Boy, she hated that pair. They were always in the middle of somebody's business. Talking about people or causing trouble. Why didn't Mr. Bartholomew kick their sorry rear ends out of school so that the rest of the students could have a little peace?

Whenever an opportunity presented itself, they terrorized Kira and her friends. Each day they invented new ways to stir up mess. Nothing was sacred. Kira's hair or her glasses or the fact that she never wore expensive gear provided daily amusement for the fashion police of Pierson High School.

Kira wished she had something on them that would get them in trouble or make them look like fools in front of the rest of the school. Show them that they weren't all that.

She lifted her head, tuning into the galley of voices. They grew closer and louder. One voice in particular made the hairs on the back of Kira's neck rise. Hurrying, she tossed the paper towel in the trash, determined to get out of the lavatory before they entered.

Paradise's voice filled the room seconds before she put in an appearance. Kira searched for a way out. With nowhere to go, she ducked inside a stall and climbed onto the seat, making certain that no part of her was visible from under the stall's door. Crouched low, Kira prayed they'd do their business and leave so that she wouldn't have to remain this way for very long.

Arms raised above her head and popping her fingers, Erin danced her way into the bathroom, singing, "Oh, right. Oh, right. Oh yeah. Oh yeah."

"Would you be quiet!" Paradise hissed. "We don't want the teachers to catch us."

"Oops, sorry. My bad. Desiree, see if anyone else is in here. Check under the bathroom doors," Erin commanded.

Desiree nodded, taking a quick peek under two of the three bathroom stalls.

Certain that she was seconds away from being discovered, Kira squeezed her eyes shut and held her breath. Fear caused her heart to pound against her rib cage as she waited. The pink plastic corners of her backpack dug into the soft skin of her back. Kira stifled a moan of pain, flattening herself farther against the wall.

She had no idea what they would do if they found her. But she didn't want to find out.

With her palm flattened against the door, Desiree pushed it open a fraction.

"We're straight."

Weak with relief, Kira felt as if she might slip from her perch on the toilet seat.

Desiree returned to the bank of sinks. She fluffed her bangs in front of the mirror. "They're empty."

Staying as quiet as she could, Kira watched the three girls through the slit between the stall doors. Slowly, she braced her weight against the connecting wall and used her feet on the toilet seat as leverage to maintain her position.

Paradise applied lip gloss before digging in her purse and extracting a comb. She ran it through her hair, fluffing her ends with her fingers. "Good. We've got a few minutes before Mr. Mallard figures out we ducked out of the cafeteria."

"Yeah," Erin added, "he's been a pain."

"Wait a minute. Mr. Mallard is cool most of the time. Why is he acting like a fool?" Desiree asked, glancing from Erin to Paradise, then back again.

Paradise huffed, flopping on the edge of the sink. "'Cause Mr. Walker got in trouble. Mr. Mallard's been on us because he thinks we know something that'll help Mr. Walker."

"Mr. Mallard needs to stay out of my business. He keeps doggin' me about Mr. Walker," Erin answered smugly. She turned to Paradise and gave her a high five. "Ain't gonna happen."

"What's going on with Mr. Walker?" Desiree asked. "Give me more details!"

"We kind of helped him get himself in trouble."

Desiree gasped, her eyes lit up like lightbulbs. "Shut up!"

Erin shrugged and smirked. "It wasn't hard. The teachers always think they're smarter than us. They're not. They're dumb. D-U-M-B," Erin spelled, brushing a lock of hair over her shoulder. "I warned him."

"Warned him about what?" Desiree asked. "Spread the love. I want to know how you got this done."

Kira's breath caught in her throat. A smile spread across her face. If Erin intended to tell all, she wanted to hear everything. Finally, she would have something on those dirty skeezers.

But she needed a witness. Without leaving the room, there must be a way to let somebody get the 411. Chewing on her bottom lip, she debated the problem.

I got it, she thought, digging into the pocket of her jeans and removing her cell phone. If she recorded their conversation, she could send it to her friend Sparkle. She aimed the Motorola V710 camera through the little slot between the bathroom stalls. Maybe she could use it to blackmail Erin. Kira liked that idea.

This was huge. She had about ninety seconds of recording time, and then she'd send a text message to Sparkle with the details of Erin's confession.

Sparkle Harris sat in her fourth-period math class bored to death. She shifted in her seat, fighting the pull of sleep as a large yawn overtook her. It took everything in her to sit up straight and fake an interest in Ms. Brown's lecture. Normally, she liked Ms. Brown and math, but today she just wanted to go home and watch videos on BET's *106 and Park*.

The cell phone in her pocket began to vibrate, causing Sparkle to jump a little in her chair. She slyly eased the item from her pocket and under the desk, checking the screen display. She glanced at the number.

Her eyebrows knitted together over surprised eyes. Kira? What did she want? She knew better than to call her while she was in class. If Ms. Brown caught her using the cell phone, the school would retain it until the end of June. Plus, her parents would have to pick it up.

For a moment, she debated against answering the call. Curiosity and defiance won out and she inconspicuously slipped the Blueteeth Wireless headset over her ear, then drew her hair across her cheek to cover it. It was a good thing she and Kira had decided to buy the same type of cell phone.

WATCH! flashed across the screen.

Erin's, Paradise's, and Desiree's images appeared. It looked as if they were in the bathroom.

Sparkle glanced toward the front of the classroom, spotting Ms. Brown at the far end of the room. She let out a soft sigh of relief. Now she could check things out without getting into trouble.

"Come on, how did you do it?"

Her gaze remained glued to the tiny screen. *Do what?* Sparkle wondered, hoping Kira had a good hiding place because Erin and Paradise would put a hurting on her if they found her.

"You know, Mr. Walker is always talkin' about helping. If he'd helped when I asked him to instead of worrying about stuff that is not his biz, he might have kept his sorry butt out of jail. 'I'm here for you,'" Erin mimicked, "'if you need to talk, come to me.'"

"Jail?" Desiree drew circles in the air with her hand. "He's in jail?"

Smiling smugly, Paradise nodded.

"Wait a minute. Slow down. Pump the brake. I thought he was sick. When we talked about this, you said you wanted to get him fired. Not put in jail."

Erin smiled, shrugging. "What can I say? My plan worked out better than I expected."

"I'd say so," Desiree muttered thoughtfully.

Perched on the edge of the sink, Erin unwrapped a grape Blow Pop sucker and stuck it in her mouth. "You know that janitor—the weird one?"

Both girls nodded.

"He told on Mr. Walker. That was soooo sweet."

Sparkle gasped. She cast a quick gaze in Ms. Brown's direction to make certain the teacher hadn't heard her. The conniving SOBs. She knew something had happened to Mr. Walker, because there was a substitute teacher in his classroom. But she didn't know that he was in jail. That wasn't right.

Mr. Walker was a good guy. He helped her get through her freshman year when her parents had told her about their divorce and she didn't know what to do. How could they treat him this way? He always helped when he could.

Sparkle returned her attention to the screen, watching Paradise perched on the edge of the sink. "You never told me. How did you get that janitor to tell?"

Erin shrugged, licking the sucker like an ice cream cone. "That was easy. I slipped in the building early and dropped a can of Coke on the floor near Mr. Walker's room. Then I put a note in the supervisor's box so that he would send somebody to clean up the mess."

"Pretty good."

"Thank you." Erin did a little curtsey. "I made sure that Mr. Walker and I were near the window so that whoever cleaned up the crap got a movie-size view when I ran out of the room crying and screaming with my clothes torn. I even had blood dripping from a cut on my forehead.

"It worked perfectly. But it worked out better than I thought. The weird janitor didn't go to Mr. Bartholomew. So he didn't look like a tattletale. It was great."

"How did you get Mr. Walker to talk with you?"

"I told him that my boyfriend was pressuring me to have sex and that I needed to talk to an adult about what to do."

"Whoa!"

"Yeah. He always wants to help. So I let him."

Their giggles rang out, filling the bathroom and sending a chill down Sparkle's spine.

"Wait, wait, wait," Desiree said. "What about your mom? Didn't she want you to stay out of Pierson?"

"Yeah. Mom never knows what's going on. She marched into the school and raised hell. Once she said what she had to say, she was done with it. If I went to the worst school in the city, she wouldn't care, as long as I went somewhere every day." Erin grinned broadly. "Besides, I know how to play her. I cried and pleaded with her and told her I wanted to graduate with my friends. That I didn't want what happened to keep me from finishing school. My mom loved that because she really wants me to graduate." Erin's hand swept through the air in a dismissing arch; then she snapped her fingers. "It was easy."

"Ms. Harris, what are you doing?"

Sparkle blinked, shocked to find Ms. Brown at her desk. The shock of discovery hit her full force. Startled, she let the phone slip through her fingers and hit the floor.

When had Ms. Brown snuck up on her? Had she been that involved with Kira's call?

Sparkle swallowed hard, slyly removing the earplug from her ear. "Ah, hi, Ms. Brown."

She was in big trouble. This was the third time Ms. Brown had caught Sparkle with her cell phone. The previous two incidents, she'd given Sparkle a warning and let her keep the phone. This time she was busted. Her good luck had finally run out.

The teacher extended her hand. "Give it to me." The girl hesitated. "I'm waiting, Ms. Harris."

Sparkle recovered, searching for an explanation that would end with her keeping her cell phone. None came. "I'm sorry, Ms. Brown. It won't happen again."

"No, it won't," Ms. Brown replied, folding her arms across her pitiful bosom. "Now please give me the phone."

The teacher reached down and snatched the phone. The earpiece was ripped from the cell phone socket and voices rose from the instrument.

Sparkle gasped, staring at Ms. Brown in astonishment. "Please, Ms. Brown, don't take my phone," she begged. "My mom will kill me."

"You should have thought of that before pulling it out." Ms. Brown glanced at the screen, recognizing several students on the screen. "You know the rules and I've been very lenient with you. I'm going to give this to the principal. Tell your parents they can pick it up in June after the last day of school."

Taking a final look at the screen before closing it, Helen Brown was shocked to hear Erin Hill say, "What can I say? Things worked out better than I expected."

What worked out better? she asked silently.

"He's in jail for attempted rape."

Laughing, Desiree squealed, "Whoa! Rape! Mr. Walker must be pissed."

"Yeah, and?" came Erin's snappy retort.

"Aren't you scared?" Desiree asked. "What if he works things out? What will you do then?"

"Nothing is going to happen to me," Erin said with a flip of her hand. "He got what he deserved. I told him I wasn't playin'."

"Okay. All that's cool." Desiree removed a stick of gum from her pocket, unwrapped it, and popped it in her mouth. Smacking loudly, she asked, "Why did you do it? What did he do to you? He always seemed cool to me."

Paradise piped in, "He tossed Jarell from the team."

"So?" Desiree shrugged. "Is that a reason to ruin the man's reputation?"

"What about Jarell's future?" Paradise answered. "There were scouts for college teams at a few of those games and Jarell missed his chance. We begged Mr. Walker to let Jarell play. He wouldn't."

"So we took him out of the mix," Erin said, giving Paradise another high five. "Mr. Mallard will probably take over and we can work on him to get Jarell back on the team."

Desiree shook her head. "You two are devil women. Smart devils, but devils."

"Hey, don't mess with us," Paradise warned.

"Yeah," seconded Erin.

"What if Mr. Walker goes to jail? What are you going to do?" Desiree asked.

Giggling, Paradise glanced at Erin, then said, "We'll send him a postcard."

Ms. Brown had heard enough. "Where is this?" she asked her student.

"I'm not sure," Sparkle answered. "It looks like one of the bathrooms on the third floor."

Nodding, she marched to the front of her classroom and pushed the intercom button. "Donna, I need to see Mr. Bartholomew right now. It's an emergency."

Chapter 33

We're in this together, Jordan mentally repeated as she dropped her cell phone into the pocket of her jacket. An electric jolt of worry slithered through her veins as she recalled Mike's call to her. Chet wanted to see him at the end of the school day and she refused to speculate on the principal's reasoning.

At 3:10 the last bell rang. She closed and locked her classroom, then marched to the principal's office. As she approached the main office, an eerie sensation of déjà vu assaulted her, tripling her already sky-high anxiety. She shivered.

In her previous experiences, administrators fired or let employees go at the end of the day. Chet's request to meet Mike after school hours fit into that mode.

Jordan didn't believe Chet planned to dismiss Mike, but why would he ask Mike to come into the building at the end of the day? When she was suspended, Chet called and asked her to come back to work on Monday. She didn't have to meet with Chet before returning to the classroom.

As she turned the corner, Mike's tall frame came into view. Worry had transformed his handsome face into a mask of conflicting emotions. One moment, he looked braced for bad news; the next, all the anguish and hurt flooded his features.

"Hi," Jordan greeted in a tone soft with concern. She touched his arm, asking, "You okay?"

Smiling sadly, he shrugged. "Yes. No. I don't know," he admitted, rubbing the back of his neck with a shaky hand.

Her heart went out to him and she wished she could shoulder the burden and leave him free of all this distress. "Whatever Chet's reason for wanting to see you, I believe this will work out."

He whipped around to face her. His eyes reflected the defeat he felt. "How? My career is ruined. My reputation is destroyed."

Without a comeback, Jordan dodged Mike's gaze, focusing on the goings-on in the main office. She glanced past Donna and into the principal's office. Moving closer, she frowned. Why was Helen Brown in Chet's office? Additionally, what did Kira Scott have to do with this situation?

Were they providing damning information against Mike? Jordan leaned closer. Her nose touched the cool glass as she tried to read the math teacher's lips. It didn't work. Frustrated, she spun away.

Jordan turned to Mike and found the same questions in his eyes. He shook his head. She slipped her hand into his and they entered the office.

"Hi, Donna." Using his free hand, Mike pointed at the closed door. "Is Chet available?"

She tipped her head in the direction of the door. "Yeah. He said for you to go straight in when you arrived."

"Thanks," he threw over his shoulder as they crossed the office. Lightly tapping on the door, they waited until Chet waved them inside.

Jordan squeezed his hand and whispered, "It's going to be fine."

Smiling down at her, he stroked her cheek, took a deep breath, and poked his head inside.

"Come in. Have a seat," Chet offered, pointing at the conference table where Helen and Kira sat.

Silence prevailed while Jordan and Mike got settled. Chet made a quick trip to his desk and returned with a green file folder. He sank into a chair at the head of the table, opening the folder and reviewing a few pages.

Fear gripped Jordan. She tried to ignore it so that Mike wouldn't sense it. Her hand shook as she sought his hand under the cover of the table while offering up a silent prayer that his career wouldn't end in this room today.

The principal cleared his throat. "Well, this has been a difficult situation to try and resolve. Finally, we've gotten a handle on what really happened between you and Erin. Ms. Brown and Kira Scott were instrumental in getting to the truth."

The room swelled with tension. Jordan's body went stiff. *What truth?* she wondered. How did a student get involved in this? And could she be trusted?

"Kira, please explain to Mr. Walker and Ms. Anderson what you learned and how," Chet suggested, leaning back in his chair and tenting his fingers, allowing the young woman to take over.

Fifteen minutes later, Kira finished her story and she and Helen Brown were dismissed, leaving Mike and Jordan stunned.

"Mike, I can't tell you how sorry I am about this." He removed his glasses and pinched the bridge of his nose before resetting the frames in the same spot. "Be assured that Erin, Paradise, and Jarell will be permanently expelled from Pierson High."

Mike scoffed, shaking his head. "Good. Erin is truly dangerous."

"That she is." Chet closed the file in front of him and studied Mike with a searching gaze.

"I should press charges, sue Erin for slander."

"Well, that's your call. Whatever you decide to do is up to you," Chet said.

Brows furrowed over his eyes, Mike admitted, "I probably won't. Suing her is more trouble than she's worth."

"Believe me, this incident will become part of her permanent record. Also, she'll be unable to graduate on time. No school will accept her for the next 180 days." The principal patted the file in front of him. "The best we can do is get her out of here."

Mike spread his hands wide and asked, "Chet, what's next?"

"You come back to work," Chet answered as if it were the easiest thing to do. "We've had a sub in your classroom and she's followed your lesson plan."

"What about the kids, don't they know about what happened?"

"Actually, they don't. Until the police completed an investigation, I didn't feel comfortable with exposing our parents to the details."

"What about the papers and the news? It was on the news," Mike said.

"You hadn't been charged with anything. An investigation was being conducted. Your name and our school were never mentioned. We made sure of that. Mike, whatever the situation, I didn't want to ruin your reputation unless we found evidence that supported Erin's claim."

"Nobody knows?"

Chet tented his fingers together and said, "There may

be a few who have their suspicions, but no hard facts. Most of the kids think that you're out on sick leave and I didn't correct them. I threatened Erin with expulsion if she breathed a word of this." He chuckled unpleasantly. "It's a good thing she's such a knucklehead."

"Didn't they see me leave with the police?"

"No. You forget. It was a half day. Our kids were well on their way home or at home watching television. And that makes it easier for you to return." Chet rose from the table and crossed the room to his desk, returning with Mike's attendance, daily lesson plan, and record books. He pushed the items toward the younger man. "All you need to do is come in tomorrow and start where the sub left off."

Relieved, Jordan let her shoulders droop. Finally, the nightmare had ended. Mike would be where he belonged, at Pierson, teaching. Her face broke freely into a smile while her heart pounded in happy expectation.

For several taut moments, Mike stared at the books. The smile faded as Jordan began to worry if he planned to refuse the job. Finally, he picked up his books, rose, and started for the door. She followed.

Chet stopped him at the door and held out his hand. Mike took it in a reaffirming handshake. "Son, I'm truly sorry about the way things happened. Understand this, in my position, I have to act quickly and investigate any incident of a sexual nature and resolve it expeditiously."

Mike nodded.

The trio strolled through the main office. At the door, Chet slapped Mike on the back. "Welcome back. This place has been a sad mountain of bricks and concrete without you running up and down the halls."

"Thanks, Chet."

Once they left the office, Jordan reached up and

cupped Mike's cheek, stroking his flesh. "You did it, Mike!"

Surprise reflected at her from his brown eyes. He lifted his hand and covered hers. "I'm not sure how this all happened, but it did and I'm grateful."

Happiness propelled Jordan into action. Without hesitation, she wrapped her arms around Mike's waist, holding him close. She inhaled the subtle fragrance of his cologne mingled with a hint of his soap.

"I'm so thrilled for you," Jordan said, burying her face against his chest.

It had been two weeks since Mike's reinstatement. Life had returned to its normal routine. No one except Jordan sensed the subtle change in Mike. The difference was difficult to pinpoint or explain. Yet it was there, partially hidden behind his pleasant exterior. She felt that he was marking time, waiting for things to settle down before he made a significant change in his life.

Returning from the Science Olympiad, Mike led Jordan through her classroom to the lab. He carried a gold and silver trophy in his hand. Once they entered the lab, he set their prize on the teacher's workstation and pulled up a stool, stretching his long legs in front of him. Silently, Jordan perched on the edge of the workstation.

She beamed happily at their award. Pride resonated from her words. "I don't know about you, but I'm proud of us. Pierson's Science Olympiad team pulled it off. We didn't take first place, but coming in second is pretty good for students who'd never worked together."

Examining their award, Mike smiled sadly. "True. The students did great. They did Pierson proud and

I loved their rap song at the end. I would never have believed they could work that into their project."

Uneasiness overtook Jordan. Although Mike spewed the right phrases, she felt a disconnection from him. She stroked his arm, asking gently, "What's wrong, Mike?"

He hunched his shoulders, glancing pensively at the trophy. "This will probably be my swan song for Pierson."

"Swan song?" she repeated.

"Yeah. This is my last big project," he answered. "I told you that I'm considering leaving education completely. My resignation will be on Chet's desk next week."

Fighting an edge of panic, Jordan swallowed hard and told herself to stay calm. Nothing would be resolved if she took a stand against Mike's choice. She ran her tongue across her dry lips. Softening her voice, she said, "I thought you had given up on that idea. I mean, we got to the truth and you were exonerated."

"That's not the point." Mike shut his eyes. "All I ever wanted to do was teach. Somehow that got tainted during the Erin incident."

All of her sympathy was with him. She understood how he felt and wished that she knew a way to help him.

He opened his eyes. She gasped. Deep misery and sorrow glared at her from his brown orbs.

"I'm tired. It's a constant battle with the kids." His voice was worn out and exhausted. "They don't want to learn. Administration ignores our cries for help and support. Plus, we have to fend off crazy parents. Work shouldn't be this difficult."

"But you love teaching and you're good at it," Jordan cried, laying her hand over his and giving it an encouraging squeeze. "I've been in your classes many times. No one doubts your teaching abilities."

"I am a good teacher," he agreed. "And I am proud of what I've accomplished in my years in this field."

"Then what's bothering you?"

Mike avoided eye contact, studying the floor and taking a great interest in the tips of his shoes. He shoved his hands inside the pockets of his trousers and whispered in a tortured voice, "I can't work like this anymore."

"I'm not the one to tell you what to do. Especially since I know where you're coming from. But I will offer you a piece of advice. Think long and hard before you do anything. Don't throw your career away because of Erin," she warned. "That girl's not worth it."

"It's not just Erin," he denied. "Although she started me to thinking about my future. There are times when I need to feel that I'm winning the battle. That I touch a life and make it better."

"You do. Every day," she insisted. "Don't forget. When I was lost, you helped me."

Shaking his head, Mike said, "I don't have any hope."

Determined, Jordan clung to his arm. "You did nothing wrong, Mike. Erin caused this. She is a vindictive little witch that's now getting exactly what she deserves. And she's gone. She's been removed from the school. Erin can't hurt you anymore."

"I know," Mike answered sadly.

Choosing a different route, Jordan said, "Look at all the people you've helped." She lifted her hand and tenderly touched his cheek, forcing Mike to look at her. "Students, faculty, your friends. You helped me find myself."

"It's not enough. Don't get me wrong. This has been a great ride. One I've enjoyed greatly. But it's time to move on."

She whispered, "Don't give up."

"I don't want to talk about this anymore. I've made

up my mind." Tiredly, he rose from the stool and headed for the door leading to the hallway. "I've got some things to do, so I'll see you later."

Watching him through troubled eyes, she wanted to call him back and talk some more. He sound so dejected, so helpless.

She refused to let him check out this way. Mike offered the students and faculty so much.

There had to be a way for Jordan to reach him. Guide him back to the classroom, away from Erin's accusation and what she stole from him. But how?

Chapter 34

True to his word, Mike turned in his resignation the following week. Over Jordan's objections, he went to Chet and they discussed a separation date. The two men agreed that Mike would not return after the Christmas break.

Left with a few weeks to change his mind, Jordan tried everything she knew to deter him. No matter the enticement, Mike refused to budge on the subject.

Fresh out of ideas, Jordan racked her brain for a way to persuade him. The semester was winding down and she felt exhausted. She hoped that an idea would materialize over the Thanksgiving holiday break.

At the tail end of her prep period, Jordan ventured into the copy room for her mail. A plain white envelope glided to the floor when she emptied her mailbox. Curious, she retrieved it, glancing at the small, neat handwriting. It bore Mike's and her names.

Her eyes widened and her heart rate doubled as she read the short note. A broad smile of approval spread across her face and she hurried from the room, intent on finding her mentor.

After a cursory knock, Jordan entered his classroom. Mike stood at his black file cabinet, flipping through files and tossing pages into the trash.

She strolled across the floor, halting at his desk. "Hey."

Mike glanced at her over his shoulder, giving her a faint smile of acknowledgment. "Hi yourself. What's up?"

"What ya doin'?" she asked.

"Checking through my stuff." He shut the drawer and sank into the chair at his desk. "I'm trying to decide what I'm going to keep or toss."

"Oh." Jordan produced the letter and dropped it on his desk.

Frowning, Mike lifted the sheet and turned it over. "What's this?"

"A letter," she answered smugly. "I found it in my mailbox. But it's addressed to both of us. You need to read it." She pulled a stool close to the desk, waiting.

Mike shrugged, his eyes clearly revealing his "not another trick" expression before he unfolded the paper. He straightened the single sheet of lined paper and began to read aloud.

Dear Ms. Anderson and Mr. Walker, thank you for letting me be part of the Science Olympiad. I know that I don't know a lot about science, but you still gave me a chance anyway.

Mike stopped, piercing Jordan with a searching glare.

She smiled and pointed at the letter. "Keep going."

Science has always been hard for me. I don't remember real good and it takes a lot for the words in the book to make sense. But when I'm in your class, it's cool.

Things come together and I feel you. You help me to get the work done. When you make examples, it makes things come clear for me. And when I make a mistake you don't let the other kids laugh at me. Thank you for that.

He put the letter down and asked in a suspicious tone, "You put him up to this, didn't you?"

"No, I didn't," Jordan answered sincerely. "It surprised me. But go on," she encouraged. "Keep reading. You're not done."

For the first time in a long time I don't feel like a retard.

Stopping, Mike massaged his forehead and blew out a large gush of air.

I never won anything in my life. I can't tell you how it made me feel to stand on the stage with the other kids and know that I was part of it all. And now we have a trophy to show for all our work. It feels like I won the lottery and never have to work again.

Mike lowered the letter. Jordan noted the moisture in his eyes before he turned away. She felt a surge of sympathy and love for this man. Unlike herself, he showed his feelings without fear or embarrassment. "I don't know if I can read any more."

It needed to be finished. She reached across the desk and removed the letter from his hands, picking up where he left off.

There's been times that I thought about quitting school because it's so hard. But you teachers helped me feel better about myself. I think I can do it.

LOVE CHANGES EVERYTHING 305

Her voice broke. She cleared her throat and started
again.

Thank you. Teachers like you showed me that I can be more. Trevien Davis.

They sat quietly absorbing the praise they received from Trevien's letter. It wasn't often that students credited a teacher with helping them find themselves.

Jordan turned to Mike. "Hey. You okay?" She touched his hand.

Nodding, he answered, "Yes."

"Want to talk about it?"

"Wow!"

She grinned back at him. "Mmm-hmm. That's how I felt."

He drew in a breath of cleansing air. "Wow! I don't know what to say. I feel so humbled by his words."

"That's sort of where I went when I read the letter."

Standing, Mike ran a hand over his face. "I made a difference and helped someone who needed me." He turned to her with a smile on his face. "It feels good, Jordan. Really good."

"I know. I'm glad."

Unconsciously, a broad smile spread across his face. "I needed this. I helped someone. No, we helped someone to learn. We showed him that he could do more, be better." He sighed, glancing out the window.

"Mike, you're a great teacher," she praised, moving to his side. She picked up the letter and shook it at him. "If you believe what Trevien has to say, he's never won anything in his life before this semester. You helped him achieve something that he always believed to be unattainable."

Mike tried to play it down by saying, "We did a little thing. He always had it in him."

"It wasn't a little thing to Trevien," Jordan responded. "We're talking about his shining moment. It proved to him that he wasn't dumb. All the things that other students said about him weren't true. He could learn."

"Maybe. I don't know," Mike muttered.

"I do. There's been a lot of disappointment in his young life and you helped him move beyond that to achieve. He feels like he can do more. Mike, he's in my chemistry class. It's almost a miracle for Trevian to receive a C on anything he does. Actually it was more like a D-plus. He thought about quitting school. But this award"—Jordan pointed at the trophy displayed on the edge of Mike's desk—"made him feel better about himself. That he had something to contribute. Don't make light of it."

She faced him. "A couple of weeks ago you believed that nothing you did changed the students or their future. I think this letter proves you were wrong."

A sheepish smile spread across his face. "You've got me there."

"Mike, you have so much to offer these kids. You're innovative, creative, and in tune with what's going on with them. They respect and look up to you. Do you know how many teachers would pay good money to have those skills?"

Glancing down at her, he chuckled. "I'm sure there are a few."

"I'd say more than a few. And I also say don't give up. You know as well as I do that the kids will fight you every chance they can, but they respect the teachers that set boundaries and have expectations."

Mike nodded.

"If you leave the job that you love, Erin's won. It

doesn't matter that she's gone or that Jarell wanted you to suffer because he wasn't picked up by a pro team. And while I'm at it, let me say this, as far as I'm concerned, Jarell's belief that he would go pro after high school was a joke. A fantasy. He's not a Kobe or LeBron." Jordan shook her head. "I'm sorry. I got off track. If you give up now, Erin's won because all the students that follow her won't have you as a teacher."

Mike ran his hand over his face. "When they took me out of here in handcuffs, I felt so ashamed. Never in my life had I been placed in a situation like that." Embarrassed, he turned away. "That day, they stripped me of my dignity."

"No. That happens only if you allow it."

"All I've ever wanted to do was help, and that girl threw it all back at me. What did I do that would make a student go to such extremes? What have I done to make her hate me that much?"

Feeling his pain and wanting to comfort him, Jordan slipped her arms around him from behind. She laid her cheek against his back and whispered, "You didn't do anything wrong. It's all Erin. She doesn't have any morals."

Jordan wished she could bear this pain for Mike so that he could move past what Erin had done to him. "I only have one more question. Do you want to quit?"

Mike turned, drawing her into his embrace, holding her against his chest so close that she could barely breathe. "No."

Jordan lifted her head and gazed into his eyes. "Then don't. Don't give up everything you've worked so hard for. Don't walk away from the life that you want."

"How do I stay?"

"You fight," she answered firmly. "Concentrate on the things that you believe in and work for change. That's the only way to live. Otherwise, you're just existing."

Chapter 35

The motor hummed softly while Jordan sat in Mike's driveway, drumming her fingers against her knee. Since his release from jail, they had agreed to put any discussion regarding their relationship on ice. Now that Mike had regained his equilibrium and his life had returned to the straight and narrow, one item remained for them to resolve. Where was their relationship headed?

This is ridiculous, she decided, switching off the engine with a savage jerk of her wrist before climbing from the SUV. There was no reason for her to be afraid. She'd been to this house many times. This time wouldn't be any different.

Her conscience corrected her. *There are plenty of reasons to be nervous. You're here to find out whether Mike still loves you and if he wants you in his life. And you're afraid of his answer.*

After arming the car's alarm, Jordan climbed the stairs and rang the doorbell. She waited nervously for him to answer. Her fingers played with the zipper on her leather jacket, zipping and unzipping the garment as she waited for Mike.

The door swung open and Mike appeared in the entrance. Surprise registered on his face. "Hey."

Jordan tried to smile, but felt the taut skin tightened across her cheekbones, refusing to give. "Hi. You busy?"

Opening the door wider, he answered, "No. Come on in."

"Thanks."

Minutes later she found herself in the living room, the aroma of oregano, garlic, and tomatoes filling the air, teasing her empty stomach. Warren Hill's sax serenaded her with his tune "Tell Me All Your Secrets."

Mike stopped along the edge of the living room. "Did you have dinner?"

Jordan shook her head, drawing in a deep breath.

Smiling at her, he said, "I can offer you a plate of angel-hair pasta with ground turkey meat sauce."

"No, thanks. I'm fine."

He pointed at the sofa. "Have a seat. What can I do for you?"

"Thanks." Jordan sat on the sofa, waiting as he got comfortable beside her. She shifted to face him and whispered his name, then stopped, unable to turn her thoughts into a coherent sentence.

Something in her tone must have penetrated, because he studied her with a frown crinkling his forehead. "Yeah?"

She sat, balancing on the edge of the sofa. "Mike, things have finally settled down. You're back on track at school."

"And I'm grateful to you for all your support. Without you, I would have made a mistake that would have ruined my life."

His admission made butterflies flutter in the pit of her belly. Unfortunately, she didn't have long to bask in the afterglow of his praise, because they had more important matters to settle.

She rubbed her eye with a nervous finger before plunging ahead. "There's one thing that we haven't found time to discuss."

He gazed expectantly at her. "And that is?"

"Us. What's going to happen to you and me?"

"Well, umm," Mike began, rubbing his hand across his neck.

Worried that he planned to dump her, Jordan panicked. She started to babble, pushing her thoughts out all at once. "I know that I hurt you when I refused to let the faculty know about us. But I was just so afraid. I acted irrationally. My insecurities took control and I made some bad choices. Can you forgive me?"

He interjected, "Jordan."

"Believe me, it's hard to be an older woman in a relationship like this. You're always concerned that you look old or foolish or that you'll lose your man to a younger woman."

Mike tried a second time, "Jordan."

Her babbling switched to full rant. "You think people are laughing at you or that you have to worry about younger women coming after your man. It's hard. People would laugh at us and maybe you'd start believing what they say. Then I'd lose you and I don't think I can survive that."

Mike placed a finger against her lips, cutting off the stream of words.

"Jordan," he shouted. She stopped. Her mouth formed a perfect O as she stared at the man beside her.

"I understand," he said. "You found it difficult and I didn't support you like I should have." He ducked his head after making that statement, but his voice maintained the warmth and strength that he'd displayed from his first sentence. "I focused on my own feelings, not on what you needed from me. Your feelings or what you might be encountering from the faculty didn't cross my mind."

Mike stood, shoving his hands into the pockets of his jeans, and added, "I'm glad you brought that up, because—"

"Wait! I'm not sure I'm ready for this." Jordan flew into a panic. She rose from the sofa and began to pace the room. This might have been her idea, but the coward in her surfaced, taking control without hesitation.

Stepping into her path, Mike grabbed her by the arms and held her in place, speaking in a gentle but firm tone. "Jordan, all I'm trying to do is agree with you. It's past time for us to talk about our relationship."

She gazed into his face and found herself drawn into the depths of those brown orbs. The questions vanished from her mind, replaced by this sense of belonging and completeness. A feeling of being home and loved filled her.

Jordan inhaled deeply and released the air from her lungs in one long stream. "Mike, I'm sorry."

"Sorry?" An uncertain smile flashed across his face. "Sorry for what?"

"I let everything get in the way. I let my fears control my actions."

"The way of what?"

Sorrowfully, she whispered, "Us. Our lives. The things I wanted with you. For letting my fears control my life and separate us. For being more concerned with what people thought rather than what was important to us. Can you forgive me?"

"I can forgive you anything," he promised softly, turning her bones into jelly. "But I don't think you have to do this."

"The truth is, I was afraid to hope that we would work out, Mike. That you loved me the way I love you." Jordan drew her tongue across her dry bottom lip, then continued. "I believed everyone who knew about us would laugh at me." She placed her hands on her chest. "This old fool trying to keep a young guy. It was difficult for me to open my heart to you while my insecurities traveled along with us. So I tried to keep our relationship a secret, just between us, hoping that however things ended between us no one would be the wiser and I could go on my way without feeling as if there was a bull's-eye on my back that read 'Look at the old fool! She thought she could hold on to a younger man.'"

His smile faded as he listened. "Jordan, nobody was laughing at us. To be perfectly honest, I don't think our being together mattered to anyone in the building. Yeah, there were some kids that thought it was funny. Let's face it, our students' lives are not that full, although they think they are." He chuckled softly. "Until today, I discounted how strongly you felt about this. I'm sorry that I didn't understand your feelings. I promise you that it will never happen again."

She shrugged, offering a sad little smile. "If you and I didn't make it, all I had was my job. I didn't want the kids or my colleagues to think badly of me."

"Nobody thinks any less of you. Self-preservation is a natural instinct. Wanting to be loved and loving someone is natural."

"I love you, Mike."

The room seemed to get smaller and she could barely breathe. But she'd finally admitted the emotions that filled her heart. Jordan glanced at Mike.

"I know."

"What?"

He grinned at her. "I've always known. Whether you said the words or not."

"I don't understand."

"You said 'I love you' each time we made love." Mike took her hands and held them between his. "You certainly proved it when you stayed at my side during the Erin incident. I felt your love." He smiled and she felt as if she'd died and gone to heaven. "As you fought to keep me in a job that I love, I knew you loved me. But it's nice to hear the words. Thank you."

"It's certainly nice to say them," she admitted, holding her breath.

"I guess it's my turn. I love you, Jordan."

Jordan shut her eyes, allowing the words to float over her like a fine mist of rain. "What do we do with all that love? Do we stay together, see what happens next?"

"How about we try marriage?" he answered quietly.

Her eyes flew open. "You're kidding, right?"

"No, I'm not. I'd never kid about something so important." He leaned in and kissed her, caressing her cheek with his hand. "Jordan Alexander, will you marry me?"

"What about kids?"

"What about them?"

She hesitated, then asked, "Don't you want them?"

"Yes."

"What if we can't?" Jordan chew on her bottom lip before continuing, "What if I can't have any?"

He cradled her hand between both of his and tenderly kissed her lips. "Then we'll be a family of two and raise a school of five hundred at Pierson."

Tears pooled in her eyes. She loved this man so much.

"Think very carefully about what I'm going to ask. "Are you truly willing to sacrifice your dreams for me?"

"There's no sacrifice. I love you. And that comes first. I'd do anything for you, don't you know that?"

Voice quivering, she answered, "There's only one answer. I love you and I want to be with you. So I say yes." She threw herself into his arms.

Grinning down at her, Mike gave her a quick kiss. "How do you propose we celebrate?"

Jordan's face scrunched up as she considered his comment. She drew close and whispered in Mike's ear, rubbing her hand along his inner thigh. "Well, you know that dinner you offered me a little bit ago?"

His brows wrinkled as his eyes followed her hand's action. "Yeah?"

"I'd like for you to serve it to me in your bed."

Epilogue

Fourteen months later

"Come on, Jordan. You can do this," Mike encouraged, wiping his wife's sweaty brow with a towel.

"No. I don't want to." Panting, she said, "I'll make a deal with you. You deliver the baby and I'll wait in the car for you to get finished."

Chuckling softly, Mike gave her a quick kiss on her forehead. "Sorry, sweetheart. I can't do this one for you. Besides, you're too close to give up now. Don't you want to meet this little guy and say hello? I mean, he's been doing the tango inside you for a couple of weeks and you promised that you'd get even with him for keeping you from your sleep."

Jordan tossed a tired hand in the air, then shut her eyes against another contraction. When it ended, she muttered, "I don't care anymore. Just get this baby out of me."

"I care. Listen to your coach. One more push, and then you can rest," Mike promised as he helped her sit.

"I can't, I'm too tired," Jordan whined. She'd been in labor for more hours than she could remember and her body didn't seem to want to spit this baby out.

"I know you're tired, but we're almost there. Right, Barbara?"

Jordan turned to her mother. Next to having her husband with her, her parents' arrival had been the best gift and surprise she could have received.

"We can see the baby's head," Dr. Lewis announced. "He has a head of curly black hair. All right, Jordan, we need one good push and that should do it."

"See, sweetheart. It's almost over. Come on, baby," Mike encouraged.

Gathering her strength, she blew out a deep breath of air as she pushed. "Mike, I hate you."

Grinning at his wife, he answered, "I know, baby. I know. That's it."

Jordan took another deep breath and pushed again.

"Mr. Walker, if you plan to catch this baby, you've got to move. It's time for you to get down here," the doctor instructed.

Giving his wife a quick kiss on her lips, he moved quickly, positioning himself. A moment later, he was holding his baby's head. "Whoa! He's almost here!" With one final push, Mike caught the baby as he slipped from his mother's body with a hearty cry. "Sweetheart, it's a boy! We have a son!" Mike lifted the infant so that Jordan could see him, then laid him on his mother's stomach while he cut the umbilical cord.

"Excuse me. I need to do a few things, and then he's all yours." Dr. Lewis handed the baby to the nurse.

Exhausted but happy, Jordan fell back against the bed and watched the nurse clean her son's airway and nose before weighing and measuring him. Throughout the procedure the infant yelled continuously and loudly.

Mike shook his head. "He's definitely got a pair of lungs on him."

"That he does," she agreed. "But he's beautiful."

"Yeah, he is." His heart swelled with love and pride when the nurse put the baby in his arms and he returned to his wife's side to lay the infant in her arms. In awe, Mike stood next to the bed, watching his family. "I love you," he whispered in her ear.

Drawing near the new family, Barbara caressed the baby's head. "Jordan, he looks like you."

Touching her baby's check, Jordan answered, "Wrinkled and red. Gee, thanks Mom."

"No, he's beautiful. He's got your nose and eyes. You can't see it yet. But in time, you will. Have you chosen a name?"

"Michael Anthony Roy Walker," Jordan answered.

"Oh, honey. Your dad will be so happy and proud."

"We wanted to name him after both grandfathers," Mike explained.

"Thank you. I'll leave you three to get acquainted." Barbara followed the doctor and nurse from the room.

"I love you, Mike. Thank you for my son." She gazed into her husband's eyes, then studied her baby. "He's incredible. I never thought I could be this happy."

Mike signed contentedly and rested a hand on his son's head. "Thank you. You've given me the life I've always wanted."

ABOUT THE AUTHOR

Karen White-Owens is a native Detroiter. She holds a bachelor's degree in sociology and is currently working toward a master's in library and information science at Wayne State University.

In addition to writing, she is a librarian at the Mount Clemens Public Library and devotes her free time to teaching the fundamentals of creative writing to young adults.

Her current release *Circles of Love* received four and a half gold stars from Romantic Times Book Club and was a Romantic Times 2004 Reviewers' Choice Nominee for Best Multicultural Romance.

Her husband of sixteen years is her biggest fan and supporter.

BOOK YOUR PLACE ON OUR WEBSITE AND MAKE THE ARABESQUE ROMANCE CONNECTION!

We've created a customized website just for our very special Arabesque readers, where you can get the inside scoop on everything that's going on with Arabesque romance novels.

When you come online, you'll have the exciting opportunity to:

- View covers of upcoming books

- Learn about our future publishing schedule (listed by publication month and author)

- Find out when your favorite authors will be visiting a city near you

- Search for and order backlist books

- Check out author bios and background information

- Send e-mail to your favorite authors

- Join us in weekly chats with authors, readers and other guests

- Get writing guidelines

- AND MUCH MORE!

Visit our website at
http://www.arabesquebooks.com